The Homeless Bishop

The Homeless Bishop

A Novel

Joseph F. Girzone

ORBIS BOOKS

Maryknoll, New York 10545

Founded in 1970, Orbis Books endeavors to publish works that enlighten the mind, nourish the spirit, and challenge the conscience. The publishing arm of the Maryknoll Fathers and Brothers, Orbis seeks to explore the global dimensions of the Christian faith and mission, to invite dialogue with diverse cultures and religious traditions, and to serve the cause of reconciliation and peace. The books published reflect the views of their authors and do not represent the official position of the Maryknoll Society. To learn more about Maryknoll and Orbis Books, please visit our website at www.maryknollsociety.org.

Library of Congress Cataloging-in-Publication Data

Girzone, Joseph F.
    The homeless bishop : a novel / Joseph F. Girzone.
  p. cm.
        ISBN 978-1-57075-925-3 (hardcover)
    1. Bishops–Fiction. 2. Poor–Fiction. 3. New York (N.Y.)–Fiction. I. Title.

    PS3557.I77H66 2011
    813'.54–dc22

                                                    2011000321

Some men see things as they
are and say why?
I dream things that never were
and say why not?
　　　　—GEORGE BERNARD SHAW

Acknowledgments

I am deeply grateful to Richard and Elizabeth Della Ratta for their patience and careful review of the various versions of this manuscript. Writing this story was a long journey, and I wanted to make it an adventure that would have meaning to a wide variety of readers. I cannot thank Richard and Elizabeth enough for their help and encouragement.

I am grateful to Michael Leach and the staff at Orbis Books for their attentive shepherding of the manuscript and their loving help and support during every step of the publishing process. Michael's editing of the original manuscript made it much more professional than my original. I am grateful to Maria Angelini and Joan Laflamme who turned the end product into a beautiful work of art.

Contents

CHARLIE

Foxes have dens and birds have nests, but the Son of Man has no place to lay his head.
—MATTHEW 18:19-21

1

Upstate New York

As I sat in the last pew waiting for the early morning mass to begin, I noticed a stranger walking into the church. As he approached my pew, a strong, musty odor wafted through the air, giving the impression the man's clothes were old, not recently washed, and probably had had previous owners; they certainly did not fit him. He was about five feet, ten inches tall, very thin, almost gaunt. His hair had not been cut, nor had his beard been trimmed recently. I immediately noticed the soiled, light-blue patch on the right leg of his dark brown pants. I sure hoped he wouldn't sit near me.

My thoughts were not charitable, much less fitting preparation for the sacred mysteries that were about to begin. I wondered what this unkempt vagrant was doing in church, and at mass time. Did he come in to get warm? It was early spring and the air was still chilly, in fact, cold. Could he be coming to church to worship? Not likely. He took a seat in a pew on the left side of the aisle, and people nearby moved away from him, which was understandable.

I breathed a sigh of relief that he hadn't chosen to sit near me and turned my attention back to the altar. Almost immediately, I was distracted again. Three of the ushers were engaged in quiet discussion. Then one of them walked up the aisle and spoke to the man, apparently asking him to leave the church. He listened without comment and then went back to his own thoughts. The usher, red faced, returned to the back of the church.

As the priest walked up the aisle to begin the service, I noticed him looking over at the bum, who returned the look with a smile. The priest continued toward the altar, singing the processional hymn with gusto. The congregation sang along, but I was too distracted by the homeless man to join in. I could not keep my eyes off him. "Why should I let this man disturb my worship of God? He has just as much right to go to church as anyone else. Who am I to say he is any worse or any better than anyone else in the church?"

He certainly didn't appear to belong in this congregation. "What is there about the rest of us that makes us fit together so well compared to this man? Maybe it's because we hide our shame, whereas his shame is apparent to the whole world. Perhaps looking at him makes us aware of the camouflage we use to hide our real selves from the eyes of others." I was beginning to feel guilty. Still, I found myself protesting, "There *is* a difference between him and me."

At the Gospel everyone stood up. I glanced across the aisle, and there was the bum–sitting, sound asleep. I watched, and he did wake up for a few minutes during the homily before he fell back to sleep again. There was no way he could be deep in meditation and not have noticed what others were doing.

Communion was the climax. I was wondering if he would go to communion. To my surprise he did get in the line on his side of the aisle. As I was in the aisle on the right side, I could watch his every move. He didn't have the same casual bearing as the others; rather, it seemed as though he was unfamiliar with what it was all about. The priest must have had the same impression, because he just looked at him for a moment when he approached to receive the Eucharist and then passed him by and gave communion to the next person on the right side of the aisle. The person immediately behind the bum nudged his shoulder. But the bum stayed there, and when the priest looked at him, the bum held his hands out to receive the host. The priest still refused. The bum then said to him, "Peace, Father." The person behind him gave him a shove and told him to keep moving so the others could receive communion.

The person who had nudged him was a colleague, a judge whom I had known all my life. He had a bad reputation, even as a kid. Just during the past week he had swindled a widow out of her house by having her declared incompetent. He had previously had the woman sign an agreement that turned her house over to his wife in return for her care as long as she was living in the house. When she was declared incompetent and committed to a nursing home, the judge's wife took legal possession of her home. Seeing this crooked judge approach the priest and piously receive communion made me stop and think. Judge and bum were treated so differently, but what were they really like?

When the priest gave me communion, I felt ashamed not because of what I had witnessed, but because I had spent my whole time at mass judging others. Still, I found myself watching and speculating about the homeless man across the aisle.

When I left the church the homeless man was just a few feet in front of me. Again, I started thinking about him. Where was he going now? Where did he live? What would his day be like? How did he stay warm? What would he find to eat? I couldn't explain why, but I felt a strong need to know more about this man. I made up my mind to follow him—at a discreet distance, of course. We walked about three miles into a seedy part of town. I couldn't believe I was following him. What was I thinking? Still, I felt compelled to continue. I saw him bend down near a bus stop and pick up something. He then went into a deli and came out with a brown paper bag and continued on his way. It seemed likely that he had picked up some money at the bus stop and used it to buy food.

The vagrant finally came to an old railroad bridge. Off to the side was a small lot, part of a yard next to an abandoned and dilapidated house. Sitting around a bonfire were five men. I watched from a distance, but close enough to hear. They knew him, because they greeted him as he approached.

"What you got there, Charlie?" Now I know his name, I thought.

"A surprise. I found some money on the street and bought us a banquet," Charlie laughed, as he opened the bag and put the contents on an old three-legged table.

"You got no class, Charlie," one of the men griped. "Here, put this newspaper on the table. Don't you know you're supposed to have a tablecloth?" The fellow spread out two sheets of paper.

Another man took out a pocket knife and began cutting the bread and the tomatoes. Not thinking, he divided the round of baked kielbasa into five pieces, as he muttered, "Thanks, Charlie, for thinking of us."

Charlie ended up with a crust of bread. He said nothing as his friends attacked the food liked hungry animals and gobbled up the few other items from the bag.

"Too bad you didn't buy something to drink, Charlie. There's nothing to wash this down."

When they finished, Charlie wished them a good day and left. I had thought he was part of their group, but apparently they were just acquaintances.

By this time I was getting hungry myself and wondered if I should start back home, where lunch would soon be ready. But I still felt a tremendous curiosity about this odd man and decided to follow him one more block. Half a block down the street he stopped at an old but well-kept brick house. When he rang the hand bell on the door, an elderly lady came out as if expecting him. She had snow-white hair tied in a bun at the back of her head and looked like one of the old-time "gentlewomen" who had lived in this neighborhood years earlier.

"Charlie, I was hoping you'd stop in this morning. I have so many things to tell you. It was quite week. Come right in, Charlie. Come right in."

The two disappeared into the house. I continued walking down the street but kept an eye on the house so I would see when Charlie came out.

"Who was that woman?" I thought. "Was it his mother? Or a friend? Or just a lonely old lady? Charlie certainly doesn't look like the kind of person this proper-looking lady would associate with. But who knows? Loneliness does strange things to people. But, there I go judging again. How do I know she's lonely?"

I glanced at my watch and realized I was late for lunch. Taking out my cell phone, I called my wife to tell her I had been sidetracked. When Maureen answered, I knew she was annoyed, and I told her I would be home as soon as I could to explain the whole story.

Right then, I saw Charlie leaving the lady's house. I surprised myself by deciding to catch up with him and introduce myself. As I was about to pass him, I turned and said, "Oh, pardon me. Didn't I see you in church this morning?"

"I'm not a parishioner, but I did go to mass this morning."

"I noticed you were bypassed when you went up to receive communion."

"It's certainly understandable," Charlie said, in a surprisingly gentle tone, which even seemed to have a hint of refinement about it. "After all, I don't make the most charming impression on people, and I realize that, so I'm not offended when people feel repulsed. Most people probably thought I didn't know about communion and just went up to get something."

To my surprise I felt drawn to this guy—a feeling I tried to resist. I certainly did not want him to become a friend, or I'd never get rid of him.

When I introduced myself, Charlie merely said: "Nice to meet you, Martin. I do remember you from church this morning. You were sitting in the back on the right side. Everybody calls me Charlie." I cringed at the thought that he might reach out to shake my hand, but he didn't.

"You live around here, Charlie?"

"Yes, been around a while. Are you from the neighborhood, Martin?"

"I moved back here about two years ago. I grew up not far from here and came back to take a job at a law firm downtown."

"You married?"

"Yes, I have a wife and two kids. And that reminds me. I decided to get a little exercise after church, and now I'm sure my wife is wondering where I am. I'm glad I met you, Charlie. Have a good day."

As I walked off, I wondered if Charlie knew I was lying and that I had been following him. What if he now followed me? He could even be a thief or worse for all I knew. I was getting anxious, and every now and then I turned around and looked in different directions to see if he was anywhere in sight. As I approached my house, I thought about something entirely different from my own concerns about Charlie. I knew he had nothing to eat. What little he had picked up at the store he gave to the others. All they left him was a crust of bread. If I were a real Christian, wouldn't I have invited him to come and eat with us? Then I thought about how he looked—and smelled—and my own worries about what kind of person he might be. I couldn't expose my family to any risk. No, there was no way I could be expected to invite him for a meal.

When I got home, everyone was angry with me. The kids' plans were upset by my lateness. Maureen had been holding lunch for me. I felt I owed everyone, so toward the end of the meal I asked if they would like to go out for dinner, maybe to a Japanese restaurant we all liked. Afterward we could see the original *Les Miserables,* which was playing for free at the library. They had loved the musical, which we had seen on a trip to New York. Everyone liked the idea.

When we finished eating, I went upstairs to the bedroom. I kept thinking about my strange morning and the even stranger man I had felt so involved with. Why on earth had I been sneaking around following a vagrant?

At that point Maureen came into the bedroom. "Marty, what is it? What happened? Are you all right?"

Embarrassed and confused at my own behavior, I didn't know at first how to explain. Finally I told her, "Something happened this morning. I can't explain it. I feel that something is happening inside of me, and I have to process it."

"But, Marty, what happened?"

"Maureen, this isn't like me. It all started when a vagrant came into church this morning and walked past my pew. He left behind a stench of old clothes that had not been washed in God knows how long. For some reason, he obsessed me. I couldn't stop thinking about who he was or what his life was like. It totally distracted me. When the guy went to communion, the priest passed him by, which also bothered me. Then John Carroll, who was behind him in the aisle, pushed him out of the way and told him to move on. That bothered me. That damned hypocrite!"

"You mean the judge?"

"Yeah. And you know how I feel about him with all the dirt in *his* life and the shady deals. Seeing the priest smiling at that hypocrite after denying Jesus to the bum, I couldn't help but be struck by the contrast. Which of the two was really better, the bum or the crooked judge? I saw I was no different. I had been making judgments about the homeless man all through mass.

"And here's what is really strange. The reason I was so late for lunch was because I felt I had to have some answers about this guy with the shabby clothes. So—you aren't going to believe this—I followed him for, well, you know how long."

"What did you find out, Marty?"

"Not much. He seems to be just what he looks like, a simple bum, maybe a bit retarded. Probably harmless. Yet, all the time I was following him, I had the nagging thought that I had seen him somewhere before, but I can't remember where. Why is this bothering me so much? I absolutely must find out more about this fellow. I feel compelled to find out just who this man is and what his background is. He may be simply what he appears to be, and that's fine. Or he may be something else. I keep feeling that I need to learn more for my own benefit. But I have to know."

"Marty, please be careful. You don't know what his past may have been. He may not be as simple or as innocent as you think."

"Don't worry, sweetheart. I'll be careful."

I pulled my attention back to the present. "Shall we leave for dinner a little before five?"

"That sounds fine. And the movie is a great idea. I love you, dear."

"Thanks for putting up with me, sweetheart. I know I'm strange sometimes."

"Only sometimes?" Maureen said with a smile.

2

THE RIDE HOME FROM THE MOVIE WAS QUIET. No one felt like talking, not because anything happened, but even Meaghan and Donald, our children, felt the need to hold on to the mood of the movie as long as they could, so deeply had it affected them. They all walked out with tears still running down their cheeks.

Finally, I asked Maureen how she liked it.

"I'm still *verklempt*, just like after the play. Do you think there are people today, in our country, who are jailed for stealing a loaf of bread? It's so hard to believe anyone would send a person to prison for nineteen years for stealing food to feed a hungry family."

"At one time I would not have believed that either, but in court one day a case came up just before my client's. A young black man had been arrested for stealing a package of hot dogs, hot dog rolls, two quarts of milk, and some medicine for a sick baby. His family had not eaten in three days. A new law had drastically cut down on food stamps, and the little money he was making at his job ran out, so out of desperation, he stole what his family needed. The judge, a very conservative Christian, doesn't believe there are any poor people, just people too lazy to work, or scofflaws; to teach him and any others like him a lesson, he sentenced the man to two years in prison. It was his third conviction. The baby died only a month after the father went to prison. I think most decent people would be horrified at what happens today, even in our enlightened country. There are still mean, self-righteous Pharisees, who have a sick need to punish others whose troubled lives they can never begin to understand, much less feel compassion for. That judge who took communion so piously this morning is that kind of judge, pious on the outside but with a heart of ice toward poor people with troubled lives. He thinks they're all potential criminals and prides himself on cleaning up this "human scum" that infects society by locking them away in prison. "Maximum John" is his nickname among lawyers. But, he'll go places because he does favors for people in high places and satisfies people's sick need for retribution. Pontius Pilate is still very much alive and well."

"Daddy," Meaghan broke in, "in the movie is Jean Valjean Jesus, do you think?"

"What do you think?" I asked.

"He was just like Jesus. He was even willing to go back to prison just so an innocent man wouldn't be condemned in his place," Donald answered.

"Yeah, and he always helped out everybody, just like Jesus did when he was on earth," Meaghan added. "I think he must be Jesus."

"He surely was a lot like Jesus. Maybe that's what we're all supposed to be like if we are Jesus' followers," Maureen commented.

"I think that was part of my experience this morning at mass," I said. "What is Christianity all about? I experienced the mysticism of our religion, and then I thought of the corrupt element in our religion all at the same moment as Jesus is offered to his Father in the mass' re-presentation of Calvary. Seeing it all at once shook me to the core. It's like the paradox Jesus was talking about when he said the kingdom of heaven is like a catch of fish; some of those fish are good, and some of them really stink. He was straightforward in his sense of reality, warning us that the kingdom of heaven on earth will always be a mystery, hard to embrace, but necessary to prepare us for heaven. I am so glad we saw the movie tonight. It is all about what I have been struggling with all day."

3

I HAD A LONG BREAK AT THE OFFICE the next day between an early appearance at court and a meeting with a client at eleven. So I decided to pay a visit to the lady Charlie had visited the day before. After my court appearance I drove down to the neighborhood and parked in front of the house.

After ringing the doorbell twice with no response, I knocked on the door. I was determined to wait as long as I had to. Finally, the lady appeared behind the curtain on the door window, and pulling aside the curtain slightly, she asked what I wanted.

"My name is Martin O'Dea, ma'am. I am a lawyer and a member of Sacred Heart parish. Yesterday, Charlie came to mass and sat not too far in front of me, and I know that you and he are friends. I am concerned about Charlie. He seems as if he could use some help, and I was wondering if you could help me. I would like to help him if he needs anything."

The woman must have felt comfortable with what I said. She opened the door and invited me inside and through the hallway into her kitchen. I took a business card out of my wallet with my name and the name of the law firm and offered it to her. She looked at it, put it into her apron pocket, and motioned for me to sit down at the table.

Hanging over the table was a beautiful lamp with a Tiffany shade, brilliant with shades of various colors. Looking around the room, I guessed the woman had been living there for most of her

life, probably since childhood, and I guessed her age to be close
to ninety. The house, no doubt belonged to her parents, whom
she had most likely cared for in their old age. Everything in the
house, including the occupant, was a genuine antique.

"My name is Susie, Susie Delaney," she said in a gentle voice.

I could tell immediately she was a refined person and sensed
she was well educated.

"Miss Delaney, you sound Irish. You must be a member of our
parish, too," I said.

"You're right. I am both. But, I have not been strong enough
in years to walk all the way up there for mass. I watch mass on
television, usually on Mother Angelica's channel. But I do miss
receiving communion."

"Would you like me to have someone from the church bring
you communion," I asked.

"I would love that."

"Once in a while my family and I could pick you up and bring
you to mass with us, if you would like that."

She had tears in her eyes. "Oh, I would love to go to mass
again before I die. I would not be able to go often with you.
Sometimes I am very weak, and I am afraid it would be too much
for me, but maybe once in a while, or on important occasions like
Easter and Christmas, and on the Blessed Mother's feast days. I
don't know how many more Easters I will have left, or Christ-
mases either. Sometimes I think I stay alive just to help poor
Charlie. He seems so helpless."

"I can tell you worry about him, Miss Delaney."

"Just call me Susie, please. No one has called me Miss Delaney
since I retired from teaching at the university."

"So she is well educated," I thought, "from an honorable old
Irish family, still with the lace curtains on the windows."

"Yes, I've worried about Charlie ever since he came down the
street over a year ago. He's not like the other homeless people
wandering around. He keeps pretty much to himself, but he stops
in once or twice a week to see if I need anything from the store.

He is so thoughtful. I try to give him breakfast, but he is so shy, he eats like a bird. I don't know how he lives. He has had an interesting background. It was almost a year before he opened up and told me about himself."

"He seems like an interesting man."

"That he is. You would be surprised what a fascinating life he has lived. So many things have happened in his life."

"He is a likable fellow, Susie, even if he is different, and you're right, he seems to be harmless, a gentle soul."

"He's been a big help to me, especially in the bad weather when I can't get out. Not that I go out often even in good weather, but when I need something for the house, or have run out of food or medicine, he always shows up sooner or later and goes shopping for me.

"How long has he been living around here?"

"About a year at most, I'd say. He wasn't here long before he got himself into trouble. It was in the papers. He was accused of stealing a bicycle, of all things. He told the police that he didn't do it, but the police pressured two men they had arrested for something else to testify against Charlie. It was near election time, and they didn't care whom they convicted, whether innocent or not. A conviction would impress the voters. The men didn't even know Charlie, but they still testified against him to get a lighter sentence for crimes they had committed. So, Charlie was indicted. The judge tried to get Charlie to plead to a lesser charge, and when Charlie said he could not confess to a crime he had not committed, the judge said he was being arrogant. Charlie told the judge that he was mistaking integrity for arrogance, which angered the judge, so he gave Charlie time in jail. He had to be released six weeks later when the mother of the boy whose bike was missing found it in the shed in their backyard. Charlie was freed immediately, though the judge never had the decency to apologize. Charlie's record was cleared, however, which was the important thing."

At that point I finally remembered where I had first seen Charlie. It was in court. All the details were coming back. I had recognized at the time that the poor wretch, whoever he was, was not guilty. The judge had known it too, but he was determined to convict him. It was clear the judge had a bad, almost spiteful, attitude toward the fellow. The man was taken away in cuffs. I felt sad for him. It appeared he had no one in the world to be there with him as support or comfort at what must have been a terrifying experience for him.

As I was recalling the details of the incident, Susie took an ancient cast-iron teapot off the stove and filled the two cups she had previously placed on the table, then sat down to continue her story about Charlie.

"And that wasn't the only time poor Charlie was arrested," she continued. "He once had a part-time job working on a farm with some migrant farmers. One day the place was raided by immigration enforcement agents, and they were all arrested, Charlie among them. Since Charlie had no identification of any kind, the judge assumed he was part of the group. He does have a slight accent. Charlie said nothing in his own defense. He was put on a bus with the others and shipped out across the country for deportation to a town just across the border in Mexico. All the way to the Mexican border they were housed in jails—every night a different jail in a different city or town. I could not help crying when Charlie told me what had happened. I guess the man is so simple he doesn't know how to speak up and defend himself. He eventually came back across the border and found his way back here by hopping trains. I guess he feels comfortable here. He's been here ever since.

"I could tell Charlie was angry about the plight of the people who felt forced to emigrate in order to survive, even though he spoke calmly and was very matter of fact. He then made a remark that made me realize that he is not as backward as I thought. He said he had heard a politician on the radio one day telling the American people that there is relatively full employment in the United States. Charlie then looked at me and said in stern, measured tones, 'If we have full employment, then whose jobs are the thirty million immigrants taking? There must be a severe shortage of labor to attract them here.' I thought that was quite an astute observation."

I then asked, "Do you know, Susie, if Charlie has had an education?"

"You're going to be shocked at this, but Charlie, I think, is brilliant, even though sometimes he appears simple. I don't know about his formal education, but I do know, at least from what he has told me, and I am inclined to believe him, that he spent the short time he was in jail teaching other inmates to read and write and even taught them mathematics. Some of the inmates ended up taking education courses and even decided they wanted to go to college when they get out. Charlie said they were very talented, and it was a shame so much of their lives had been wasted."

"I am surprised you were able to get so much out of Charlie. He seems like such a private man."

"Oh, I had my ways. I had to be subtle and gentle with him, but little by little I was able to wheedle it out of him. He has become like a son to me, the son I never had. I took care of my father and mother all my life and lived here with them when they got old. Now that I am old, and most of the neighbors are long gone, Charlie is all that I have, and yet he is really a stranger. I don't even know where he lives. I have a sneaking suspicion he may be sleeping in an abandoned house somewhere in the neighborhood. He must be terribly lonely, though he doesn't seem to be. I think he lives in his own world, where he may be happy and very much at peace, though I don't know how he survives the bitter cold winter in these parts."

"Susie, maybe we can all go to mass together next week. If Charlie would like to come with us, we can all have brunch afterward. Do you have a phone? If you do, I will call you and check with you."

"That would be wonderful, Martin. I do have a phone. I'll have to make sure Charlie looks presentable. I think we'd all be embarrassed if we didn't clean him up. Oh, and could you do me a big favor before you return to work? Would you mind picking up a box of gas mantles for me?"

"Gas mantles? What are they?"

"Don't you know? I guess I'm getting too old. They are those little wire webs, like tiny fishnets, that were used on gas jets in old houses. There, see? There's one on the wall near the door," she said as she took a match out of a box and lighted the jet.

I was wide eyed. I had never seen such a phenomenon. "Where would I find those gas mantles?" I asked.

"The nice man in the local hardware store five blocks from here keeps them in stock for me."

"I'd be glad to get them for you."

I couldn't help but laugh at her sense of reality, in spite of her age, and was impressed with how much she cared for Charlie. I was sure he was one of the few people she ever saw. His visits probably gave her something to live for, knowing there was at least one person in this world who needed her. I walked out feeling her loneliness, wondering what kind of a teacher she had been and what subjects she had taught.

I had never imagined I would have been so thoroughly entertained by an old lady well into her nineties. I wondered if Charlie was just taking advantage of this vulnerable woman; certainly, she was intelligent and frugal enough to have squirreled away savings somewhere. Maybe he was after her money. Then I felt guilty for again judging him so rashly. Charlie seemed too honest to even think of something like that, but then, a harsh voice seemed to whisper in my ear, maybe he just pretends to be that way and is really cunning. There was no way to know. I felt ashamed for being so petty. "Why can't I just accept him as a simple innocuous victim of life's fortunes? Another example of *Les Miserables*? Someone with a story I cannot even fathom?"

4

AT THE HARDWARE STORE I HAD NO TROUBLE getting the gas mantles. The man knew just what I was looking for and even knew where they were going. "Say hello to Miss Delaney. She sure is sharp for her age. She was a great teacher! My son had her for science in college. Quite a woman! She worked with that Italian guy—what's his name?—the one who worked on the Manhattan Project."

"You don't mean Enrico Fermi?"

"That's the one. She was very involved in that kind of stuff. No one would ever believe that a woman who was involved in putting together the atomic bomb was living right in our midst in a rundown part of town. She's such a modest person, you would never know she is an important person."

"That's amazing. I never imagined her being involved in something like that. She is so unpretentious and so humble. She just looks like a nice old lady."

"That's the way she likes it. I guess she's not too proud of how the government used her work. She told me she prays every night for the victims of the atomic bombs. She went to Hiroshima and Nagasaki after the war and apologized to the people in the area for what we had done to them. She was furious when she found out that there were no extensive military installations in those cities, at least not of the level that there were in other places. She was even more upset when she found out from

20

Franciscan priests in Nagasaki that the two places bombed were the only places in Japan where Catholics had lived for the past four hundred years while surviving the cruelest persecutions from hostile Japanese emperors. She cried when she told me how guilty she felt, especially since she was Catholic. She later became friends with a priest here whose father loaded the atomic bombs on the planes. It troubled him for the rest of his life as well."

"Do you know that fellow Charlie who is Miss Delaney's friend?" I asked.

"Yeah, he's harmless enough, like a little kid, really. Comes in occasionally to get things for Miss Delaney or for some other people he visits. A very honest fellow. I once gave him too much change, and after he counted it, he told me I gave him twenty-five cents too much. I told him to keep it for himself. He was thrilled."

Leaving the hardware store I went down to the old lady's house, proud as a little kid who had gotten the things he had been sent to get for his mother. Needless to say, Miss Delaney was pleased. She wanted to reimburse me for the gas mantles, but I wouldn't hear of it.

I wanted to ask her about her work on the Manhattan Project but thought better of it, knowing that the subject would be painful for her.

"Martin, thank you so much for getting the mantles for me. I'll show you how they work."

She then proceeded to demonstrate the whole operation for me, explaining where the gas came from, and how she attached the mantle to the gas jet. I was fascinated watching her set up the simple operation. When she lighted it, I was surprised how much it brightened the room, which had been dark because the shades were down.

Then as we sat and chatted, discussing the adventures of Charlie, I could not help but wonder if the stories were all true or just fantasies. And yet Miss Delaney certainly seemed to have clear enough judgment to discern reality from fiction—or the fantasies of a wandering hobo. *She* certainly did not look upon him as such; that was clear. Perhaps it was the accuracy of the details about these strange places so far away that convinced her that what he was saying was true. He could not have made up the names of the cantinas and the various churches and shrines and market-places he visited in Mexico if he had not been there. Nor would he know the types of clothes and shoes the people wore. She described how Charlie cried when he told of how haughty and aloof many priests were in those places and how so many in America were just as self-important. This made me wonder even more about this wandering stranger.

Susie told me that Charlie could even sing some of the songs the Spanish people sang when they gathered for parties and dances. And he was able to sing them in their native tongues. As she went on, I found myself drawn to the world of this human oddity. The one thing that troubled me was *why* I was allowing myself to be sucked into this whirlpool. I was, after all, Marty O'Dea, the sharp lawyer who always demanded facts and proof for everything and was so cynical about people and even about life.

When I left Susie that morning, my head was spinning. She certainly was not the simple old lady I first thought she was. She was quite intelligent and a fascinating woman besides. The stories she told me did not, as I had hoped, resolve my questions about Charlie, however. Instead, they intensified my curiosity about him. "Why can't I just let this whole thing go away and get on with my work? Who is this Charlie, and what is he here for?"

5

THAT NIGHT I TOLD MAUREEN ABOUT MY VISIT with Miss Delaney. The kids were eavesdropping and pestered me to let them hear all the details of what the elderly woman had related to me. I was happy they cared, even though I was surprised they were so interested. But it was clear we were all hooked on the daily events in these two strange people's lives, though I did wonder whether it was just morbid curiosity. What was there about Charlie and that brilliant old lady, who was as obsolete and irrelevant at this point in her life as the bum who came to visit her?

The next time I visited Susie, she was in a happy mood. She was excited about going to church the following Sunday morning with me and my family.

"Martin, how have you been?" she asked, as we enjoyed freshly baked lemon scones and hot tea.

"Very well, thank you, though I have to admit, I have been confused ever since I met that friend of ours."

"You mean Charlie?"

"Yes. I can't get him out of my mind. Even my family keeps pestering me for more information about him."

"Well, Martin, you are not alone in that. While he seems to remember some things clearly, like all the experiences he has had in different places and what the people were like and how they lived, he doesn't seem to remember other things, like his own name."

Susie shook her head slowly. "I will never forget that story he told me about his forced trip to Mexico with all those migrant farmers who had been deported for being in the country illegally. I told you briefly about that experience, but there was more to it.

"When Charlie arrived in Mexico he had nowhere to go, and no family. The people were very nice to him and took care of him. Though they themselves were poor and had little room in their homes for any more people, one family made a room out of a little shack in the back of their own simple house and let him live there, sharing with him what little food they had.

"Charlie learned a lot during the time he was in Mexico. He even learned to speak the common people's language, and this is what totally convinced me that he really did have all these experiences. When he came back to the United States, he was still wearing traditional Mexican clothes, complete with a huge Mexican sombrero that had belonged to an old man who had recently died. Charlie seemed totally oblivious to how ridiculous he looked. When I first saw him, I broke out laughing and couldn't stop. At first he was embarrassed, and then, realizing how ridiculous he must have looked to me, he started laughing too. After that he went back to wearing his own clothes, including the brown pants with the light-blue patch near the knee.

"While he was in Mexico, he learned much about the lives of the people there. He felt comfortable among them, because they seemed as simple as he was, and they all trusted him because he was so simple. The people in the village had little to eat and no medical facility to go to when they were sick. Charlie felt sorry for them, and when they shared their simple meals with him, he usually gave most of it to the children sitting near him when the grownups weren't looking.

"The people were in desperate straits. Charlie thought he should do something to help them, since they gave of what little they had to keep him alive. But he did not have the slightest idea what to do. He decided to see if there was any place where he could find a job.

"On one of his treks he came across a huge estate on a steep hillside. He got past the gate and found access to the mansion, where he was stopped by the guards.

"Approaching him with their weapons drawn, one of the men asked him how he got inside the gate.

"'I just walked in while the guards were chasing some kids away,' Charlie said in broken Spanish. 'I was hoping I could talk to the owner.'

"The two guards laughed aloud. 'Talk to the owner? Now why would such an important man like you want to talk to the owner? I am sure you must have a thriving business of your own,' one of them said, mocking what must have appeared to them a modern Don Quixote, a pretentious fool.

"'Because I think we can talk business,' Charlie said, totally unfazed by their ridicule. He had a purpose and would not be put off. Charlie was getting nowhere with these fellows until the owner happened to walk out of the house and ask what was going on. Charlie spoke to the owner in Spanish, perfect Spanish this time. The man invited Charlie inside and asked what he could do for him. Charlie told the landowner that there was a family he was visiting who had a small vineyard, with three different varieties of wine grapes that produced one of the best wines he had ever tasted. He told the man that he had grown up in southern Italy and was familiar with excellent wines, and that he had come from Italy to get to know the common people in the Americas. He suggested to the man that since he was aware that the local soil was excellent soil for wine-making grapes, he could develop a very lucrative wine business.

"The owner was impressed, and during the next two weeks Charlie arranged for his peasant friends to meet with the owner. He himself worked out the legal details of the deal. The owner, who turned out to be a decent man, would form a company, and

Charlie's peasant friends would own 25 percent of the business and receive 25 percent of any profits. The owner agreed to set aside three hundred acres of his huge estate initially for wine-grape growing and for the winery. The owner was sold on the idea when he sampled the wine the family made. He was greatly impressed and realized the great marketing potential.

"I could tell," Miss Delaney told me, "that Charlie felt proud that he was able to help his poor friends who had done without in order to help him. Charlie contacts the owner on occasion to find out how well the business is doing. They now have expanded to five hundred acres and have been very successful in marketing the wine not only in Mexico but in neighboring countries."

I had a difficult time swallowing this story, as there was no way I could imagine that simple creature pulling off anything like a character in a Frank Capra movie.

"Ever since his experience with the migrants," Susie continued, "he has had a feeling for those people. He insists that they are not illegal immigrants, but rather refugees fleeing starvation and destitution. The experience made him think differently about many of the nice things he had previously believed about America."

"He sure is difficult to understand," I told her. "I don't know why I have such an interest in knowing more about him."

Then I asked, "Susie, is 'Charlie' his real name?"

"I have no way of knowing for sure, but I don't think so. I'm not even convinced that he knows. When I asked him once, all he said was, 'Everybody calls me Charlie, so that must be my name.' Maybe he has had an accident or an illness at some time or other, and it damaged his memory. He never talks about anything personal. At times I think his simplicity is his way of hiding his identity."

"I think that is why I am so curious about him. I guess his apparent detachment from reality makes me feel I have to keep an eye on him, maybe protect him. Does he ever talk about relatives or family?"

"I once broached the subject, but I didn't get anywhere. It caught him up short, and he thought for a minute. It was as if he was trying hard to remember but could not come up with anything, so I just changed the subject. I could tell he was embarrassed, as if he should know whether he had family or not. I have to tell you, Martin, I got a surprise visit one day. Out of a clear blue sky, two men came to visit me looking for information about Charlie. Once Charlie started coming here, they apparently became interested in him and checked him out quite thoroughly.

"It was interesting how they did this. They got his fingerprints off the door knob, and, after having them processed, were able to find out interesting pieces of information about him, though the information was not complete because records of his fingerprints go back only as far as the first time he was in trouble with the law. But in time they found out from various individuals that Charlie was in training in a special college in Rome, although they could not get sufficient information about the location and nature of the facility. Then they told me something very shocking." She paused. "I'll share it with you, Martin. His real name is Carlo Brunini, and he was raised in southern Italy. He also studied canon law at one time—the official law of the Catholic Church. He was quite widely respected for his learning and his talent, but then something happened, and he seems to have just fallen off the map. There were rumors of former colleagues having spotted him on occasion, but they were not certain it was the same person; they could not imagine that the shabby homeless individual they saw could be the same person they had known.

"When these men came to visit and shared all this with me, they also asked how I knew Charlie. They smiled at the story I told them and were assured there was no reason for them to be concerned. When I asked them what they knew, they were quite straightforward and told me what I just shared with you. They also mentioned that Charlie liked to take rides on railroad cars, his favorite way to travel to distant places. There are records of him doing this in a number of cities, though the police never pursued it because he seemed harmless enough."

I was beginning to see that this simple vagrant who had walked into church that morning was a fascinating character, and I was now feeling quite proud of myself for having the insight to notice as soon as I saw him that there was something unusual about this particular drifter. Now I was enjoying the pursuit of his identity and his real life. It was becoming an adventure unlike anything I had ever encountered before.

"Susie, I am so grateful for your kindness and your patience in telling me all these things about our friend. Have you had a chance to talk to Charlie about all of us going to church this Sunday?"

"Oh, yes, I have, as a matter of fact. He was surprised when I talked to him about it, but then he brightened up and said that would be exciting, and he would be looking forward to it. So, if you don't mind picking us up Sunday morning a little before time for mass, we will be ready. And I will make sure that he is properly dressed."

After a few more minutes of small talk, I thanked Susie for being so gracious and left.

Needless to say, my family was surprised when I told them we were going to take Miss Delaney and Charlie to mass Sunday morning.

When Sunday arrived, we drove to Miss Delaney's house, picked up our guests, and continued on to church. Though Charlie's hair and beard looked trimmed, his clothes were the ones he always wore. Still, they were ironed, and the pants had a crease in them, which made me smile, because it looked so incongruous with the blue patch near the right knee.

As we entered the church, people moved politely away, and when we took seats in one of the pews in the rear, people gave us plenty of space. When everyone sat down, Charlie stayed kneeling, with his elbows on the back of the pew in front of him and his face buried in his hands. He stayed that way for the long-est time. Since he was different anyway, no one thought anything of it. "He probably doesn't know what church is about," I thought, "and is just trying to show he's interested. Or maybe that's the way he sleeps when he goes to church."

At communion the priest passed him by again and without making a fuss, Charlie humbly walked on. A deacon who was assisting with communion saw what had happened, and he walked over to Charlie with his ciborium and quietly called to him and gave him communion. Charlie was deeply touched and smiled as the deacon said, "The Body of Jesus." He responded without thinking, "Grazie a Dio." Charlie took the sacred bread, kissed it, and put it in his mouth. Looking at the deacon, he smiled. "Thank you. One day you will be a priest." Mystified, the deacon went back to his place and continued giving the Eucha-rist to the others who were waiting in his line.

After mass I looked at Charlie and bluntly asked him, "What was that all about with the deacon?"

"It was nothing. I was touched by his concern. He offered me communion, and I thanked him."

"Charlie, you're an enigma. What strange behavior. Why didn't you just do what everyone else does?"

"That was a special moment," Charlie said. "In a flash I saw that deacon's future."

"You saw his future?" I pursued, without thinking that I was intruding on his privacy.

"Yes, he will not always be a deacon." Then he stopped and said no more.

I had arranged for brunch at a local restaurant. When we got there, we had more fun than we could have anticipated. Even Meaghan enjoyed herself and was surprisingly pleasant during the whole meal. The biggest surprise was Charlie's enormous ap-petite, as if he had not eaten in days. He finished two servings of pancakes and sausages, a dish of fresh fruit, and then strawberries dipped in a white chocolate sauce, along with two cups of coffee. Everyone was delighted to see the big happy smile on his face when he finished.

"Thank you for the wonderful meal. I wish all my homeless brothers and sisters at the railroad yard could enjoy such a feast."

"Those homeless people have really become a family to you, haven't they?" Maureen asked. "But it is such a dangerous way to have to live."

"Life is dangerous. For a homeless person, going to sleep at night is dangerous. Getting up in the morning is dangerous. Walking around the streets is dangerous. The homeless are shunned. They are hated by many well-to-do people because they think they're scum feeding off society, a drain on the resources of upright citizens. They are fair targets for some mean-spirited police, who harass them and brutalize them whenever they get a chance. They are sometimes targeted by ambitious cops and district attorneys when they need a quick conviction for a murder they can't solve."

"So, Charlie, why are you homeless?" I blurted out.

"I suppose you could say things just happened, and I found myself in a predicament where I really had no other choice."

"I think we all are learning from your experiences, Charlie," I responded.

I paid the tab, and we all left. After dropping Miss Delaney and Charlie off, we drove home.

I had no idea where Charlie went after we dropped him off with Miss Delaney. He never accepted the kind old lady's continued invitations to stay at her house, even though there were extra rooms. Since he was familiar with the railroad, it had an attraction for him, as well as for other homeless people, who often gathered along the tracks. They stayed away from the nearby "nice" people and put up a tent or built a little shack in an isolated place where they could have a fire.

Later I discovered that Charlie spent many a night along the tracks with others of "his kind," as he had come to think of himself. He was one of those souls destined by God to understand just how little and insignificant they are, even though divine love makes them important to God. But, they never have the joy of knowing that they are important. Society will always prevent that. They are just unwanted nuisances pricking the consciences of people who wish they would just disappear.

Although the transformation took time, Charlie must have finally come to the realization that he was one of the unwashed, unwanted homeless people who meant nothing to anyone. He had become what everyone *thought* of him and others of his kind. That experience brought with it a compassion and love for the outcast that passed all understanding.

Although I didn't realize it at the time, Charlie would soon leave us for the life he had abandoned and for the new life he was meant to live. One day I would understand the mystery of Charlie and know that it was the greatest mystery of all.

CARLO

*So now you are no longer strangers but
are citizens with all of God's holy people.
You are members of God's household.*
—EPHESIANS 2:19

6

Palagiano, Italy

ONCE A LITTLE VILLAGE ON THE OUTSKIRTS of the Roman port of Tarentum from which Roman ships left for the far-flung ports of the empire, modern-day Palagiano is a growing if still poor part of Italy. Only three years earlier the village celebrated the appointment and consecration of one of its own as bishop and soon as archbishop of Taranto.

Since his childhood, Carlo Brunini was different from the other children, not in a strange way, but in his serious yet humorously boyish ways. He was the middle child of a family of seven children, and by the time he was ten years old, he was expected to help with the cooking and caring for his younger brother and two little sisters, who adored their big brother. He worked after school, running errands for neighbors. The tiny amount of money he made was a help to his parents, and he was glad to help his neighbors.

He excelled at school. He was blessed with a memory that was flawless, but even more important, a mind that could penetrate complex people as well as complex problems. His playful, self-effacing humor disguised his intelligence and enhanced his popularity, especially with the girls in the village. By the time he was thirteen, he had four girlfriends. Because he loved them all so much and could not marry all of them, he told them one day he had decided to become a priest. Carlo entered the seminary at fourteen and was ordained to the priesthood at twenty-five. Remarkably, he was immediately sent to the Vatican diplomatic college to be trained for service as a Vatican diplomat. While studying he also worked in parishes, and six years after ordination was appointed and consecrated bishop of Taranto at the age of thirty-one. Two years after that was made archbishop. The Vatican had been watching his progress carefully, ever since his seminary rector made them aware of what an exceptional student and deeply spiritual young man he was and what an asset he could be to the church.

Now, on the brink of a decision that would not only upset the Vatican officials but might destroy the rest of his potentially brilliant career in the church, he had asked for a special audience with the Holy Father, which was readily granted. The pope was concerned about the crisis troubling this young archbishop. The Vatican could ill afford to lose a cleric in whom it had invested so much education and training with the hope that he would one day fill an important role in the church.

On his way to the Vatican, Archbishop Brunini stopped at Palagiano for a brief visit. He was not sure whether he would have another occasion to visit his family and friends before embarking on a personal mission that would be either of great spiritual benefit to him personally or the beginning of his downfall—or maybe both.

His mother was only in her sixties, and her health was relatively good. She was constantly busy with her children and grandchildren. She had always been Carlo's confidante, and now he wanted to share his plans with her and assure her that what he was about to do was no reason for concern.

So the two could be alone, he took her for a walk in the garden and, sitting under the grape arbor, told her in a general way the startling plan he intended to present to the Holy Father.

"My son, are you sure this is what you really feel in your heart you should do? There are so many people who love you and depend on you for leadership and support in these very difficult times."

"Mother, I have thought this over for a long time. I need to learn about people and situations that are lacking in my experience. I need that experience in order to be a good shepherd, as Jesus wants his priests to be."

"But, son, you are a good shepherd, the best we have ever had. If ever a bishop was like Jesus, it is you."

"No, Mother, I try, but I am still lacking, and I know God wants me to be more prepared than I am for what my work demands of me and will demand in the future. I have to do this, Mother. Trust me. I will be careful, and I know I can count on your prayers. Since God always hears your prayers, there is nothing to fear. Give me your blessing, Mother, before I leave, and know that I love you."

"May the Lord always bless you, Carlo, with Jesus' heart and mind, so you will always see things through his mind and love his sheep with his heart."

The next morning at the entrance to the Vatican, Carlo passed the colorful Swiss Guards and proceeded to the pope's office. The pope's secretary announced his arrival: "Padre Santo, l'arcivescovo Brunini è qui per il suo appuntamento."

"Come in, come in, my dear archbishop. I have been waiting anxiously since your call."

When Carlo attempted to kiss the pope's ring, the pope instead gave him a big hug. The pope gestured for Carlo to sit in an armchair as he seated himself opposite his guest.

Carlo calmly explained his plan, asked for the pope's approval, and sat back while the pope considered his most unusual request.

After a long, reflective silence, the pope responded. "My dear Carlo, I cannot say I am thrilled about this. I have serious reservations about your plan. But because of my trust in your reputation for prudence, I am asking you to explain yourself in more detail. If I have a better picture of what you have in mind, perhaps I'll feel more at ease with this rather surprising request."

"Your Holiness, please know that I have not made this decision lightly. I do not come from a wealthy family. We have struggled through life, and my family sacrificed much for my education. Now that I have been so honored by the church and entrusted with serious responsibilities, I am having a very difficult time with all the honors and adulation people show me, even those people who I know detest everything we stand for. There is something unhealthy about this show of obsequiousness. I do not feel at all comfortable with the way people treat the hierarchy. I often get the feeling that many good Catholics don't feel comfortable with it either. We may be inclined to look upon their show of respect as acceptance of what we say and what we teach, but I feel in my bones that their values and thoughts are far from what is sacred to us. I sense a bitter resentment in many. They show us superficial respect but do not share our values because in many ways our values are not theirs. I feel a need to live the way people live, and not just ordinary people, but the poor, the homeless, the victims of injustice and contempt. I want to be treated the way they are treated, to feel what they feel, to live the way they live, so I can understand what it is like to be held in such contempt by society, including many Christians. Among my own flock there are the poor and the homeless, as well as the anticlericals in southern Italy, and they come to me with their problems and their hurts and their feelings of injustice. If I am to be a good shepherd after the heart of Jesus, I have to get to know my sheep, not just in fantasy, but in real life. I need to feel their pain as Jesus did and respond to them with the feelings Jesus had because he understood the loneliness and the fears and the pain that his sheep were suffering."

"That is very noble, Carlo," the pope responded, "and I am deeply touched by your sentiments, but are you being realistic?

If everyone wanted to do what you want to do, we'd have no one to run the church. You already have a reputation as a saintly priest who loves his people and is caring for them. What exactly do you intend to do if I grant you the leave you request?"

"Holy Father, I intend to live the life of a homeless man. No one will recognize me. An unkempt beard and shaggy hair and old clothes will be camouflage enough. If you are anxious, perhaps I could start on the streets of Rome. If you hear anything that gives you concern, Holy Father, I will immediately abide by your judgment.

"Carlo, my dear Carlo, you amaze me. You have the heart of the street actors I see wandering around Rome. Your words pour out like honey. But I know you are sincere, and I am interested in seeing what happens. I am willing to give it a try. But be prudent and be careful! There are enough cynics in Rome who would love to hold us up to ridicule if they ever found out that an archbishop is going around Rome masquerading as a homeless beggar. Can't you just imagine the headlines?"

Carlo could not avoid laughing at the thought, and though the pope was serious, he too chuckled.

"Holy Father, I promise I will be most prudent."

"Carlo, I will call your vicar general and assign him to oversee the archdiocese during your leave.

"Thank you, Holy Father!"

"You have my permission, Carlo. Please be careful."

"May I have your blessing, Holy Father?"

"My son, may the Lord bless you and keep you in his care and watch over you, especially on cold and dangerous nights, and bring you back to us safe."

The two men embraced, and Carlo reiterated his promise as he left. "I will not cause you or the church embarrassment, Holy Father. Of this you can be sure."

7

AFTER LEAVING THE VATICAN OFFICES, Carlo directed his secretary, Monsignor Agnelli, to drive him to the Via Appia so he could visit the Basilica of St. John Lateran, the ancient Roman church originally built by Constantine in 316 to honor St. John the Evangelist. It had since become the official cathedral church of the bishop of Rome. Carlo wanted to spend time there praying for God's help in his new endeavor.

After that visit Monsignor Agnelli drove him to the Catacomb of St. Sebastian, on the Via Appia, so Carlo could pray for his favorite saint's intercession that the Lord would look kindly on his undertaking and bless his pilgrimage-retreat among the poor.

One of the most colorful of the early Roman martyrs, St. Sebastian was supposedly born in Narbonne, Gaul, and raised a Christian. He entered the Roman army as a young man and was later made tribune and commandant of the Praetorian Guard, the emperor's private security force. When Emperor Diocletian found out that Sebastian was a Christian, he had him condemned to be target practice for the Mauritanian archers, who left him for dead. When some noble Roman women came to bury his body, he was still alive. They took him into the imperial palace where they lived and nursed him back to health. He later confronted the emperor for his persecution of Christians. Thinking he was seeing a ghost, the emperor was at first shocked, but then he had

Sebastian beaten to death. It was this saint to whom Carlo prayed for protection.

When Carlo emerged from the catacomb, he was like a butterfly that had turned back into a caterpillar. He was no longer wearing his clerical robes but was dressed in the clothes of a poor man—wrinkled dark pants, old workman's shoes, light-brown shirt, and a worn and peeling brown leather jacket fitting down to below his hips.

Once in the car he directed Monsignor Agnelli to take him to the main railroad station, where he knew he could meet some of his new companions.

"Are you sure you want to do this, Excellency? You know it might hurt your whole career."

"Mario, I have to do it. I'm just afraid that I might not have what it takes to endure what the poor endure day and night, every day. It takes more than courage. Pray for me."

"Every morning at mass, Excellency."

"Thank you, Mario, and I will pray for you as well, and for your dear mother that she may get better."

"Grazie, molto grazie, Padre."

As Carlo exited the car at the station, he accidentally tore a hole in the right leg of his trousers.

"You had better get back in, Excellency. There's a patch in a little courtesy packet in the glove compartment, left from your last plane trip."

Getting back in the car, Carlo retrieved the packet and nervously tried to patch the tear.

"Here, let me do it. I do this all the time."

"See, Mario, I have a lot to learn."

"About things that matter little."

"It's the little things that do matter, the little things that are so important in people's lives. I have so much to learn about what is important to people."

"There, but not like brand new. The blue patch doesn't match with brown."

"Well, it's real."

They both guffawed at the ironic situation. Then Carlo hugged his friend and walked off into the oblivion of the busy station. Mario watched him for a minute or so until horns started honking; then, with a tear trickling down his cheek, he gave a last look at the ragged man walking slowly into the crowd to become one of the least of Jesus' brothers.

No sooner had Carlo begun his venture than he had his first shock. He met a man in even shabbier clothes at the entrance to the railroad station who seemed to recognize him. "Don't I know you, sir?" he said to Carlo.

"I doubt it, Signore. I'm new around here. I just drifted in from out of town."

"Oh, my mistake. I thought you were a friend I knew years ago, who grew up with me near Naples."

"Nothing happens by mistake," Carlo said. "I no doubt will see you around. What is your real name?"

"Peppino, just Peppino."

"Mine is Carlo."

"Carlo, yes, Carlo. Are you sure I do not know you?"

Carlo could feel the perspiration pouring out under his arms as he tried to recall any time or place where this man could possibly have known him or even casually met him. But he kept his expression calm.

"I am quite sure," Carlo responded. "Otherwise I would have recognized you. I never forget a face, especially the face of a friend. I have to say, though, you are not just an ordinary beggar. You are well bred."

The man started to cry. "Yes, I have not always been a beggar. I was a priest. I had a falling out with my bishop, and he took away my faculties to function as a priest in his diocese. Now I roam the streets, trying to be a priest to the abandoned and the outcasts. I hope God has mercy on me."

The shock was almost too much for Carlo. The very first homeless beggar he meets is a priest, prompting him to wonder how many priests have become homeless beggars, perhaps not of their own choosing. Maybe God was already teaching him something he needed to know. What would drive a priest to become homeless? Maybe God wanted him to take a look at the plight of some priests as well as the plight of the poor.

"Peppino, I am sure God loves you and has a special work for you. You think you know me. Maybe if I knew your name, it might help to jolt my memory."

"Giuseppe. Giuseppe Anastasi. But they call me Peppino."

"No, that is not familiar. But I promise I will never forget that name, nor will I ever forget you, Father. You are still a priest, still doing Jesus' work among the most rejected of society. You are a good shepherd, Father Peppino. I won't forget you. Would you give me your blessing?"

Carlo bowed his head as the priest rested his right hand on his head and recited the blessing, "Benedicat te Omnipotens Deus, Pater, et Filius, et Spiritus Sanctus. Benedictio ejus descendat super te and maneat semper."

"Molto grazie, Padre," Carlo said, thanking him, noticing tears in the priest's eyes.

"That's the first time I have given anyone my priestly blessing in four years. It felt good."

"Come on, Peppino, you are still a priest and a good priest. Don't forget that. Keep your mind and heart open to grace and don't be afraid to follow where God leads you."

"You should be a priest yourself, Carlo. I think you'd make a good one. You care. Many don't care."

"Thank you, friend. I wish I had an address to give you, but I don't have one either. Hopefully, we'll meet again. If you need me, ask around for Carlo. I have a feeling all we beggars are like a family. In time we get to know one another and the special places we hang out."

"Sounds like you're new to the road. Do you have a place to eat?"

"No, Peppino."

"A nice place is Il Forno. An old lady owns it. She acts tough, but she's got a good heart, and she helps us a lot. Her name is Margherita. She may give you a little job, but it's not much, just enough to save your pride. Then she'll fill your belly up with a hot meal. She's an angel. Her place is not far from here, only a few blocks down on Via Macchiavelli. Eleven in the morning is good. So is two in the afternoon. She's not too busy at those times, and she can use a little help picking up after tourists' lunchtime."

"Thank you. I appreciate your help. It's all kind of new to me."

Carlo reached out and, in spite of the odor, hugged his new friend and kissed his cheek.

"Ciao, Peppino."

"Ciao, Carlo. Good luck."

As Carlo shuffled down the street, the priest watched him, still wondering where he had seen him. He felt there was something unusual about this man. He did not seem like a beggar, too re-fined perhaps. He noticed the newly sewn patch on his pant leg. Turning around to walk in a different direction, he said a short prayer for whoever he was—or had been.

Carlo walked along, thinking in much the same vein. He re-alized he had not eaten since breakfast and was hungry. For the first time in his life, he did not have the wherewithal to buy food, even something simple. A tinge of panic touched him. He had never had this feeling before. As he walked along he saw a man selling fruit from a cart. The man, if he was a kind fellow, might have given him a few grapes, or maybe a bruised apple, but Carlo's pride kept him from asking. Then a thought struck him. "When the man looks the other way, I might grab an apple or a banana." The thought frightened him. He realized that his first tiny taste of hunger had brought him close to becoming a thief, a crime that could have him arrested and put into jail. "How fine is the line between a highly respected archbishop and a common thief?" he wondered.

As he walked along, passing one restaurant after another, the delicious smells of garlic and onions, tomato sauce, and pork and chickens roasting in the kitchens sharpened his craving for something to satisfy his increasing hunger. Suddenly, the thought of the starving leper outside the rich man's villa in the gospel became very real.

As he was approaching Via Sforza Pallavicini, he thought of stopping at the home run by the Carmelite order. "They will surely give me a meal and treat me with respect." But no, that would not do. He had just begun his pilgrimage-retreat, and he was already beginning to look for an easy escape. Finally, seeing a small restaurant with only one old man dining, he decided to ask the owner if he needed any work done. He would be glad to do whatever work was needed.

"What do you want, a handout?" the owner snarled at him

"No, no. I am hungry, but I don't want something for nothing. I would be glad to do some work for you for just a little something to eat."

"You beggars are all the same—good for nothing, too lazy to do a good day's work, or keep a steady job like the rest of us. Yeah, there's something you can do. Come with me."

The man led Carlo to a room behind the kitchen, took a pail and poured soap into it, and filled it with water. Then he got a brush and gave it to Carlo. "There, you can scrub the floor in the dining room before people start coming in. Make sure you wash all that crud off the floor around the tables or you'll walk out of here with nothing. And hurry it up. I don't want good people to see the likes of you hanging around my place."

Used to constant respect as an archbishop, it was painful, very painful, to be treated with such contempt. "Would it hurt a laborer who had lost his job as much?" Carlo wondered. He realized it would be humiliating for anyone, no matter who or what the person was.

Starting in the corner of the dining room, Carlo got on his hands and knees and scrubbed the dirt-caked tiles beneath each table. It was more strenuous than he imagined it would be. "What if I don't have the strength to finish?" It was only his severe hunger that drove him to continue.

"Jesus, I don't know whether I can go through with this," he prayed. "This is humiliating. I have never been treated like this in my whole life. Whatever possessed me to think that there would be a sort of glamour to being a homeless beggar?"

The loud voice of the owner shocked Carlo from his reverie. "Hurry up. I don't want you here when people come."

Carlo worked faster, then emptied the pail, and filling it with clean water, went over the floor again with a mop. When he finished, he brought the pail back into the utility room, cleaned the mop, washed out the pail, and put the mop upside down to dry.

As he come out of the room, the boss had already looked over the floor. Although he didn't show any approval of the job, he gave Carlo a meatball sandwich and a paper cup full of beer from the tap. Carlo politely asked if he could have a cup of coffee instead.

"You damn bums. Beggars can't be choosy, you know."

Grabbing the paper cup, the man splashed beer all over Carlo's shirt. He gave him the coffee and told him to take his food and eat it across the street.

"Thank you, Signore. I am very grateful for your kindness," Carlo said, though inside he was almost on the verge of tears from the humiliation. For the first time he began to understand why Jesus had such compassion for the poor. Jesus could identify with them because they were treated with the same contempt as the religious officials and the law-obsessed hypocrites treated him.

Walking out into the street, Carlo saw a bench across the way. It felt good just to sit down while he ate his first supper as a homeless beggar. An odd feeling of accomplishment came over him, and for some strange reason lifted his sagging spirit. Blessing himself and looking at his meatball sandwich and cup of stale coffee, he thanked God that he had something to eat.

No one noticed him. He felt invisible, as if he did not even exist to all those people who passed by. Most did not want to notice him sitting there, afraid that he might ask for a handout or just look them in the eye. Only a few hours into his first day and he already was beginning to feel he didn't matter, that he was some kind of invisible creature in the sea of humanity swirling around him. Even when he tried to smile at people, they would avert their eyes, which made him realize that he no longer meant anything in the eyes of society. He was nothing more than a piece of human trash. He was beginning to understand what happens to these wretched street people and why Jesus felt the way he did about how his followers treated them.

A deep sadness enveloped him like a dark cloud. The sadness was like a drug, making him sleepy and weary. His paper cup fell to the ground, his head drooped, and he fell into a sleep so deep that he dreamed of nothing and felt nothing until a tap on his shoulder woke him. He heard a voice asking, "Are you okay, Signore?"

Looking up, he saw a stately carabiniere bending over him, concerned.

"Yes, sir, I must have fallen asleep."

"You don't want to sleep here," the policeman said to him in a kind voice. "There's a little pocket park not far from here. You can rest better there than on this busy street. It's safer. I will be walking past every now and then, and I'll keep an eye out to make sure you're okay."

The carabiniere stooped down and picked up the paper cup, which was partially crumpled, and put it in a nearby trash container. Then he took some lira notes from his pocket and placed them in Carlo's hand, asking him to pray for his sick daughter. He then walked on.

"Grazie, molto grazie, Signore. Pregherò per voi e la vostra famiglia. Yes, I will certainly pray for you and your family."

"That man has faith, great faith," Carlo thought, "asking a beggar to pray for his sick daughter."

The man sounded as though he cared, and it made Carlo feel as if he found a friend, but he knew the carabiniere would not be his friend. He was just a good man who cared. As the officer left, Carlo saw it was getting dark, and a chill was in the air. He realized that he had picked the wrong time to make his pilgrimage-retreat. The weather would soon be cold. "What do the homeless do when winter comes?" he thought.

Carlo knew where the park was and walked toward it. It was early, so there was a chance he could find a vacant bench where he could sleep. He had passed that place many times when studying in Rome. He knew just the place to spend the night, which was near a clump of trees, providing a safe shelter. He wished he had a blanket to cover himself and a pillow too. But these were comforts he would not have, so he might as well not even think about them or he would fall into a sinkhole of self-pity. That was the last thing he needed.

Not being able to break his habit of saying his prayers on his knees, he knelt in front of the bench, blessed himself, and prayed with a humility and a loneliness that he never had experienced before, wondering as he prayed if that was the way all the homeless felt.

"Father, I have to admit I am frightened. Homeless people are attacked and killed almost every night somewhere. I am now one of them. My motives for being one of them may not even be pleasing to you. I don't know how you feel about it. But I hope I can learn something about Jesus and about how he feels toward the poor and the homeless. I want to know what he saw in their lonely lives that made him always so caring of them.

"Father, please don't look away from me, or think badly of me. I need you, and I know I need my guardian angel, whom I have rarely thought of before tonight. Make sure my angel protects me. I have never slept in the streets before. Nor have I ever felt as frightened and insecure as I do tonight.

"Be with me each step of the way and help me to understand what it is I must learn. Then this pilgrimage-retreat, as difficult as it may be, will be worth whatever I have to bear.

"And, dear mother Mary, be near me. Your sweet love will be my solace and my comfort as it always has been, especially in difficult times. St. Athanasius, St. Sebastian, St. Ignatius of Antioch, St. Thérèse, St. Catherine of Alexandria, St. Joseph, and St. Francis, pray for me and be my companions. Your lives were not easy. What you endured encourages me and gives me strength. Good night then. I love you all."

For the first time in a long time, Carlo did not sleep well.

8

A CAWING CROW WOKE HIM before the sun rose. He was filled with panic. For a moment he wondered where he was. Then he realized he had forgotten his breviary, the official prayer book of the church that priests were supposed to pray each day. The thought crossed his mind that God had planned it that way, but he was so used to praying from his breviary each day at certain hours that it might be difficult to adjust. One more deprivation that identified him with the homeless—not having the comfort of the church's beautiful and comforting prayers!

Carlo's next concern was how he would wash, brush his teeth, and take a shower. And where would he find something to eat? It seemed he had just eaten, but he was so hungry. He hadn't eaten much, just a sandwich. Already his stomach was growling. He walked past a church, and it would have been so easy to stop at the rectory and beg. "After all, an endless run of beggars stop at rectories all day and sometimes at night. Why not try it just this once? But suppose the priest recognizes me; then my retreat will come to a sudden end."

Another homeless man was walking toward Carlo. He decided to ask him if he knew the priest in that rectory.

"Friend, my name is Carlo. I'm new here, and I am very hungry. Can you tell me if the priest in that parish across the street is a kind man?"

"Welcome to Rome! I never met him, but one of my friends told me he's new here, just transferred from one of the mountain villages."

"Thank you."

"If he's from outside the city," Carlo thought, "there's no way he could know me. I might as well give him a try."

Walking up to the entrance, he rang the bell. After what seemed a long time, the door opened. A balding man, overweight, wearing a two-day growth of beard, looked angrily at him.

"Not another bum! Now what the hell do you want this time of the day?"

Frightened by the rude outburst, all Carlo could get up the courage to say was, "Just a little something to eat, Father, and maybe a cup of coffee."

"Do you think I run a restaurant? The cook hasn't come in yet. If you weren't too damn lazy to work, you wouldn't have to bother decent people. Get on your way and don't ever stop here again."

The slamming door shocked Carlo. He felt both anger and humiliation. "How could a priest who had dedicated his life to Jesus treat a human being like that? I wonder how many souls have been turned away from God by such meanness. But now I am judging him. My judgment may be even more offensive to God than his meanness. Maybe my being out in the streets is not my choice. Maybe this is where God knows I belong. Maybe in God's eyes I am not worthy to be one of his priests. Maybe my motives in becoming a priest were not pure, unselfish, and authentic. Perhaps I am the despicable person that priest saw in me."

The day had just begun and already Carlo was traveling down the psychological road of all other homeless beggars, the road to self-degradation that occurs so naturally from the way others treat them. Even St. Paul, wounded by the rude treatment of some Christians, began to feel that he and others like him were nothing better than despised outcasts. Paul, in his shame, would no longer depend on others for support. He supported his ministry by plying his previous trade as a tentmaker, selling his goods in the marketplace. Carlo, after not even a full day, was beginning to doubt himself and his relationship with God and to feel that he was a homeless beggar unworthy of any better treatment than he was receiving, even from God.

Now, not knowing where to go or how to find something to eat, he realized he had forgotten what had always been the most important part of his day—his early morning prayers and meditation, and offering mass. "I am so sorry, Lord. For the first time my stomach was more important than my need to spend time with you."

Walking back to the church he had just passed, he entered and knelt down in the back pew. Mass had just begun. It had been years since he had attended mass as a parishioner in a pew, and the first time from a back pew. The baroque interior of the church brought a feeling of prayerful peacefulness. On the left side of the sanctuary, on a side altar, was the statue of St. Sebastian, his friend, which helped him feel at home.

"Glory to God in the highest and peace to his people on earth! Lord God, heavenly King, almighty God and Father, we worship you, we give you thanks, we praise you for your glory."

These words had new meaning for Carlo as a homeless person. For the first time, he had to ask himself what he was thankful for. He had been rudely treated, still smelled from the beer that had been splashed on him, had had a rectory door slammed in his face by one of God's representatives, the same man who was now offering mass on the altar. "Lord, couldn't some other priest have said the mass this morning? It is not easy for me to praise you and be thankful to you while he's officiating. But I guess there are a lot of people who have had difficult encounters with rude priests and have no choice but to attend their masses. Maybe, Father, this is one of the lessons you are teaching me, a lesson I need to know if I am to learn how to be a good shepherd who understands the many kinds of anguish suffered by your flock. But I can already see that it is not going to be as romantic an experience as I thought it might be. It is already far more painful than I had imagined, Father. Please give me the grace to persevere."

As the priest began the words of consecration, Carlo spoke them in a low voice, concelebrating with this priest he already did not like and realizing his prayers were being accepted by Jesus as he was presenting the sacred offering to his Father.

Time for communion came. Carlo was almost too frightened to consider approaching this priest for the Eucharist. However, he walked up the aisle with the other parishioners, mostly women, with only seven or eight men among them. He had never felt so ashamed and humbled. As his turn came for communion, and he held out his hands to receive the sacred host, the priest looked at him, hesitated, and then placed the sacred host in his hand. The priest looked at him as if something powerful had struck him. Was it the delicate refinement of Carlo's hands, waiting so reverently for the host to be placed there? Those hands, with their finely manicured nails, clearly unused to hard work, contrasted sharply with the coarseness of his clothes and his unkempt appearance. Perhaps the priest was wondering, "Who is this man?"

Forgetting to respond, "Amen," the proper response, Carlo simply looked at the priest and said, "Thank you, Father." Jesus had not rejected him.

During the rest of the mass the priest hardly took his eyes off the beggar in the back of the church. He was deep in prayer, still kneeling with hands folded and head bowed, while the rest of the people were sitting during communion meditation time.

When mass ended, a few pious women stayed and quietly prayed the rosary together. Carlo stayed kneeling, still deep in meditation. When the priest took off his vestments and went back into the sanctuary for his thanksgiving after mass, he noticed the beggar still kneeling, with head bowed, still motionless, as if his spirit was in a world beyond. When Carlo finished praying and rose, then genuflected, and left the church, the priest rushed down the aisle to catch up with him. Carlo was already walking down the street, as the overweight priest chased after him, his huge body bouncing with each step.

"Young man, young man. Wait, wait!"

Carlo turned around and saw the priest running after him.

As the priest approached, he was filled with apologies. "I am sorry for being so rude to you earlier. Please forgive me."

"That's all right. I can imagine you must be pestered day and night by people like me. I can understand."

"That is no excuse, especially for a priest. I know you haven't eaten yet, have you?"

"No, other than my communion."

"Would you honor me by having breakfast with me?"

"Father, I am so ashamed. I stink from beer a man splashed all over me last night, and I am so embarrassed."

"Please come. It will be good for my soul for the way I treated you earlier."

"I can't thank you enough. I am so hungry," Carlo responded.

The two men walked up to the priest's house, entered, and sat down for breakfast. "My name is Father Giacomo Pallini," the priest said as he extended his hand to Carlo.

"I am Arch . . . Archimede Bruno," Carlo responded, quickly covering up an almost fatal slip. "You offered mass very beautifully this morning, Father. I was impressed with how respectfully and thoughtfully you prayed."

"It is not easy for me to be pious. I come from a rough family. None of us is very refined. In fact, we're rugged and tough mountain people. Even the priesthood doesn't do miracles to change what we are and how we've been raised. I guess I slipped back into my old ways this morning in the way I treated you. I felt so bad afterward, but you had already disappeared down the street. When I saw you at mass, I was glad you had come, even though I still had difficult feelings."

"I can understand, Father. Please don't feel a need to apologize. I am really not an important person."

"Would I be prying if I asked you to tell me about yourself?"

Carlo, for one of the few times in his life, was stumped for words.

"Father, I guess all I can say is I am what you see, just a homeless beggar, spending my time trying to keep alive."

"Where are you from?"

"A little village down south near Taranto. It's hard to get work down there, so I thought I would have better luck if I came farther north. So far, jobs are hard to find here as well. But I am not concerned. I am enjoying what I see in the big city."

When the two men finished their breakfast of eggs scrambled with greens and prosciutto, cheese, bread, and coffee, Carlo thanked the priest profusely and asked for his blessing.

He knelt before the priest. "Benedicat te, Omnipotens Deus Pater, et Filius, et Spiritus Sanctus." One who knew the reality would have seen something remarkable–a brilliant archbishop dressed in rags being blessed by a coarse, rugged, but goodhearted fat and balding priest,

"Thank you, Father." Carlo said, as he shook the priest's hand and followed the priest to the door.

"Archimede, wait just a minute. I have something I want to give you."

The priest came back shortly with a small leather bag containing a piece of *soppressata* (a dry, cured salami), a wedge of cheese, a small loaf of fresh-baked bread, and a little flask of wine. "Just a little something to tide you over until you get acquainted with the neighborhood. You can keep the bag in case you happen to have a little more food than you can eat sometime."

Carlo was delighted when he looked in the bag and saw the contents.

"Thank you, Father, and may God bless you and your people."

"Thank you for allowing me to share my breakfast with you."

As Carlo left, the priest stood there watching this strange beggar as he walked down the street, more baffled and bewildered than ever over this wanderer who had none of the trappings of a "professional" beggar. His beautiful hands and carefully manicured nails indicated a person of elegance and distinction. "Could he be Jesus?" the priest wondered, and then turned pale as he realized how rudely he had first treated him. "Never again will I treat anyone like that, never again," he swore to himself.

Carlo continued down the street in a much happier mood. He felt a little more like an respectable human being again, for a short time anyway. But the day was still young, and the time passes very slowly when life is hurtful. Hours drag on slowly; minutes are like hours; days seem endless.

Carlo noticed he was wandering closer and closer to the Vatican, and he realized that might not be the most prudent thing to do. He suspected a contingent of the Swiss Guard in ordinary dress had been assigned to shadow him, for his own protection as well as for Vatican intelligence. He knew his every move would be reported to the Vatican security office, and the information relayed to the Holy Father. So, it would be wiser for him to stay in Rome for as short a time as necessary to convince the pope that his pilgrimage-retreat was being conducted in a careful, prudent manner and would not create a scandal.

Since it was a warm, sunny day, he thought it would be pleasant to wander through the Villa Borghese to see the gardens and the museum and art gallery. It was a good hour's walk, but with a bag full of food he felt secure enough to take a chance that he would have the energy to make the trip. Skirting the Vatican, he started toward the quiet, peaceful little paradise where he could wander, pray and meditate, and think about what he would do for the next few days. The gardens would be a peaceful place to get his bearings, especially as he was fast learning that he had to have a plan.

As he walked, he thought about his plans to leave Rome. Before he had even considered this retreat, he had wondered how

the homeless lived in the United States. The European press often described the way the poor and minorities were treated in
America. With that in the back of his mind, he had brought his
passport with him when he left Taranto as well as an open airline
ticket that he had purchased only a week before his meeting with
the pope. He had expected the pope to honor his request to take
an extended leave. He had considered that it would be unlikely
for him to be recognized in the United States. He knew he should
leave Rome and go to the States as soon as possible. He already
had his visa, and he just hoped that no overly zealous Catholic
at the embassy would inform the papal nuncio in Washington
that the archbishop of Taranto was on his way to the States. Carlo
was fully aware of the Vatican's intelligence system, which was
often more professional in its network of personal contacts than
the diplomatic network of many secular governments.

As Carlo passed through the entrance to the Borghese Gardens,
he was like a child going to Disney World. The carefully sculpted
shrubs and artistically arranged flower beds were breathtaking.
There were not many visitors, so he relaxed and nibbled on his
soppressata and cheese, which he cut into small pieces with a tiny
knife on a key chain. Passing a stunningly decorated pool, he
went back under the nearby trees and sat down while he finished
his carefully rationed lunch. Then, resting against the tree trunk,
he fell sound asleep.

It was early afternoon when he awoke, and wandered across
to the Borghese Villa, a combination museum and art gallery that
contains the largest private art collection in the world. This was
the dream of Cardinal Scipione Borghese, who wanted it to reflect an ancient Roman villa. Both the gallery and the museum
are on the ground floor of the villa.

When Carlo reached the entrance, he was told he needed a
ticket. Not having one, he looked at the attendant and said, "Oh,
I'm sorry. I don't have the money for a ticket." He turned
slowly to walk away. A voice from inside the building called to

the attendant, and whatever it told him, the attendant quietly called Carlo and gestured with his head for Carlo to go inside. Carlo smiled and thanked him and walked into the building.

Having such a refined taste for beautiful things, his eyes feasted on every masterpiece he viewed, especially those by Titian and Raphael. He wondered why he had never allowed himself the luxury of visiting this place in all the time he was studying in Rome.

The museum also gripped his imagination with all the statues and relics of times long past. What impressed him most in the museum was Bernini's sculpture of *David* and Ruben's *Pieta.*

As sophisticated as it is, the Borghese Villa is a playground for the local residents. Besides the gallery and the museum, there is a theater, a biology park, a lake and ice skating rink, and—as in every place in the Western world—kids skateboarding. The villa is at a higher elevation than the Piazza del Popolo, which it over-looks, and is a secret oasis of green and refreshing pools of wa-ter isolated from the busy streets of Rome.

Carlo managed to stay on the grounds of the villa for two days. Then he decided that before he left the country he would wan-der up the Janiculan Hill, one of his favorite spots as a student, and get one last breathtaking view of Rome and the Vatican from the top of the hill.

Carlo continued his walk up the Gianicolo and reached the spot he intended to visit. He sat there for the longest time with much to ponder as he viewed that site. Not only was he looking down upon St. Peter's Basilica and the whole of Vatican City, but he could see all of Rome spread out as far as his eyes could see. The view reminded him of Jesus' experience when he looked across from the Mount of Olives and viewed the glorious site of Jerusalem and the gold of the Temple shining in the sunlight. Now Carlo was viewing the new Jerusalem and the glorious monument built to the glory of God. The vast church and its pi-azza with its open arms so symbolic of Jesus reaching out to embrace the world! The Vatican, the center of Christianity, embracing over a billion and a quarter people, all so different in culture, race, language, in dreams and visions, with liberals and conservatives, progressives demanding constant change, and traditionalists frightened of even the slightest change threatening their cherished customs and memories of the past, and of values held dear from childhood. All of these people with their varied demands struck Carlo as a large family of children wanting attention. The seeming impossibility of it made him wonder how the church could ever make a decision involving even the smallest and most insignificant change that would not upset at least ten million of its members somewhere. This makes any radical change almost unthinkable. Carlo saw the church and the Vatican in a new light, understanding more about what would be needed in church leaders in order for them to be faithful to God in carrying out the mission Jesus gave to Peter and his church.

Those few hours had a profound impact on Carlo and turned out to be a most important part of his pilgrimage-retreat. He fell asleep while still absorbed in meditation on the vision spread out before him.

What Carlo experienced on that little hill would affect him for the rest of his life. He left there the next morning with the strong impression that the Holy Spirit had spoken to him in a way that he could not completely digest immediately but would in time decode all the messages God had given to him that afternoon and far into that night.

The next morning he walked into the lower part of the city, which eventually brought him near the perimeter of St. Peter's Basilica. As he turned a corner, he ran into two cardinals whom he knew—and who had never been particularly friendly toward him. One looked at him and nudged his companion, who turned to look at Carlo. But Carlo's shaggy appearance was a perfect camouflage. Carlo kept walking as if they meant nothing to him. He did not know it but, as he continued walking, the two clerics turned and watched him for a few seconds. The close call shocked Carlo and convinced him he had to leave Rome quickly.

It was time for him to go to a place where he could learn about people and a culture that was far different from the European culture that had saturated his whole life. His passport, visa, and ticket enclosed in a thin pouch taped to his waist underneath his clothes, Carlo made his way to the airport.

At the airport Carlo confirmed a flight, called a friend in New York, and, with little explanation, asked if he could pick him up at Kennedy International Airport the next morning.

9

THE LONG FLIGHT FROM ROME to New York City in a cramped
seat next to the lavatory was uncomfortable, but Carlo's excitement about his new adventure overrode his discomfort. As the
captain announced their approach to the city and pointed out
major sights that were within view, Carlo became like a child,
trying to identify every building he saw, trying to remember
their names from photographs he had seen in books and maga-
zines and on television. The Statue of Liberty was beautiful, and
the Empire State Building easy to identify. He was surprised at
the size of Long Island. He could not wait to explore this new
place.

But once on the ground and in the airport he found it was not
a hospitable world for a homeless beggar. Although he knew
English very well, and could speak the language with only a
slight accent, the airport signs were not familiar. Just walking
around Kennedy was confusing. Fortunately, when he walked
out the front exit, his friend's car was approaching.

Father Frank Labito was quite certain it was Carlo standing
there, because there was no way a real homeless person would
be standing so confidently at the entrance of such a busy airport.

When the car stopped, Carlo bent over and looked in the open
window. Excitedly he greeted his friend, "Francesco, my dear
Francesco, what a relief to see you. I don't know what I would
have done, if you hadn't come to pick me up."

"Carlo, I love your new outfit! You look like a million lira. Throw your backpack into the back seat, and jump in before security complains."

Carlo climbed in, hooked his seat belt, and made himself comfortable. Soon they were driving away.

"Carlo, you have to bring me up to date. I couldn't understand what you were telling me when you talked about your pilgrimage-retreat. I never heard of such a thing."

"It was too much to explain over the phone."

Carlo then told him the whole story, knowing that he could trust Father Frank, who had been Carlo's dogmatic theology professor in the seminary and also had taught him the Sicilian dialect. They had been good friends for years.

The two men arrived at Father Frank's residence in mid-afternoon. Frank asked the cook to prepare a light meal for his guest. While the two sat at the table, they made up for lost time; it seemed they had a thousand stories to share. Father Frank had not known that Carlo had been sent to the Academia for diplomatic training, and seeing him now in his homeless clothes, he could not resist laughing. "You look like quite a diplomat in that outfit."

Carlo laughed, knowing well how ridiculous he must look, and told his friend about the blue patch.

The cook put a tureen of minestrone and a platter with cheese and crackers on the table, along with two soup bowls and silverware. Then she took a bottle of homemade wine out of the buffet and set that on the table with two glasses. "Buon' appetito!" she said, as she retreated into the kitchen.

"Thank you, Mildred. It smells delicious," Father Frank replied as the swinging door closed behind her.

Carlo was hungry and ate two full bowls of the soup. The cheese was imported from Italy, and the bread was homemade Italian, so he felt very much at home. "Oh, how good it is to be living in an ordinary house, so peaceful, so natural," he thought.

When they finished the snack, Father Frank invited him to stay at the priests' residence, but Carlo felt that he needed to be on his way. Father Frank then gave Carlo an envelope and a backpack. He said they might be useful on cold nights when Carlo was having a difficult time finding a place to sleep.

Carlo thanked him profusely, gave the elderly priest a hug, kissing him on both cheeks, and then followed him to the door. Father Frank offered to drive him wherever he was going, but Carlo declined. They agreed to keep in touch.

Once out on the streets again, in a strange city in a strange country, panic began to edge around the corners of Carlo's mind. Out of curiosity he opened the backpack the priest had given him. To his surprise, it contained a lightweight, insulated sleeping bag as well as a lightweight insulated tent in which he could sit or lie down. There was also a map of New York State and a New York City subway map. But what he saw was worse than the maps of Italy. Everything on Long Island was complicated and compact.

Spotting a subway station across the street, he decided to make his way into Manhattan. He entered the terminal and hesitated at the turnstile until an impatient commuter behind him swiped him through, gave him a push, and muttered, "Go!"

Before long, he realized that where he was going was no less confusing than what he was leaving. Arriving at 59th Street, he found himself in another completely different world. It was early evening, and fortunately he was near a huge park just across a beautiful circle dedicated to Christopher Columbus. Looking at his map, he saw it was called Central Park, and he could see it was vast. He decided that he had done enough walking for the day. Not wanting to deal with the issue of food, he just stopped in a deli and asked for a glass of water. The woman at the counter saw that he was probably hungry, wrapped some cold cuts and a roll, put them in a bag with a small bottle of water, and gave them to Carlo.

"Thank you so much. You are so kind," Carlo said in a low voice that only she could hear.

She looked at him and could see he was not a common, everyday kind of vagrant. She thought he was probably an unfortunate fellow who had recently lost his job. "Pray for me, and good luck. Don't get discouraged."

"I will not forget you, Señorita. You are a very special person."

Too tired to even think of exploring any of the magnificent sights all around him, not even Broadway with all its bright lights or the Lincoln Center just across the Circle, he wearily headed for the park. He hoped he could find a secluded place where he could enjoy some peace, if not quiet, for the night. Dragging himself far enough inside the park, he found a private area under a small grove of close, low-lying trees. Opening the package containing the tent and sleeping bag, he sat down, ate part of what the lady had given him, and after washing it down with a mouthful of water, he set up the tent, closed the flaps, and bedded down for the night, saying a brief but heartfelt thank you to God for his safe arrival, for his priest friend, and for his safe "escape" from Long Island. "Dear Father, bless Father Frank for giving me this tent and sleeping bag. It is so warm and comfortable." As he drifted off to sleep, the last sounds he heard were raindrops bouncing off his tent. It was surprising how warm it was in his new shelter and sleeping bag, though on colder nights they would probably not be adequate to keep out the frigid air.

It was late when Carlo woke the next morning. Emerging from the sleeping bag, he peeked out through the flap and could see people already wandering around in the park. He knew he must have slept long and hard. His first reaction was a feeling of guilt, as if he was still on a work schedule. He relaxed when he realized that in his new life situation he had nothing to do except get himself up and moving. He prayed softly:

"Thank you, Father, for the restful sleep. Dear Mother, keep me close to Jesus today and protect me from harm. Holy Spirit, guide me so I can learn to understand Jesus and what he tried to teach us."

Suddenly he remembered that Father Frank had given him an envelope. Hopefully, he hadn't lost it! He reached for the backpack, and at the bottom he found the envelope, which he must have put in there without realizing it. Opening the envelope he was shocked to see the contents—five ten-dollar bills. It was as if someone had given him a fortune. His eyes came to rest on the map, and he opened it to get a better understanding of where he was. Noticing he was not far from St. Patrick's Cathedral, he decided to attend a late-morning mass.

The rain had stopped completely. Apparently it had been just a sprinkling during the night. After packing up his tent, he looked around and saw a man much like himself walking down the path. Putting his arm into the strap of his backpack, he approached the stranger and, in a friendly voice, greeted him, "Good morning, sir! Can you tell me where I can find a place to wash up?"

"Yeah, there's a church way down the street. Just ask people where St. Patrick's Cathedral is. There are restrooms there, with warm water. I go there sometimes."

"Thank you. I appreciate your help."

"Glad to help a comrade."

Carlo did not feel comfortable in this huge city. Everything was fast and frenetic, and the sound of horns and gridlock in the streets made him feel uneasy and anxious. He would have to find a place where life was more relaxed and the pace slower. He knew there were homeless people in New York, as in all big cities, but a homeless person would have to live in this city for a long time or grow up here in order to move around comfortably in the midst of such chaos. For Carlo, being homeless as part of a retreat was one thing, but to start out as a novice in one of the most crowded cities in the world would test his sanity, and that was not an intended part of his retreat. "But maybe that is what happens to the homeless," he thought, "this feeling that they may be losing their mind."

Entering the church, Carlo was impressed with the peace and quiet of the place. The interior was totally soundproofed from the noise and bustle of the streets. He recalled the stillness and serenity of a little village church he often visited in the mountains of Italy. Walking up to the last pew, he genuflected, knelt down, and rested his face in his hands. He became lost in prayer, a luxury for a homeless beggar. The tinkling of a little bell roused him, and looking up, he saw a priest and an elderly man entering the sanctuary to begin mass.

"Oh, thank God. I miss you, dear Lord. I know you are always with me, even when I cannot feel your presence. Thank you, dear Lord, for this mass today. It may be just a coincidence, but I still think you arranged it for my comfort and as a token of your love. I pray, dear Father, that you grant similar tokens of your love and tenderness to my fellow homeless who may have never had the joy of knowing that you care for them. And blessed Mother, be a mother to the homeless. Give them the tender compassion they must crave."

In that quiet, majestic church Carlo experienced a warm feeling of devotion, a sense that God was near. He had not had such a sense of closeness to God since he started out on his pilgrimage-retreat. It was affecting him deeply, because he thought his feeling of distance was God's way of telling him that what he was doing didn't meet with God's approval. Still, this sense of the divine presence, whether it was from God or just an emotional response to the serenity and soft lighting created by the stained-glass windows, brought Carlo a feeling of peace.

After the gospel reading the priest gave a short homily. "As you look around, you can see clutter the workmen left around, and the scaffolding at inconvenient places, and other things that are disturbing. This is a symbol of the church itself. There are always things about the church that are disturbing, clutter, and customs and practices long out of date, people who trouble us, priests whom we find difficult to like. This shows that the church itself has to be renewed and renovated at times. Sometimes our religious leaders don't have the courage to make change or perhaps the vision to understand the need for change, or they may think that loyalty means putting up with things the way they are, in spite of people's clear need that things be different.

"I see all the poor homeless people wandering the streets, for example. I am sure many of them are Catholics. Why don't they come to mass and receive Jesus in communion? They surely need his presence in their lives as much as anyone. Perhaps they think they will not be welcome? Would they be? We have to change sometimes, so we can more faithfully represent Jesus and be living evidence of his resurrection. We need to show others that Jesus is still alive and well."

The priest's comments stirred Carlo's heart. He had never allowed himself openly to criticize faults in the church. This priest did not impress him as discontented. He was calm and deliberate, simply stating what he had observed in the daily lives of his people. Carlo's thoughts turned inward. He knew he was treated with great favor by church officials. "Has that blinded me to serious defects in this sacred institution?" he asked himself. To have criticized the church would have jeopardized his future. Suddenly he felt fear that his love for the church was not pure, that it had prevented him from being loyal to Jesus himself. "If I were really loyal to Jesus, I would be more adamant about church officials being sensitive to the feelings of the people, like this priest is. We need to notice the church's shortcomings, which are offensive to Jesus and insensitive to our peoples' pleas for change. Jesus loved his church and called it a precious pearl, but then on another occasion referred to it as a catch of fish, some good and healthy, and others that stank to high heaven. If I really felt the way Jesus does about his church, wouldn't I notice that there are stinking fish and want to do something about it?"

The priest's homily had cut Carlo to the quick, arousing a sense of shame in an area of his life where he had never felt shame before. This simple message from an unknown priest–in a nation considered by his own people as secularist and materialist–had pointed out to him that he had been ignoring the hurt in people's hearts, their hunger for spirituality, the insensitivity of their shepherds. He was not the good shepherd he thought he was, or tried to be. He had overlooked a most important aspect of a good shepherd's concern–the spiritual pain in people's souls. For a good part of his ministry he had looked upon people complaining about the church's inattention to their concerns as "things to handle." Now he saw their complaints as desperate pleas for help, which he had glibly cast aside. He was not the caring, sensitive priest he had always imagined himself to be.

When he went up to communion, the priest gave Carlo a second look after placing the host in his hand. Perhaps, as with the priest in Italy, it was Carlo's beautiful hands, which did not fit the stereotype of a homeless beggar.

After mass Carlo waited while the priest was taking off his vestments. He stood near the doorway of the vestry until the priest finished, then nervously approached. The priest turned and greeted him, "Good morning! What can I do for you?"

"Would you be kind enough to hear my confession, Father?"

"Of course. Come over here and sit down. Do you want to make your confession face to face, or would you rather do it privately?"

"Face to face is good."

Carlo sat down, and the priest put on a purple stole and sat facing him. Carlo began to perspire. He had never been nervous before when he went to confession.

"Bene . . . ," he began, nervously speaking in Italian. He stopped abruptly and continued in English, "Bless me, Father, for

I have sinned. I am a priest, and while I listened to your homily this morning, I realized that I have not been the good shepherd I thought I was. I have never allowed myself to deal with faults in the church and always defended it against the complaints of people. Your homily made me realize that people's complaints are often a plea for help, an expression of their caring and their craving for greater intimacy with God. These pleas fell on my deaf ears, and I failed to nourish them. The financially poor are not the only people who are poor. Spiritual poverty is even more painful, and I have failed to recognize that in my people. This I humbly confess. I am deeply sorry, and I ask God's forgiveness and that you give me absolution."

The priest was shocked at such a sensitive and profound confession from an apparent vagrant. He knew that before he could decide upon absolution, he had to probe deeper to understand what this extraordinary confession was all about.

"I have to admit I am totally baffled. You certainly do not look like a priest. Are you really a priest?"

"Yes, I am, Father."

"You have an accent, and you started to say your confession in Italian. What diocese do you belong to?"

"Father, I belong to the archdiocese of Taranto in Apulia."

"Father," the priest said, "I have to admit I am very confused. You appear to be homeless. I have to ask you if you are still a priest in good standing or if you have left the priesthood."

"I am a priest in good standing, but I am on a leave of absence. I am trying to understand the poor and the homeless, so I am on what you might call a pilgrimage-retreat, living the life of a beggar among the homeless. I am learning what I need to know to be a much better priest when I return to my diocese."

"I'm sorry I had to pry, Father, but I had to assure myself of your sincerity before giving you absolution. I admit I am shocked, but if what you tell me is true, I admire you. For your penance, spend ten minutes before the Blessed Sacrament, meditating on the sanctity of your priesthood. Then, if you are hungry, you are welcome to come over to the rectory and have breakfast with me."

"Thank you, Father, but it's better that I move along."

Carlo then expressed sorrow for his sins, while the priest said the words of absolution, "God, the Father of mercies, through the death and resurrection of his Son, has reconciled the world to himself, and sent the Holy Spirit among us for the forgiveness of sins. Through the ministry of the church may God give you pardon and peace. I absolve you from your sins, in the name of the Father, and of the Son, and of the Holy Spirit. Go in peace, Father."

"Thank you," Carlo said. Then he went back into the church to do his penance.

Outside the church Carlo took out his map and checked possible routes to Albany. He had been told that Upstate New York was similar to the area around his hometown in Italy. It might be helpful to begin his life among the poor in an area that was familiar. It would take a week to walk to Albany. If he hitchhiked, it might take only a few hours. "Is it worth the risk for me to hitchhike?" he worried.

The problem was solved when a police officer approached and saw Carlo looking at his map.

"Can I help you?"

"Yes, please. I'm trying to figure my best way to get to Upstate New York."

"How far up?"

"Albany."

"The best way to get there is by train. A one-way trip is about forty dollars. Or you could take Metro North almost to apple country, sort of a rural area. That's about ten or fifteen dollars."

To Carlo, that made good sense. "Thank you, officer. You solved my problem. Where can I get the Metro North?"

"Not far from here," and he proceeded to give directions.

"Thank you so much. I cannot tell you how much you have put my mind at rest."

Carlo headed for Grand Central Station. His new insight into himself, triggered by an American priest whose name he did not even know, along with his regret and desire to reform his thoughts, gave Carlo the enthusiasm to go wherever the Lord would lead.

10

THE TRAIN RIDE ALONG THE MAJESTIC Hudson River was breathtaking. The Palisades on the New Jersey side were fascinating, and farther north there were rolling hills, stately mansions, and other points of interest, like lighthouses on little islands right in the river. Looking at his map, Carlo located West Point Military Academy and vaguely remembered some of its history. Soon he was in apple country, and it was time to end his relaxing train ride.

He had no trouble locating an apple orchard, though he had to find a bridge to cross over to the west bank of the river. The orchards spread for miles along the highway, and they all needed help badly, since new immigration policies had cut off the supply of workers from Jamaica. As a result, fruit was falling from the trees and rotting. When Carlo entered an orchard store, he immediately asked for the manager. The lady waiting on the customers asked him, "What do you want to see him about?"

"I would like to apply for a job, if you need help."

The lady phoned the manager, who appeared a few minutes later. He was middle aged, with a ruddy complexion, and dressed in overalls. Approaching Carlo, he asked, "Are you the one looking for a job?"

"Yes, I am."

"I'm Joe Abbruzzese. I manage our family farm."

"My name is Carlo. We have an orchard back home in Italy."

"What part of Italy are you from?"

"Palagiano, near Taranto, in Apulia," Carlo responded.

"My family is from Bari, not far from Taranto. But to the matter at hand. Our orchard is large and the work is hard. Are you used to hard work?"

"I have always enjoyed work."

"You start at seven in the morning and work till four in the afternoon, five days a week. I'll pay you $8.75 an hour. If you work on Saturday, I pay extra. I also provide room and board. It's already the second week in September, so if you work for the next six weeks you should do well."

"I can work steady for a few weeks, and then I will have to move on. But I'll work hard during the time that I am here."

"Whatever. Steady workers are hard to find today. Americans don't want to do this kind of labor. When can you start?"

"Right now if you like."

"Come with me." Joe led him out to a nearby section of the orchard where three Latino men were working.

"Tomas," Joe called out.

"Si, Señor."

"I have a new worker. His name is Carlo. He will be working with you. Will you show him what has to be done?"

"Si, Señor."

Tomas took Carlo through the various sections of the orchard, and explained what had to be done. Carlo learned that Tomas had come from Mexico many years ago and over the years had become close to the Abbruzzese family. He went to church with them every Sunday morning and celebrated birthdays and other occasions, both happy and sad, with the family. Tomas hadn't intended to stay in America, and for the first few years he returned to Mexico at the end of the fruit harvest to be with his family. After only three years he was able to build an impressive home in Mexico with earnings from his work at the orchard.

Eventually, he decided that life in America would be more stable and healthier for his family, so he brought his wife and four children, as well as his parents and his wife's parents, to the United States, where they worked for the Abbruzzese orchards. After a few years they applied for citizenship.

During the time he worked at the orchard, Carlo developed a close friendship with Tomas and his family and with the Abbruzzese family. He was grateful for the help they gave him. Even though he was just a homeless drifter for all they knew, they all treated him with respect as a human being. He was glad the Abbruzzese family provided him with a place to sleep each night, although he said that he would be willing to sleep in his tent and sleeping bag, as the weather was still quite moderate. But Joe told him it was unnecessary. As long as he was working for him, he would have a decent place to sleep, for which Carlo thanked him profusely.

Carlo proved to be a very entertaining guest at the orchard, and everyone liked him for his humor and ability to tell stories of his adventures, always being careful to avoid saying anything that might reveal his identity.

It was during his time at the orchard that Carlo and several other workers were deported to Mexico, and it was while working his way back to the United States that Carlo met the peasant vineyard workers for whom he organized the vineyard arrangement with the estate owner.

Upon his eventual return to the United States and to the orchard, Carlo was warmly welcomed by the Abbruzzese family and the other workers, but after several more weeks, Carlo once again decided it was time to move on.

The Abbruzzese family and the other workers were sad the morning Carlo left. Joe would also miss him because Carlo was fluent in Spanish and could communicate with all the Spanish-speaking workers. Knowing that he could not carry much with him, the workers all contributed what they could afford and gave him a gift of money. It wasn't much, but for them it was two hour's pay each, and for Carlo it was a precious amount. "The poor never have so little that they don't have enough to share," he observed. "Many others, who have much, never have enough to share." Carlo was amazed at the generosity of these poor people. He hugged them all and left. They shouted their goodbyes, and he turned and waved to them, calling loudly, "El buen Señor bendiga, en el nombre del padre y del hijo y del Espíritu Santo."

Tomas remarked, "He blessed us like a priest. I wonder who he used to be." Those poor, simple laborers felt that they had been blessed, as though God had come to live with them for a few beautiful days. Faith sees things to which others are blind.

Carlo felt sad at losing the companionship of his new friends and thought about how fortunate Americans were to have immigrants in ever-increasing numbers blessing their country with their presence. He realized that as hard-working and industrious as they are, they would in time raise the spiritual level throughout the whole country by sharing their deep faith, their gentle, unselfish spirit, and their beautiful family life.

Carlo walked north along Route 9W. After almost an hour a car stopped, and the driver asked if he wanted a ride.

Carlo was only too happy to accept and got inside.

"Where are you on your way to, fella?"

"Just upstate."

"I'm going as far as Coxsackie, if that's okay."

"That's fine. That will be a big help."

"Where are you from?"

"I was working at an orchard, but now I want to see what it is like around Albany. I really appreciate the ride."

"Glad to help. That would have been a long walk."

"In good weather it's not bad. It's difficult when it rains, but I have my little tent."

"You speak good English, but you have bit of an accent. Are you Mexican?"

"No, I'm Italian."

"You seem educated. What kind of training do you have?

"Well, I just spent time harvesting fruit."

"Do you have any skills? The reason I'm asking is that I own my own business. I manufacture machine parts. Have you had any kind of experience with machines?"

"No, I don't think I'd have any skill at all for that kind of work."

"That's too bad, because I could hire you if you did. It's hard to find workers, and I have to admit the jobs can be pretty boring."

"I appreciate your kindness, and I'm sorry I have no ability at all in anything practical like that."

"Well, whatever you do, or end up doing, I wish you luck. It's a tough time to be out of work."

"I know, and I feel sorry for people who have families to support."

"You never married?"

"No, I'm content being by myself. Gives me time to think."

"You're an interesting fellow. I don't think I ever met anyone so content with having nothing. Are you a spiritual man?"

"No. I just have few needs."

"Free and uncomplicated."

As the two men rode along the long monotonous highway, the time passed quickly. They enjoyed each other's conversation. The two men could understand each other, though they were living in worlds apart.

After a while, the man asked if Carlo minded if he listened to a favorite program. Carlo had no objection.

The program started with the announcer saying, "This news is coming immediately from Moscow, Russia." He was speaking in Russian.

"So, you speak Russian," Carlo said, also speaking Russian.

Shocked, the man replied, "Yes, I was born in Leningrad. I came over here as a kid. Where did you learn Russian?"

"I learned it at college in Rome," Carlo replied.

The man was impressed. The two spent the rest of the hour enjoying the news and conversations on the Russian program. When it ended, they spent the next hour conversing in Russian. By that time they had arrived at Coxsackie, and the driver had enjoyed the ride so much he offered to take Carlo the remaining twenty-some miles to Albany. Carlo agreed.

Carlo thanked him profusely, not only for the ride but for the pleasure of chatting in Russian. The man gave Carlo his business card as he got out of the car.

"Thank you, and God bless you for your kindness," Carlo said in Russian before closing the door."

"You also. It is truly a small world."

11

Upstate New York–Charlie

CARLO, OR CHARLIE, AS HE CAME to be known, wandered around Albany, eventually ending up in that little old section of Albany, not far from a railroad and the old Erie Canal, where over a year later he would meet Miss Delaney and Martin O'Dea and all the other people he would come to know.

During that time Carlo became more and more the homeless man he appeared to be. He lost his few possessions and any desire or capability to keep his clothes and person clean. His mind wandered as much as his body. Eventually he seemed, even to himself, to be truly the homeless Charlie. The urbane archbishop he had once been seemed only a distant memory.

Upstate New York–The O'Dea Family

After Marty and his family took Miss Delaney and Charlie to mass and then out to dinner at a restaurant, they dropped off Miss Delaney and Charlie outside her house. They pulled away, but Marty stopped the car no more than a block away and got out. He asked Maureen to drive home because he wanted to find out where Charlie lived. He hadn't gone into the house with Miss Delaney but went off on his own. Marty intended to follow him to find out where he lived.

Maureen took off with the children, and Marty rushed back down the street to catch sight of Charlie. In a few moments he saw him walking down the side street, going south to an old long-abandoned area along the railroad tracks. The homeless used to gather there during the Great Depression in the 1930s and build little shacks for themselves. It was like a little city of homeless poor. Charlie approached the area, where there were now only a half-dozen shelters, mostly small, but one larger one with a thin trickle of smoke indicating a small fire inside.

Marty didn't go any farther. He got a glimpse of the little community, and once he saw where Charlie was living, he slipped quietly away and walked home, thinking about the strange life of this eccentric man. "These homeless men are his family," Marty thought. "He shares whatever he receives during his daily travels." Marty realized that those five men in the abandoned lot—the ones whom Charlie fed on the day Marty first saw him—were part of Charlie's family.

Now that he knew where Charlie lived, he decided that he would visit Charlie's family when Charlie was absent, bringing with him a good supply of food. If he could get acquainted with them, he might gradually find out more about Charlie. They probably knew more about him than anybody. He arrived home in a happy frame of mind, knowing that he was finally putting together the pieces of his puzzle on Charlie's life.

Walking into the house, he called to Maureen, "Sweetie, I finally found out where Charlie lives."

Maureen came down the stairs into the kitchen.

"Guess where," Marty said.

"I'll never be able to guess. Where does he live?"

"In a little homeless village. There's a little family of them. Reminds me of what the early monks must have been like when they gathered around a St. Benedict or a St. Francis. First chance I get, I'm going to bring a box of food down to them, so they don't have to beg."

And that is just what he did. He brought a box full of assorted foods: meats, bread, juice, coffee, vegetables, fruit, cheese, cans of sardines, and a few bottles of wine.

At first the men were suspicious, but when Marty told them he was a friend of Charlie's, they relaxed and welcomed him. On his first visit Marty was careful not to ask too many questions. The men might suspect he was after Charlie for something. But on later visits, he felt he could casually ask about Charlie. What the men revealed was startling.

They told Marty that Charlie was a big help to them. He understood them. When they were having problems, or were depressed, or were missing their families who would have nothing to do with them, they always went to Charlie. One man named Nick, who had been homeless for many years, talked freely about Charlie. "He's a great listener, truly interested in the rest of us. He's a patient guy and just lets us talk, and sometimes he asks us questions that make us think. He doesn't say much, but somehow he helps us to understand how we got ourselves into this mess. There used to be others here with us, a good number of veterans. With Charlie's help, several of them were reconciled with their families, and we see them only when they stop down for a visit every now and then."

Another fellow, whom the men called Rudy because of his big red nose, added, "On cold nights when we all gather around the stove in Jake's big shack, Charlie gives us talks when we ask him to. He tells us that being homeless is nothing to be ashamed of. 'Remember,' he said once, 'even Jesus had nowhere to lay his head, and often slept out in the hills, wrapping his cloak around him. He rested his head against the root of a tree and would fall asleep, just like us.' He told us things about Jesus that made us feel good about ourselves."

When Marty asked them if they knew what Charlie did before he became homeless, they had no answer. But one of the men, a quiet fellow named Mickey, said something revealing. "One night, a bitter cold night, when we were all sitting around the stove, listening to Charlie and asking him questions, it was very late and we were getting sleepy, and Charlie was tired too. Matt asked him if he knew any big shots who were kind to homeless people, and Charlie, half asleep, made the comment, "Yes, my driver, Father Agnel . . . " and then he immediately woke up and didn't say another word, surprised at what he had already said. We all looked at each other mystified, but, because we loved this man so much, we never asked him to finish what he was going to say. We let him keep his secret, whatever it was. But we all know he is a good man, and to us he is like a saint, the saint of the homeless, because he is one of us. If you are his friend, we hope you will have the same respect for him that we have and let him keep his secret."

"I promise," Marty said. "I too know he is a good man. I knew there was something special about him from the very first time I saw him come into church. He was so forgiving when the priest refused to give him communion. I can tell he has suffered much at the hands of others and yet has never become bitter or lost his serenity. There is a dignity about him that draws one to him."

"You see in him what we see in him, and that is why we love him," Mickey said.

Another fellow in the group told another story about Charlie. He held the whole little group spellbound, even though they had all witnessed what had happened. "As you know, Charlie likes to be free. He likes to work for his food, but if he's hungry enough, he'll beg for something to eat. Wandering around the way he does, just about everyone on the streets knows him. When we said that Charlie gives us talks, they were jealous and asked if we thought Charlie would give them talks too. Well, we all talked about it and talked to Charlie, and he seemed happy to go along with the idea. It took us at least two weeks to make arrangements because we didn't know where we could all gather in one big group like that. Those kinds of things don't usually happen among us.

"We finally decided to have the little retreat in the city park along the Hudson River near downtown Albany. We started gathering at about 9:30 in the morning. A few of us got there early to help set up the little affair. Most were there by 9:45, though some drifted in later. We had about two hundred of our city-wide family, both men and women. Almost half of us were veterans of one war or another. Charlie helped us set up, which was not a big job because we didn't have much to set up. We had all saved some of our food for a few days so we could have a picnic. We knew some would come without anything, and we wanted them to be part of the picnic too. Some brought soda. Out of respect for Charlie, there was no alcohol. We didn't want guys walking around drunk and upsetting everyone else. And that easily could have happened.

"Jake was asked to introduce Charlie, and he did a wonderful job. He said that because of Charlie, we all felt our lives were not a waste. We could still accomplish good by caring for one another and doing whatever we could to better the lives of others or ease the pain of those who were suffering in any way. Because of Charlie, he went on to say, some of us started visiting sick people in the hospitals, even though we make the nurses uncomfortable, and some of them kick us out.

"After saying all the nice things about Charlie, he asked Charlie if he would please come up and talk to us. Charlie stood up, and went up to the front of the group. We were all sitting on the warm, dry ground. Charlie started his talk with the words, 'My dear homeless brothers and sisters. I feel so honored to be one of you and so humbled that you think enough of me to ask me to speak to you all. It is not as if I have never spoken in public before, but I have never before been lost for words. It is not easy to talk to you people. You probably know more about life, real life, than most people. You never really know what life is all about until you have suffered and been humbled and beaten down by life. Then it all of a sudden becomes very real.

"'Jesus did not understand what life was going to be like for him, and he was God, until he went off on his own. He also was one of us, a homeless beggar with nowhere to lay his head. His clothes were not clean. They were wrinkled and soiled, and his hair was never combed. I'm sure he never carried a comb around in his pocket. He loved parties, but for the most part he wandered around from village to village, eating whatever was available along the way, which wasn't much. Some people were kind and gave him and his apostles food. Often all they ate were berries or fruit or the heads off ripe grain. Most of what they ate swam in the river, or grew on bushes or trees. Occasionally someone would give them a loaf of bread or a skin of wine. He ate the way we eat–whatever he could get. He knew, like us, that even scraps taste delicious when you're starving.'

"When he talked to us like this, Charlie made us feel very close to Jesus, as if Jesus was one of us. Charlie should have been a priest or something. He's really different. He shouldn't have to be a tramp like the rest of us. He's too good for that. But he's never depressed or discouraged. He's got a happy spirit, and we learn a lot from him. If we give him enough time, he'll have us all back on our feet again."

Marty listened, stunned by what Jake said about Charlie. "Maybe that's what I sensed in Charlie from the first day," Marty said. "There was something different about Charlie. I didn't know what it was, but he just didn't seem to be what he looked like. He sure does have class."

"That he does, that he does," Rudy chimed in, and the others agreed.

"I'm grateful I had a chance to spend some time with you gentlemen," Marty said. "I know Charlie's in good hands with loyal friends like you. And I appreciate your sharing with me. If you don't mind, can I stop down again to visit? And I won't come empty-handed."

"How can we say no to that? We're not always here, but you're welcome if you're in the neighborhood," Jake said.

Marty had a good walk home. What the homeless men had to say answered many of the questions Marty had about Charlie. He had also learned much about the homeless. They weren't odd people but were like everybody else, just down on their luck, with all their options used up. He wondered how they could get used to living with no family, only memories of family in times past, good memories, painful memories, probably memories saturated with guilt.

Marty had come to an entirely different conclusion about Charlie. And he was grateful to be his friend.

12

CHARLIE BECAME AT EASE IN HIS NEW LIFE and chose to make another trip to Mexico. During the journey he reminisced about the past months. Some of his experiences were happy; others were devastating to his ego and feelings of self-worth. It seemed impossible to think of himself as an archbishop; he had for so long been forced to look upon himself in the mirror of other people's view of him as a shabbily dressed and dirty homeless person. To many people he was one of society's contemptible good-for-nothing nuisances cluttering the streets, either too lazy to work or an addict of some sort. He now understood what too many Christian people had done to the least of Jesus' brethren. Charlie knew that his extended retreat had forever altered his life in a way more dramatic than he could have ever imagined. He knew it was time for him to think of returning to Italy.

So, when he arrived back in Albany, he knew his stay would be short. He had with him a sack of presents from the vineyard workers to his homeless friends. The freight train pulled off on to a side track, and as it was about to stop, not far from his friends' village, the door of the empty box car slid open and Charlie hurriedly let himself down to the ground, grabbed his big sack of packages, and headed for the cluster of shacks. One of Charlie's homeless colleagues spotted him and yelled out to the others, "Hey, it's Charlie! Charlie's back. He just got off the train, wearing a big Mexican cowboy hat!"

The others gathered around and gave Charlie a loud welcome, cheering and hugging him, glad he had decided to come back "home."

"How was your vacation, Charlie?" Jake asked him.

"Wonderful. I'll tell you all about it tonight."

Then Charlie opened the packages and spread the contents out on the paper they spread out on the ground. "These are presents for all of you. They're from people who know you and love you. I hope you can use them."

"Charlie, no one else has ever done anything like this for us before," Nick said.

"Well, there are many people whose lives and future depend on you, too, even if it is only for your prayers. Remember that! You are very special to God, each one of you. And if it is only a smile given to a person walking down the street, that smile to those people from a homeless person will imprint an indelible mark on their memory and touch their hearts in a way they will never forget. Your presence in the streets is a living message to people. You have dignity, my friends. You are silent prophets who preach merely by your presence and how you act. So do not shortchange yourselves. You are important to God; that is why God makes the salvation of all of us dependent on how we treat the poor and the homeless."

"Charlie, what is this picture supposed to be?" a man named Bobby asked about a small painting.

"That's a picture of Jesus' mother that is sacred to the Mexican people. There is one there for each of you. About three hundred years ago a Mexican peasant was out in the hills, and he had a vision of Jesus' mother. She told him to deliver a message to the bishop of the place. The man did as Mary told him. When he went to the bishop and delivered the message, the bishop gave him a hard time. He did not believe him until the man was leaving and the bishop saw that image of Jesus' mother on the back of the peasant's cloak. The man was shocked when the bishop asked him about the picture because the man didn't know it was there. Then the bishop believed that the message was from Jesus' mother. That may not mean much to people here, but it is a treasure to those Latino people, and they wanted to share those pictures with you. There are gloves that they made by hand for each of you, and they will really keep your hands warm. The sweaters are all hand woven by your friends, who wanted you to be warm in the cold weather. The hats too are handmade."

Rudy looked at the gloves he had picked up and asked, "And the people who made all these are poor people?"

"Just as poor as we are, Rudy."

As callous as these men seemed, they could be very sensitive to such a show of affection from people they did not know and whom they would never meet. They had never seen this kind of caring from their own people, and to receive such thoughtful handmade gifts from poor people like themselves, who lived thousands of miles away in a foreign country, overwhelmed them. One of the men turned to walk a little away from the others, so no one would see his tears.

Jake asked Charlie if he could write a nice letter to these people, with each one of them saying something to express his appreciation. Rudy suggested they try to send some simple gifts to show their gratitude. They all wanted to do something, and agreed to plan on it. Nick, who was good-hearted, but a little simple, suggested, "Since we don't have anything, maybe each of us could steal something from the stores and put it all together and send them a package."

"What, are you nuts, Nick? Then we'd all end up in jail. We all learned our lesson about that stuff, and we agreed it would never happen again."

"Sorry, just trying to help."

Rudy said, "I can carve. Maybe I can carve some figurines and send them. Another fellow name Paul added, "And I can paint. Maybe I can paint pictures on wood, and we can send those."

Everyone wanted to do something, so they decided to think about it and come up with a plan. Then they all went into Jake's big house and sat around the pot-belly stove to warm up, as there was still a chill in the air. They asked Charlie to tell them all the things that happened while he was away.

Charlie had much to tell them, and as they were family and had little contact with the outside world, he could share many things with them that he dared not share with anyone else. They were his family.

"You're not going to leave us are you, Charlie, the way you left the people in Mexico?" Rudy asked.

Charlie looked at him, and for a moment was lost for what to say, as he could see that Rudy was becoming frightened that he might lose his dear friend, whom he had come to love.

Charlie said to him, and to all the others, "Sadly, I do have to leave. I have to go back where I came from. I have a lot of responsibilities."

"Charlie," Rudy broke down and could not contain his grief, "what kind of responsibilities do you have that are more important than your responsibilities to us who have come to love you? You are the only one on this earth who cares for us."

Tears flowed down Charlie's cheeks as he walked over and put his arms around Rudy and told him, "Rudy, and all of you, I must leave. You will one day understand. But when I do leave, I will write to you, and I will send you a special phone so that we can talk as often as you like, and the phone will be all paid for, so it won't cost you anything."

Jake, who had just been listening and analyzing, then came out with the question, "You are not really a homeless beggar, are you, Charlie?"

"Yes, I am, Jake, but I became homeless by my own choice so I could become one of you and learn what your life is all about and try to understand the plight of the homeless people around the world, and understand why Jesus loves you so much. You have all taught me a lot, and now I must go back home and do what I can to relieve the plight of the homeless in whatever way I can. You have taught me so much. I can never adequately tell you what that means to me."

"Charlie, be honest with us. Who are you?"

Even knowing that that question would arise sooner or later, Charlie still was not ready for it. Stammering for a minute, and then realizing he had to be totally honest with these loyal friends, he decided to tell them. "I'm a bishop. My name is Carlo Brunini. I am the archbishop of Taranto in southern Italy."

"Oh, my God," Nick exclaimed. "Do you think God sent you to America to be with us, Charlie?"

"I like to think so, Nick. Whatever, I am a better person, a better priest, and a better archbishop because of what I have learned from you, my special family. I'll tell you, I now know why Jesus called himself the Good Shepherd. It was because he had such a deep and beautiful feeling of love for people like you, and among all the people he knew in Palestine, they were the ones he loved and worried about the most. And he made treatment of you and those like you the basis for how he will judge people when they die. He will say to people who are kind to you, 'Come, blessed of my Father, into the kingdom of heaven, because when I was homeless and hungry and naked and ill and in prison, you cared for me. As long as you did this for the least among you, you did it to me. So come into my Father's home, and those who are not kind to you, God will give them a hard time, a very hard time.'"

Carlo's little family of homeless people was devastated by the prospect of his leaving. They had come to look upon him, even though he was much younger than most of them, as their father. They had learned to go to him when they had problems, when they were depressed, when they received bad news about their families, when one of them got sick and had to go to the emergency room. He worried about each one of them. He was of greatest help to them was when they had a serious medical problem. Carlo made sure they went to a doctor, if they could find one who would help them even though they had no medical insurance. When they needed costly medicine prescribed by the doctor, Carlo then was not just a homeless beggar for himself, he begged for money to buy medicine for his sick friends. He always carried their prescriptions with him to show people he was sincere, because often the medicine was not cheap. He was surprised how many really generous people there were among just ordinary people, though some insulted him with their hateful attitude. It was just like back home.

He would often care for his friends when they became ill, especially in miserable weather. He would beg for special food from store managers and cook the food himself when he went back "home" to their village along the tracks. He was fast learning what Jesus meant when he said that the Good Shepherd always worried about the sheep and went around looking for them and caring for them.

The thought of their dear friend now leaving filled them with memories of all that he had done for each of them. This made their grief all the worse, and as one of the men said, worse than the grief he felt at his divorce. When they asked when he was going to leave, he told them within the next two weeks. He still had some unfinished business, especially with Marty and Miss Delaney. Rudy asked if they could all come to the airport with him and see him off. Charlie told them he would be honored.

As soon as Marty found out that Charlie had returned from his trip, he went over to the village of the homeless and invited Charlie and any of the others to go to mass the next Sunday with his family and Miss Delaney. Everyone at the village accepted—thirteen in all—not so much because they were dedicated Catholics—over half of them were anything but Catholic—but more as an expression of solidarity with their friend and protector, who would be leaving them forever.

When Sunday came and the crew of them piled into the church, the consternation was evident on the part of the very conservative old-time parishioners. Were it not for Marty and his family, whom everyone knew and respected, there might have been a scene, but after the original shock, the people settled down and the mass commenced. At communion only a few of the homeless accompanied Marty and his family, and Charlie, to the altar to receive the Eucharist. Again the priest passed over Charlie. This time the deacon was not there to make up for the pastor's rudeness. The other homeless who went to receive were in another aisle, and the eucharistic minister gave them the Eucharist, so they didn't notice their friend being slighted by the priest.

Realizing that the priest had refused Charlie, Marty broke his own communion in half and gave half to Charlie, which was observed by the pastor, very much to his annoyance. Fortunately, the other homeless men did not even notice what had taken place, or they would have been deeply offended to see something like that happen to their friend. Charlie, however, accepted what had happened as a welcome experience in his retreat to learn about the homeless poor, and their treatment by society, even "very Christian" society. Such treatment did, however, add to the gradual deterioration of his self-image and to his growing realization of his own personal unworthiness of God's special concern for him. He had for all those months on the road come to the understanding of himself as no better and in fact sometimes, even worse than some of the homeless, many of whom he had learned to recognize as beautiful persons because of an innate simplicity and innocence, and humility, of which he found only too little in himself.

After mass Marty took the whole crew to a restaurant, where the waiter discreetly ushered them to a quiet corner where they would not become the main attraction. Maureen and the kids enjoyed the whole experience, especially since some of the homeless turned out to be real stand-up comedians, particularly Willie, who had actually been a comedian in the past. He had only recently fallen on hard times and was totally destitute of every material possession, except for his talent as a comedian, which came to life halfway through the brunch.

"Can you imagine," Willie started out, "what a job we could do if we had our own restaurant? If the Three Stooges could make a go of it, imagine the name the Thirteen Stooges scrawled all over the front of the shop. People would come in just for the show, out of sheer curiosity, and then, with Jake's cooking, nobody in the county could compete with us. We could even advertise, 'Cooking like you never had in your whole life.' No other restaurant can possibly cook like Jake, or serve the kind of food that Jake cooks. 'Come and taste Jake's delicious cuisine. Guaranteed, you'll never be the same.'"

Willie had to wait until the guys stopped laughing.

"And once we put you guys' picture in the newspaper ads, that alone would draw the first big crowd; just to see you all in real life, because nobody would believe it. What other restaurant would have waiters and staff like you guys? It would be real class in camouflage. Nobody could compete with what you would offer. People would come from all over, just for the experience. And of course the entertainment would be free. And the drinks, half of you could take turns being bartenders, and with all those years of experience behind you, you could stump the experts. Nobody could handle that stuff like you guys."

By that time, the manager, hearing all the laughter, quietly walked over to see what was going on. When he saw the show, he realized he had a real live one there right in his restaurant. He said nothing then, but when the group was leaving, he cornered Willie and asked if he would like a job working at the restaurant four nights a week. He told the manager that he would have to discuss the matter with his agent, Marty O'Dea. Before they all left, Marty and the manager made arrangements to meet the next day to discuss details for a contract. Two days later Willie had a job. The rest of his buddies were speechless.

After the Sunday brunch, everybody parted. Charlie, however, had some unfinished business with Marty. He now had to

share with Marty and Miss Delaney what he had already told
the others about leaving soon to go back home. Charlie's homeless friends easily accepted whatever he told them, but Marty
was more cynical than the simple homeless people and would
require a more detailed explanation. So when Charlie told
Marty that he had important news to share, Marty invited him
and Miss Delaney back to his home and led them into the privacy of his den. Then Charlie began to tell them his amazing
story.

"Marty, I have already shared with my homeless family that
my time here is coming to an end."

"Coming to an end? You're not dying are you?" Marty said in
shock.

"No, no, nothing like that. My stay here is coming to an end.
I have been a homeless beggar for the past year and a half, and
it was a great learning experience for me. I was, however, a
homeless beggar by choice, not by necessity, and now it is time
for me to go back home and back to work."

"What do you mean, by choice? And where's back home,
Charlie?"

"In southern Italy."

"In southern Italy? But, you speak perfect English."

"That was part of my training."

"Training for what?"

"Marty, you may have trouble believing this, but I was trained
by the Vatican for the Vatican diplomatic service. I am really a
priest, an archbishop, to be precise. My real name is Carlo
Brunini."

Marty's jaw dropped open.

"I am the archbishop of Taranto in southern Italy," Carlo went
on. "The pope gave me special permission to live as a homeless
person so I could see how the poor are treated. I felt this was
necessary if I was to understand why Jesus, as the Good Shepherd, was so concerned about the poor. My pilgrimage-retreat
was a very important learning experience for me, and I have

learned much not only about the poor, but about myself and how we as priests too often look upon the poor and, more important, how we should treat the poor. My life will never be the same. I realize, Marty, it was not fair to keep my identity hidden from people and to let them treat me like any other homeless beggar, but for those who were kind to me, like you and your family and Miss Delaney, and my family of homeless friends, I have the warmest feelings of gratitude for your genuine goodness and caring. I promise to remember you always."

Miss Delaney just sat there speechless, hardly believing what her ears were hearing. In all her years as a loyal Irish Catholic she had never heard of an archbishop demeaning himself by resorting to such strange behavior. It was very hard for her to accept.

Marty fell back in his armchair in total shock. "My scraggly, homeless beggar friend Charlie, an archbishop! I am almost beyond shock. I can hardly believe what you are telling me. I have had vagrants tell me all kinds of stories, and when I was younger I fell for them, but this has to top them all. I have to be honest, Charlie, I have a hard time believing you. Do you have any evidence whatsoever of what you are telling me?"

Charlie, with a broad grin and quiet laugh, opened his shirt, reached under his t-shirt, and took out the leather pouch containing his important papers. Opening it, he showed Marty his passport and the Vatican document certifying him as archbishop of Taranto. Marty could only look at these obviously authentic credentials and realize that all that was happening to him was an incredibly real-life movie episode.

"Well, Charlie, or Bishop, or whatever I have to call you from now on, I have to admit I am totally lost for words. Would you mind if Maureen and the children came in, so you can tell them what you just told me? After you leave, there is no way they will believe this story if it comes from me, with no verification from you."

"Go ahead, Marty. I owe it to them."

Marty called out to his wife and told her to bring the kids into the den for a surprise. A few minutes later, they were all in the room.

"You'd better all sit down, because you are in for one hell of a shock," Marty told his family. "Would you believe me if I told you that Charlie is not really a homeless beggar, but in reality is a bishop, and not just an ordinary bishop, but an archbishop?"

"No way!" Donald burst out in a laugh, and the others chimed in with the same startled exclamation, "No way, no way!"

Meaghan was the most perplexed. "What's this, a joke or something? You certainly don't look like an archbishop to me. Yuk! You have to be kidding."

Charlie laughed, recognizing the preposterous picture of a scraggly bum being an archbishop. Charlie really liked Meaghan; she was real and down to earth. Every time she opened her mouth, she said just what was going through her mind, revealing her true self, and that was refreshing.

"What will you do when you go back to Italy?" Maureen asked.

"My secretary will pick me up at the airport and drive me to the Vatican to make my report about my pilgrimage-retreat to the Holy Father. Then I will go back to my diocese and resume my work as archbishop. All that people will know is that I had been on extended leave. Everyone will probably presume that I was on a special assignment for the pope, since I had been trained for diplomatic work."

"How are you going to get to Rome from here?" Marty asked.

"I already have my ticket and my passport. It's just a matter of getting to Kennedy Airport in New York."

"And how are you going to get to Kennedy?" Marty pressed him again.

Charlie laughed. "Time is short now, so I have to take a flight from Albany to Kennedy."

"I'd be happy to drive you, if you like. Maybe we can all go with you, all except Meaghan. I don't think she'd want to come."

"Oh, no, you're not leaving me out. If you're going, I'm going, too," she said to her father. "I wouldn't miss this for the world."

"Okay, so that's settled. When are you leaving, Charlie?"

"My flight is Wednesday morning at ten o'clock. My little family wants to accompany me to the airport, too, so we'll have to make arrangements for them."

Marty broke out in a belly laugh. "Charlie, when you do something, you really do it in a big way. And now it's my turn. I've got the perfect solution. This will have to be done in grand style. I am going to rent two limousines to take us all to the airport. Miss Delaney, your homeless friends, my family, and you."

Even Charlie had to break out into a guffaw at the absurdity of such an arrangement. "Wait until everybody sees us homeless bums getting out of two limousines at the airport. We'll be lucky if Homeland Security doesn't take us all in as suspects."

"Now what about clothes and a shave, Charlie?"

"Just the way I am is fine. No one will recognize me this way. And as soon as I exit from the gate at the airport in Rome, my secretary will recognize me by the clothes, especially by the patch here on my right pant leg, which he sewed there when I tore my pants getting out of the car. If I shave, I will be too easily recognized, since I am not totally unknown in Italy, so the beard will do fine. In fact, I kind of like it."

Meaghan had one last question, "If we're going to be riding in the car with you, you *are* going to take a shower before we go, aren't you?"

"Yes, Meaghan. Just for you."

With that, everything was settled. Marty took Miss Delaney home and dropped Charlie off at the village of his homeless family.

The next few days were sad days for everyone at the camp, but they were busy making presents for their friends in Mexico, so they could keep in touch with them. The phone Charlie was giving them would be well used. He arranged this with Marty, and he also asked him to help the others send their presents to Mexico. They were Marty's friends now, too, like he was taking Charlie's place.

Charlie's presence with his homeless friends had created bonds among them all and molded them into a real family. They cared for one another and lived for one another, as it was centuries ago. It wasn't planned. It just happened that way. One big concern among all of them was how Charlie would manage to keep in touch with them. This created a problem because they had no address. Jake suggested they make a mailbox, or buy one if they had to, and set it up on the road and tell the mailman about it to make sure their mail would be delivered. They executed that project in two days and asked the postmistress at the post office what their address would be. When she told them, "1 Dead End Street, Albany, NY 12201–1111," they all laughed and then went home and put it on the mailbox. They made a post from an old dead locust tree trunk and fastened the mailbox on top. Then they dug a hole and secured the post in front of their little village. The mailman got a big laugh when they showed it to him. "What a strange group of homeless people you guys are, with a real address for your shacks. Unheard of! You guys have sure changed since I first delivered mail down this way."

Wednesday arrived and the two stretch limousines showed up at the village of Charlie's homeless friends at precisely seven o'clock. They packed themselves into the cars with Marty's family and Miss Delaney and Charlie and took off for the airport. It was not a long drive, taking little more than half an hour, and they arrived in plenty of time.

Before Charlie went through security, they all hugged one another and were bawling like children. It was a long time since any of them had cried or been emotional about anybody. The lives of that little group, including Marty, Maureen, the children, and Miss Delaney, would be changed forever. And as different as they were, from that day on, they bonded into one grand–if odd–family, going to church together and caring for one another.

When the rumor about that scraggly beggar and his true identity spread around the parish, the pastor asked Marty if it was true. Marty assured him that it was. From that day on, the pastor spent much of his free time caring for the poor in his parish and visiting Charlie's homeless friends.

13

IT WAS 4:00 IN THE AFTERNOON when Carlo's plane landed at Fiumicino Airport, a half hour's car ride from Rome itself. When Carlo came out of the gate, he walked straight to the entrance and sure enough, his faithful secretary, Monsignor Agnelli, was waiting, having just arrived after circling around the loop for the third time.

As Carlo walked to the car, the secretary got out and opened the back door for Carlo to enter.

"No, no, Mario. I'll sit in the front with you."

As soon as they got settled in the car, the secretary's phone rang.

"Hello. Yes, Your Excellency. It will take about forty minutes. Thank you, Your Excellency. The secretary then turned off his cell phone.

"The Vatican, Mario?"

"How on earth did you know? The Holy Father wants you to come to his apartments immediately. Your Excellency, do you want to change into your clerical clothes? They are in the back seat. I thought you might want to wear them in case we had to meet with the pope."

"Mario, I think I would like to go in looking just like this. I am sure the Holy Father has been wondering about my appearance as a homeless beggar and how I protected my identity. I think he'll break down laughing when he sees me."

The drive to Rome and the Vatican was pleasant, especially as Monsignor Agnelli pumped Carlo with a thousand questions about his pilgrimage-retreat.

"Mario, I learned a lot. I think I know now why Jesus had such a tender spot in his heart for the poor. It takes great faith and simplicity of spirit to be poor and not despair. It takes enormous courage to decide to keep on living. The homeless are remarkable people. Their very life is a prayer—desperate, silent, unspoken pleading with God to keep them alive. And by some miracle, no, not one miracle, but by a continuous chain of miracles all day long and all night, they do stay alive, especially on freezing cold days and nights. It is so hard to sleep when you are freezing. I learned that firsthand. For them to survive, they have to be on God's mind day and night, as he watches out for them. I can now understand why God has such love for them, Mario. But, tell me, how are things in our diocese? Is everything quiet and peaceful? No disturbances? No scandals?"

"It's been good, Your Excellency. The people like the vicar general who took your place. He is very quiet and easy going. Everything just flowed smoothly, as if you had never even left. He let everything go on as usual, so you could feel comfortable when you returned. I think you'll be pleased when you get back and see all is ready for you to take over the reins again and pick up where you left off."

They finally arrived at the Vatican, and when they approached the entrance, the Swiss Guards were totally mystified at the sight of a beggar expecting admission to the Vatican offices. However, they recognized Monsignor Agnelli, who told them that nothing had changed except the actor's makeup. The guards insisted on calling the office to request instructions as to whether they should grant access to Monsignor Agnelli and a homeless beggar. The official inside was shrewd enough to ask no further questions. All he said was, "The Holy Father is expecting them." There were no salutes this time, just bewilderment.

When the two arrived at the pope's office, the secretary announced their arrival, and ushered them into the room, and immediately withdrew.

The pope had been anxiously awaiting them but was not expecting the sight that stood before him. Caught totally off guard, he broke out in a loud laugh, "So this is what the distinguished Archbishop of Taranto really looks like! Carlo, Carlo, my dear friend! I have to admit, this is really a shock." The pope gave Carlo a welcoming hug and could not resist commenting, "Archbishop, you have an odor, and it is not the odor of sanctity!" Holding his breath, the pope still hugged him and patted his back, but pretended to gag.

"Sit down, sit down, and tell me all about your adventure."

"Holy Father, it was the experience of my life. I learned more about Jesus during the past year and a half than I learned in the whole rest of my life, including seminary. I have finally come to realize why Jesus has such a passionate love, yes, a passionate love for the poor and the outcasts. He could see clearly how an arrogant and self-righteous society had stripped millions of his poor of their dignity and pride as God's children and reduced them, even in their own eyes, to nothing more than unwanted trash. Now I understand why he took pride in identifying himself as the Good Shepherd and homeless himself, because he himself was treated by the leaders of his own people as trash to be eliminated. I now feel firsthand what that kind of daily treatment does to a person. And Jesus also knew it firsthand, and it finally makes sense why Jesus could identify with the poor and the poor with him. Whatever you do to the poor, you do to me."

"Carlo, I am proud of you. I know it must have been humiliating, but you kept your dignity and acted with prudence. We almost had to intervene when you were detained with the Mexican migrant workers, but you handled the situation so adroitly we decided you could take care of yourself, and so no one was the wiser as to your identity. I found myself looking forward to the reports from those who kept an eye on you from time to time. It was like watching a television series. I particularly enjoyed your escapades traveling in box cars as you went from place to place across the country."

"Holy Father, I'm glad I didn't know you knew. It was a life-changing experience for me. I felt very comfortable being one of them, and I will from now on always have that image of myself as one of them. Whenever I look in a mirror, I will see not a fancy-robed archbishop but a shabby homeless beggar. They have a goodness, a humility, and a spiritual dignity that Jesus could see in them, and I felt proud to be among them, especially in the end, when we had become a family and were caring and concerned for one another."

"Well, Monsignor Agnelli, what do you think of the prodigal returned?"

"He looks just fine, Holy Father, more a bishop than ever, the kind we should see more often."

"That is precisely why I think it is so important for him to return to his diocese immediately before the aura of this newfound sanctity wears off. Are you ready to get back to work, Your Excellency?"

"Yes, Holy Father. I think I have an entirely fresh understanding of what Jesus really expects of me from now on."

"No more shocks, I hope, Carlo. This one was like an earthquake. But you did handle the whole experience with great care. I am sure you will continue administering your diocese with the same discretion."

"That I will, I promise, with God's help."

"Carlo, one last thing. You make a fine-looking homeless beggar, and I want a photograph of this before you leave. Another thing, I don't want you leaving here looking like that. I'll have my barber come up and cut your hair and give you a good shave. And while you're waiting, you can take a shower in my bathroom. I want you walking out of here looking like an archbishop. There must be robes around here that will fit you. They'll be on the bed when you finish your shower. And I'll have the house-keeper throw those clothes out."

"No, no, Holy Father. These clothes I must keep as a reminder of just who I am. They are a treasure to me."

"Carlo, you are an enigma. I'll have them washed and ironed so Mario won't get nauseated on the drive home."

"Thank you, Holy Father."

As Carlo went into the bedroom to prepare for his shower, the pope spent a few minutes talking to Monsignor Agnelli. "Mario, we are both blessed to be friends with the most saintly person I have ever come across in my life."

"I know, Holy Father, and he's the only one who doesn't know it. He still feels he is not worthy. I worry about him so much. He is so vulnerable and so innocent."

"That's what makes him what he is, Mario. His life is going to be very different. I know you will be his wise confidante."

"Thank you, Holy Father. I will try."

An hour later Carlo emerged like a new man, totally trans-formed from a straggly, homeless beggar to the tall, distinguished archbishop. He even smelled like an archbishop. He was carry-ing a tiny suitcase containing his "treasure."

"It's like a resurrection, Your Excellency!" the pope commented.

"Thank you, Holy Father. And thank you for being so kind to me. I will do my best to justify your faith in me."

"God bless you, Carlo, and please be careful and go slow. And pray for me."

"You are always in my prayers. And I know I have yours."

"May God go with you, Carlo, and you too, Mario.

The pope walked them to the door and watched, deep in thought, as they walked down the hall.

The pope's secretary approached the pope and reminded him of his dinner appointments.

"Thank you, Monsignor. I would have preferred to have dinner with those two."

The monsignor did not ask what happened to the homeless beggar who had entered an hour before.

FATHER

Jesus then said, "Let the little children come to me, and do not stop them; for it is to such as these that the kingdom of heaven belongs."
—Matthew 19:14

14

Taranto

BY THE WEEKEND CARLO HAD MADE the unlikely transition from beggar to archbishop. Phone calls and meetings with staff and recent piles of mail were reduced to a manageable level.

Before him now was the Sunday mass, which he knew would be packed with well-wishers, friends, and many who would come out of curiosity.

The cathedral was filled to overflowing. He began the service by telling them he was happy to be home and that he had missed all his dear friends in his vast diocese and had prayed for them every day. He then became quite personal in sharing with his flock the purpose of his absence and all that he experienced.

"My dear friends, the reason I took time off was for a long retreat, which I know I needed. It was to understand why Jesus is so concerned about the poor that he made our eternal salvation dependent on how we treat them. You know those words of Jesus, 'Come, blessed of my Father into the kingdom prepared for you from the beginning of time, for when I was hungry, you gave me food, and when I was thirsty, you gave me drink,' and so on. I felt a need to understand why Jesus is so insistent on how his followers treat the poor, and the only way I could find that out was if I became one of them.

"So, for all that time I was away from you, I lived the life of a homeless beggar. And I learned in a very painful way what it is to be poor and homeless. I was made to scrub restaurant floors for a meatball sandwich and then kicked out so the restaurant's customers wouldn't see the likes of me. I was refused communion by a priest. I was arrested and put in jail because a district attorney needed a suspect for a crime that, as it turned out, was never committed. And I was arrested with a group of migrant farmers and shipped off to Mexico. When I finally re-crossed the border, I got in a box car and traveled by train across the United States back to where I had been previously. In this long and painful experience, my image of myself was totally destroyed, and I was made to feel like my fellow homeless, not a blessed child of a loving God, but a piece of human trash. And for the first time I saw through Jesus' eyes how his followers treat his image in the poor. They totally destroy their pride and dignity as human beings and reduce them to useless and unwanted outcasts of society. So, now when I look at myself in the mirror, I do not see a respected archbishop but a shabby homeless beggar, a feeling I don't think I will ever get over. Now that I am back home and among you, my family whom I love, I appreciate all of you more than ever, and I hope that you pray that I will always understand and appreciate each and every one of you as a precious child of God. Please don't see me as bishop but as *father.*"

After mass, Carlo was overwhelmed when he went outside to greet them. It was over an hour before the crowd thinned out and he could go back to his residence to rest.

Later he wrote letters to Marty O'Dea and Miss Delaney and his family of homeless friends, and he made sure a cell phone was provided for them.

On Monday, Carlo had Mario handpick a special committee to come to the chancery to meet with Carlo for the purpose of identifying all the homeless people in the city of Taranto. By late Thursday morning, twenty-five people showed up for the meeting with the archbishop. Over a light lunch the archbishop explained his plan to the group. He wanted to know every homeless person in the archdiocese and know them by name. They were his wandering sheep, and he needed to know each of them by name.

"Bishop, there are hundreds," a woman explained.

"I know, so I am going to have to sharpen my memory," the archbishop replied. He continued, "I would like you to break up into teams and go three or four at a time to each section of the city. Work together; and as some of the neighborhoods can be dangerous, be careful. As you contact them, tell them that the archbishop invites them to the cathedral hall on next Tuesday at noon. That will give you plenty of time to find them and contact them, and tell them to spread the word to others whom you may not be able to reach. I know that many of them, if not most, are from North Africa, not Catholic, and not here legally, but they are God's children and within our care."

The committee did its job well. By Saturday, the teams had tracked down over four hundred homeless people, men and women of a variety of nationalities. There were people from Morocco, Algeria, Tunisia, and Egypt, as well as local Italians and Italians who had come from the north to the warmer southern climate. There were Muslims as well as Christians, and no doubt some with no faith. The archbishop was surprised by the large number from North Africa. The homeless themselves were wary about the purpose of the gathering, but they gradually relaxed and eventually felt quite proud that the archbishop wanted to get to know each of them. They liked that.

On the following Tuesday, close to 450 homeless people showed up at the cathedral hall. The archbishop was already there, waiting to welcome each one as he or she entered. As more and more entered, the fragrance of the place became more and more ripe. Some of the archbishop's staff members had to excuse themselves.

When the last of the stragglers came in, the archbishop suggested they all relax and sit down. As soon as they were seated, he told them the purpose of the meeting, and said he would explain it further, but thought that they should eat first. He invited them to share the simple lunch that had been prepared for them.

They were all very orderly and respectful. They filed up patiently to get their food and then returned to their places. While they were eating, the archbishop told them that from now on, they did not need to be homeless. The cathedral was their home, and at noon each day they were welcome to come and eat in the hall. Also, there was an ancient building that was part of a farm the archdiocese owned and that was not being used. If they were willing to work together and fix up that building, there would be plenty of room for everyone to live there. The building had been built over three hundred years before and like an old castle could easily accommodate four hundred and fifty homeless men, women, and children.

"Are there any stone masons, carpenters, plumbers, electricians, and other craftspeople among you?" the archbishop asked. "I would like those with management ability and with contracting experience to meet with me afterward so we can take a ride over to the site and begin plans to renovate the building."

Hands went up all over. There was more than enough talent to handle the undertaking.

When lunch was finished, the archbishop told them that lunch would be ready at the same time the next day. They all clapped and in one voice yelled out, "Thank you, Bishop."

As soon as Carlo's lawyers and architects presented their plans to the city officials, calls started coming into the chancery from shadowy characters who controlled practically all new construction and renovations in the city. Their first overture was very low key and involved one of their emissaries approaching the archbishop and offering the organization's people to handle all that had to be done. When they were told that the archbishop already had his architects, engineers, and workers lined up, the attitude changed. A note was dropped off at the chancery by a stranger, telling the archbishop that the labor force for the project was not negotiable. Either the organization's people, which was in reality the Mafia, would do all the work, or there would be nothing done.

Carlo was furious. Father Mario had never seen the archbishop so angry. He was always calm and thoughtful when confronted with a crisis. This, however, was the first time the archbishop was challenged by the criminal element in his diocese. They had thrown down a gauntlet, demanding that he cooperate or else. It was not a lightly veiled threat. And some of these were his own parishioners, who dared to go to church and walk up to the altar to receive the Body of Jesus Christ on Sunday mornings.

The secretary did not know how to handle his superior's reaction, which was a deathly silence. The archbishop stood on the spot motionless, his ordinarily gentle features now looking like steel. For the first time Mario glimpsed the smoldering volcano that drove this man in everything he set his mind to, and he knew that the challenge by the Mafia was going to be a drama such as the city had never witnessed. He knew the archbishop was shrewd, and he could be as cunning as a cobra when threatened. Each move would be well calculated and accurately timed. He could see the archbishop's brilliant mind already plotting the war plan. While the Mafia used intimidation and death threats as weapons, the archbishop would counter with cunning intellect and flawless stealth that would eventually send the Mafia reeling, wondering what had happened, because there would be no tangible evidence of a single move made by the archbishop.

For a time the secretary stood there not knowing what to do. Finally, the archbishop came out of his trance and said, "Mario, the war has begun. I should have known they would be this way even with the church. These people are brutal and ruthless. I don't want you to say a word to anyone not even your family. From this point on we have to plan every move carefully and plan it well. We cannot afford to make a mistake, and we can trust no one. No one, Mario. The Mafia has spies in every family, on every street corner, in every bar, and they must never know our next move beforehand. In fact, they must not even know we are making a move. Everything we do must be unexpected, with no tangible evidence of our involvement. I am not cold blooded, Mario, but I have to protect my people, and I can't afford any errors. If I make a mistake, it will be the homeless who will pay the price, because they will be the victims of the Mafia's revenge. We will win this battle with God's help and sheer cunning, Mario."

What Carlo did not share with his secretary was the ultimate weapon he intended to use to checkmate the organization. To share too much with his secretary would make Mario vulnerable, because, knowing how the Mafia works, it would only be a matter of time before it approached the secretary and threatened harm to his family if he did not cooperate. The less his secretary knew, the safer he would be.

After much thought, Carlo finally decided that he would share with his secretary only those things that, if they were revealed, would in no way compromise plans known only to himself or betray in any way his covert strategy. Hopefully, the ruthless intimidation techniques of his enemies would be no match for the archbishop's brilliant, strategic mind, camouflaged by his peaceful, friendly personality.

The first round of the contest commenced as soon as the archdiocesan architects and engineers presented the plans for rehabilitating the structure as living quarters for the homeless. The presentation was made by Giulio Alesandrino, an architect, and Giorgio Marchione, an engineer. Both men were known for their impeccable integrity and strong character. Their lives had been threatened before by the Mafia, but they still offered their services to the archbishop for this job, knowing that it would be many times more dangerous than anything they had taken on previously. Both men went to mass and received communion daily. They knew that God would always protect them and their families.

The chancery waited patiently for two months for the government's response to the presentation of the plans—a response that came only after numerous phone calls from the archbishop. All that was needed was approval of the concept and the plans for use of the building. The response came in the form of a formal letter from the city planning department. The response was negative, but the chairman said he would be open to discussion with the archbishop, which he would relay to the other members of the department. The archbishop agreed to the meeting and suggested it be held the following Wednesday at the chancery. The chairman was adamant that the meeting be held at his office as a way of humiliating the archbishop. Carlo's humiliations as a homeless beggar paved his way for accepting the chairman's demand and could in no way be taken as a sign of weakness.

On the day of the meeting Carlo arrived at the chairman's office promptly at 1:00 p.m. as the chairman demanded. At 1:35 the chairman entered the room with no apology for his gross tardiness. The archbishop very graciously rose when he appeared, receiving no recognition at all for his courteous gesture.

The chairman, Vito Malatesta, took his seat behind his desk and brusquely asked, "And what is it you are here for, sir?"

"At your request I have come to discuss with you the matter of the proposed construction for the building owned by the archdiocese."

"Oh, yes. I presume you know why you were turned down?"

"I have no idea," the archbishop replied.

"I have been informed that you intend to use your own workers. Is that correct?"

"Yes, and I appreciate your telling me that, Mister Chairman, because you have revealed something very important."

"And what is that?"

"The people with whom you are intimate and who make the decisions."

The chairman turned red, partially from embarrassment for being so lax in saying what he did, and partially in anger that the archbishop knew from his own lips that he was taking his orders from the Mafia.

The archbishop sat perfectly straight in his hard chair and looked intently into the chairman's eyes. From that point on the chairman was in an awkward position and found it uncomfortable to look directly at the archbishop. He looked over the archbishop's left shoulder every time he raised his eyes to speak.

"Why do you insist on using your own workers?" the chairman asked.

"For one simple reason. Because the people who are going to live there are capable of doing their own work. They are all well qualified but are at the present time unemployed and homeless. To me, it seems a very simple thing to understand that if a poor family has nowhere to live, and the family members are knowledgeable enough to build themselves a house, why would anyone require them to hire others at exorbitant prices to build the house for them? It is just plain common sense."

"I will judge what makes sense. The law requires that licensed craftsmen must be hired to do any construction work within the city and the surrounding area."

"I did not realize that, Mister Chairman. I am very well aware of who works on the homes of important people in the community, and *they* are not licensed craftsmen."

"You seem quite aware for someone who is out of touch with real life."

"Perhaps the blind see more clearly than those who see."

"Clever, Priest, but not wise. You still have not given me reason why your project should be approved."

"For one very simple reason, and a very good reason, Mister Chairman. Because poor members of your own family will be living there, relatives whom you have long ignored. The news-papers would love that story."

The chairman was about to go into a rage but knew that he would be ceding defeat to the enemy, so he reluctantly calmed down. He was fast realizing he wasn't dealing with some ignorant priest from out in the mountains, but rather a shrewd fox who had his own intelligence as to what was going on in the commu-nity. Now he was wondering who in his own family would know that he was giving the archbishop a difficult time and was respon-sible for denying the children of his own younger brother and cousin a place to live. Some of his family were already furious with him because of his rudeness to relatives, which had become a festering boil within the whole family. Now he had not only the Mafia to deal with, but members of his family as well.

"Priest, I can see you have thought out your strategy well and have not come here unprepared. I will discuss this matter with other members of the department and send you the final decision within a few days."

With that, the archbishop rose and, without extending a hand, merely said, "I wish you well with your conscience, Mister Chair-man, as even you are answerable to a higher chairman someday, and he is not blind!" He then walked out, unescorted.

Priests are often treated with similar rudeness by those who are educated beyond their intelligence, and Carlo had long since become used to such treatment, as anti-clericalism is rampant throughout many parts of Italy, especially in the south, where there is so much poverty and where many priests have not dealt kindly with the people.

When Carlo returned to the chancery, Father Mario was cu-rious as to how he had made out with the chairman.

"As I expected, my dear Mario, poorly. Would you come into my office? I have some things to discuss with you."

The two men went into the archbishop's office and sat in two comfortable chairs. Carlo always had his guests, even chancery workers, sit in comfortable chairs, treating them as friends rather than clients or subordinates when he chatted with them.

"Mario, the chairman of the planning department, Vito Malatesta, is surely well named [*malatesta* means "headache"], and you have known his family from childhood, haven't you?"

"Yes, Excellency." Mario always became formal when the archbishop was keyed up over important business.

"Can you share anything with me that might help in getting our construction project approved?"

"Bishop, Malatesta and I have never been good friends. In fact, when we were kids, we never got along. He was always a bully and not very bright. When he grew up, he joined the Communist Party and has been a member ever since, but lately I think he's under the thumb of the Mafia. It pretty much dictates what he can do and what he cannot do. He runs the planning department, because the other members are afraid of him because of his contacts with the Mafia, so they do whatever he wants. You have to be very careful, Excellency, because these guys can be ruthless. They may not be bright, but they can be really mean, cruel."

"Do you know the Malatestas who were here at the luncheon last week?"

"You really do have a good memory. Yes, Bishop, they are relatives of Vito. They are the children of Vito's younger brother and the children of his cousin. Their parents were good Catholics who would not join the Communists, even when Vito threatened them, so he made their lives miserable, using his contacts to have them laid off from their jobs and kept out of work until they lost their homes and were forced to live among the homeless. I think it was the heartbreak and humiliation of losing everything that killed them, and they left behind eight children, who are homeless. Vito could easily take all of them in, and support them, but he's a *testa dura*, a hard head, and he won't do a thing to help them."

"Do you know them well?" Carlo asked.

"I knew their parents. We all grew up together. They would be honored to know that you even know them and are concerned about them."

"Tell them that I would like them to have lunch with me. Since they will wonder what it's all about, I don't want them to be suspicious about anything. Just tell them you had said so many nice things about them that I wanted to meet them."

"I'd be glad to do that, Bishop. That's kind of you."

Mario did as instructed. When he tracked down the homeless members of the chairman's extended family and told them the archbishop would like to invite them to lunch, they were surprised and happy.

Mario was shocked at how young they were. There were eight of them in all, the youngest merely seven years old. When they learned they would be seeing the archbishop, they were thrilled.

When they arrived, right on time, the archbishop himself met them at the front door. They were shocked and didn't recognize him immediately. He was wearing old clothes and pants with a blue patch in the right pant leg. When they looked up at him, they saw it was the archbishop.

"Bishop, why are you dressed like that?" asked Elisabetta, the older of the two girls.

"I am one of you. I learned to live like you for a while just to see how people would treat me. It was horrible, but I learned the homeless are beautiful people, and I wanted to put you at ease and let you know that I am one of you and am still your archbishop."

Carlo hugged each of them warmly, then ushered them all into the dining room and seated them one by one. Making small talk and joking with the children, he seated the girls, one on each side of him, and then after offering a prayer, started serving each of them their soup. When he finished serving the soup, he put the bowl of olives and celery and the pasta at the opposite end of the long table, so they could start nibbling. Sausage and peppers were next to the pasta.

"We don't go to church very often, Bishop," Elisabetta said. "We're too ashamed, but now that we know that you are really one of us, we'll come every Sunday from now on and sit right up front, proud that we are there with you."

"Thank you."

They were all pleased when the archbishop called each one by name. "Let's see if I've got this right. On my right side: Carla, Giuseppe, Radolfo, and Eugenio. And on my left side: Elisabetta, Marco, and Vito." When he called Vito's name, the little fellow said immediately, "I was named after my uncle, but I don't like him. He's not nice."

Everyone laughed and agreed, "That's right, Bishop, he's not nice."

Then the archbishop looked at the last one and said, "And you are Francesco, the oldest of all, at eighteen, and you are like a father to all the others, aren't you?"

"Yes, sort of, Bishop. I look after them all."

"Well, I want all of you to know that from now on you are all like my little family."

"And you are *our* friend, Bishop," Francesco replied. "We are grateful for your generosity."

"It is not generosity, Francesco. You deserve a home. And you can help make this cold, abandoned building a home for all of us, if you wish, and a symbol to the people of the archdiocese."

The children looked at each other in amazement.

"Now, let's eat!" Carlo said, "and then I will show the young ones their rooms at the other house."

After offering thanks to God and asking his blessing, they all dived into their food as if they had not eaten in weeks.

Carlo was moved by how these children had responded with simplicity and called him their friend. He thought of Jesus and how happy he was that the poor clung to him. After years of study and the priesthood, but not really learning about Jesus,

Carlo was beginning to understand the heart of Jesus, and it brought tears to his eyes.

"Why are you crying, Bishop," Elisabetta asked him as she offered him a tissue from her pocket. Elisabetta was a beautiful girl, tall for a twelve year old, with rich blond hair and dark brown eyes that held your gaze, and a lively spirit.

"I am crying because you have accepted me as your friend"

The children continued eating. "This soup is delicious, Bishop," Marco said. "Please tell the cook she did a good job."

Carlo smiled, and said, "Thank you. I will tell her."

"I don't think the cook made this soup. I think the bishop made it," Carla said.

Carla was much younger than Elisabetta. She had a quick tongue and could be a scrapper if someone crossed her. She was short, with curly brown hair, dark complexion, and hazel eyes.

"Did you make it, Bishop?" Eugenio asked.

"Yes. I wanted to. Last year it was the homeless people who were kind to me. Many others were not so nice. They didn't know I was an archbishop because I was dressed like this."

"What a story, Bishop! Will you tell us about your adventures?"

"Yes, if you like, but not right now. I want you to tell me all about yourselves."

"There's not much to tell," Elisabetta said. "Our lives are the same every day. We just wander around hoping people will give us something to eat."

"Yeah, even our families don't want us," said Eugenio. "Our parents died a year ago, and some of us are cousins, and their parents died, too, so we became good friends, and we like each other, which makes it easier to be homeless because we at least have friends we can trust."

"Do you go to school?" Carlo asked.

"Well, we used to go to school. We were smart and got good marks, too. But when our parents died, that all ended," Vito said. "We have some relatives, an old aunt and some others, who are nice to us, but they said they have enough to do with their own kids and really can't handle any more."

"But they do give us food when we visit them, and we understand that they don't want any more kids. We wouldn't be happy with them anyway. They're not like us at all. We're happy the way we are, but it's difficult on cold nights," Marco said.

"How old are you?" the archbishop asked.

"Radolfo is nine, Giuseppe is twelve, Carla is ten, Elisabetta is twelve, Marco is fifteen, Eugenio is sixteen, and me, I am eighteen," Francesco said.

"And don't forget me. I'm seven," Vito added.

"No, don't forget Vito," the archbishop added.

"How can we forget him? He's named after our mean uncle whom nobody likes!" Carla said.

As they were finishing their dessert, the archbishop asked them, "Did you see that little house at the end of the garden when you came in?"

"Yes, Bishop, but it's not a little house. It's a big house," Vito said.

"I always dreamed of living in a house like that," said Elisabetta.

"Well, your dream is going to come true. That's the house you are all going to be living in," the archbishop asked.

"Really? You mean it? All of us?" Francesco said.

"Yes, and you will go to school, and you can make our home and property look as beautiful as you want it to be. You can help take care of the grounds and keep everything looking nice. And when people see what beautiful work you do, you will have more business than you can handle, and perhaps someday you will have to hire people to work for you. My groundskeeper, Professor Alessandro Giuliani, will be your mentor, and he will train you to do professional landscaping–how to plant vineyards and grow orchards and make beautiful flower gardens. People will eventually come from many miles around just to see the loving work you will be doing under his direction. And if you bring joy to your work, you will be starting what can be a life-time profession for you, since we Italians love gardens and vineyards and orchards."

"Do you really mean we can live in your house and work for you, Bishop?" Eugenio asked.

"Yes! I will bring you over to the house when we finish. I already made sure that the housekeeper got everything ready for you, so you can all have your own rooms and live like a family. I am busy during the day, so you will have to arrange your own breakfast and lunch. There's enough food in the refrigerator and in the pantry. We can have supper together when I am home, though sometimes I have meetings or I may have to travel, so you will have to cook for yourselves. And on Friday, after work, you will all receive a little stipend so you will have some money to buy the food you like and clothes. I suggest you save a little each week, even if it is not very much, as we never know what the future will bring."

"I'll do the cleaning," Elisabetta said clearly.

"And I'll help Elisabetta," Carla chimed in.

"I'll do the cooking," Francesco said, "since I am the oldest, and Vito can help me. He's my sidekick."

Before they left they all had jobs. The archbishop accompanied them to their new house. The children could not believe that they were going to be living in this beautiful house.

"Look at the beautiful fireplace!" Carla said. "I can make the fires and keep them going."

"And I'll help," Radolfo added.

"Here is a key for each one of you, and remember, no fighting. Make sure you respect one another and share the work *willingly*," the archbishop warned them.

"Thank you so much, Bishop. You are like a father to us. We will not disappoint you," Elisabetta said, as she ran over and hugged him, then rested her head against his chest, not being tall enough to kiss him.

All the others crowded around and hugged him, and they all laughed.

"All right, now. I have to get back to work. Make yourselves at home, and after you get settled, go outside and find Professor Giuliani. He's ready to meet you and be your teacher. We will have supper at seven o'clock."

The children went through the beautiful miniature villa in no time. After minor squabbles over who would get which room and who would room together, they finally settled down in the room with the television. They plopped on the large rug in front of it and in no time had all fallen asleep, a luxury they had not been able to enjoy for a long time.

Over the next few days the children adjusted to their new home and their new life. They liked Professor Giuliani the moment they met him. He was a gentle man with a kind smile, a neatly groomed beard, and a full crop of white, wavy hair. He was an actual professor who had taught paleobotany and horticulture at the University of Rome and had a distinguished reputation for identifying pollen on the Shroud of Turin as being identical with the pollen, and therefore plants, common in Jesus' time and where Jesus lived. Being able to help these homeless children was a dream fulfilled for him, as he had always hoped to have a large family, but at fifty he was still alone.

Professor Guiliani asked the children no questions but showed them around the grounds and told them the names of flowers.

15

"Hello, the Archbishop's office," the receptionist answered.

"Give me Brunini."

"Do you mean the archbishop?"

"Whatever you call him," was the brusque reply.

"May I tell him who is calling?"

"This is the chairman. He'll know who I am."

"The chairman of what? Please, sir, be a little more specific. The archbishop has to be careful, as there are a lot of strange people with high-sounding titles who call, and it is my responsibility to protect the archbishop."

The chairman got the message, namely, that to the receptionist he was one of those angry people who hated clergy, so his tone changed. "This is Vito Malatesta, the chairman of the city planning department. May I speak to His Excellency?" It hurt to say that.

"Just one moment, please, Mr. Malatesta, while I transfer your call."

"Hello, this is the archbishop. May I help you?"

"Yes, this is Malatesta. I hear you've put some of my family up in one of your buildings. Are they your hostages now?"

"No, Mister Chairman, they are not hostages. My secretary knows those children, and to tell you the truth, I was deeply troubled when I found out that they were living in the streets and that you refused to help them. If you cannot see value in them, then I will treat them with the dignity they deserve as God's children. This is not a ploy, Malatesta. They're welcome to live here as long as they wish, and we will train them so they can make a living for themselves in horticulture and landscaping, if they so choose."

"If you are trying to pressure me, let me tell you bluntly, it won't work."

"I have no intention of pressuring you. But if you choose to be impossible to work with, I will do what I have to do."

"You're threatening me again? I'm warning you, it will do you no good!"

"I am not threatening. I will use only legal means to accomplish the good I am determined to accomplish since you and your people allow homeless families and children to wander the streets like they were unwanted animals. I know you are not a Christian, and that's fine, but you are not even a decent human being. To threaten you would be to demean myself. To be honest, I feel contaminated every time I talk to you."

"Then don't expect to get a permit!"

"If I don't get my permit legally from a Mafia stooge, I will get it through other legal means. Then see how your puppet master can protect you."

The chairman slammed the phone on its cradle.

Monsignor Agnelli was in a small room outside the archbishop's office and could not help overhearing what the archbishop had said. He was flabbergasted. Never had he heard the archbishop talk to anyone like that, and he was shocked at the bluntness of his words. A lesser man would be afraid to antagonize an already hostile person in high office, especially a person in a position to grant or deny a needed permit. But he realized that the archbishop must be certain that his alternative plans to get the permit would be successful, otherwise he would not be burning this bridge to ash. The secretary decided that he was happy the archbishop didn't share too much of what he was doing, otherwise he himself would be a nervous wreck.

Carlo knew he had rattled the chairman, which is just what he intended to do. It mattered not one bit what Malatesta would do next, but two days later the chairman and the whole planning department, as well as the mayor, received notices from the archdiocesan lawyers suing them for their denial of a permit to which the archdiocese was legally entitled. War was joined, and it was not going to be pleasant.

No sooner had the officials received the notices than the archbishop received a call from the Vatican. "This is Bishop Wosnicki. The Holy Father would like to speak with you. I will transfer the call to his private phone."

"Thank you, Bishop," Carlo replied.

"Carlo?"

"Yes, Holy Father."

"I have received phone calls from officials in Taranto complaining that you have sued practically all the city officials."

"They are being melodramatic, Holy Father."

"Explain."

Carlo, not trusting the phone lines, began immediately speaking in Russian.

"There are more than 450 homeless people in the city. Having been one of them over the past year and a half, I know the condition to which these people have been reduced. On our property there is a building that is presently not being used. It is adequate to house all these homeless people. Among the homeless are many craftsmen, and women too, who are well able to do all the renovations necessary to fit the building for this purpose. But when I applied for a permit, I was told that we had to use certain workers if we wanted to obtain the permit. I am sure, Holy Father, you are aware what that means. Besides that, the chairman of the planning department, although he is a Communist, is himself taking orders from the organization.

"When I told him outside workers would be extremely costly and in any case were unnecessary since the homeless themselves were expert enough to do all the work, he still insisted that if I wanted the permit, I had to hire the specified workers. Holy Father, there is no way I can let the church cave in to the demands of the Mafia, or to an anti-clerical Communist, and deprive the homeless of taking a stake in their own home."

"Carlo," the pope replied in Russian, "I understand completely, and I admire your bravery. This can be an important test. I trust you to be prudent and make each move judiciously. In dealing with people like this, I have learned that often it is necessary to have outside resources to provide the legal muscle you need, if you understand what I am trying to say. In this I can be a help to you, but for your own sake be careful because these people can be vicious. You have my blessing and my prayers, Carlo, but don't get yourself killed!"

"I promise to be careful, Holy Father. Thank you for your confidence in me."

Carol was relieved that the pope felt comfortable with the way he was handling this delicate situation. The pope knew full well what it was like to be in predicaments like this, and he too did not believe in submitting to the demands of such criminals whose demands undermine society itself.

It was not long after Malatesta had talked to the archbishop that news of the property struggle made the papers, and pressure from the chairman's own family reached the point where, as callous as he was, his life had become so miserable that he knew the situation would only grow worse. His family had been upset enough about his becoming a Communist and became even more upset when they found out that he was being used by the Mafia. It was a dishonor to his family. But the crisis reached the breaking point when his family learned that he had turned against the popular archbishop. They accused him of going out of his mind. No one in the family would have anything to do with him. His family members were not only good Catholics, but they loved the archbishop and would not tolerate anyone in the family doing anything to hurt the church.

The chairman knew he had to make up his mind. If he could patch things up with the archbishop and work out a compromise between the archbishop and the Mafia, that might get him off the hook.

He humbly called Carlo's office and asked if the archbishop would allow him to come and talk with him, to which the archbishop agreed. Malatesta arrived at the chancery and was ushered into the archbishop's office. He was greeted warmly, unlike the rude treatment the archbishop had received at his office.

"What can I do for you, Mister Chairman?" Carlo said kindly.

"I am in a very awkward position, and in fact, a very dangerous position."

"How is that?"

"My family is extremely upset with me. My relatives have much respect for you, and they can make my life a hell if I don't help you. So can we possibly come to a compromise?"

"Is that what you want?"

Malatesta burned. "Yes, Your Excellency."

"What would you like?"

"If you could agree to allow a number of workers of the organization's choosing, maybe that would satisfy them."

"I could agree to that as long as there are no more than twelve. I don't want them to have any kind of leverage."

Malatesta didn't like it, but he didn't think twice. He bowed. "Thank you, Bishop. I am put to shame by your kindness."

Later that afternoon the chairman approached the head of the organization and was rudely rebuffed. The boss refused to budge in the slightest. The organization would not tolerate the church dictating the terms of any agreement. The archbishop would have to use their workers exclusively, and that was it.

The chairman was now desperate. Afraid, yet unwilling to make what he knew would be a fatal break with his family, he also knew that he could not survive if he crossed the Mafia. His only hope was to seek protection from the archbishop, which was humiliating, but at least he had a chance of staying alive.

He made arrangements for another visit with the archbishop and told him frankly the dangerous predicament he was in. He said he had made up his mind to talk to the rest of the board members and get them to approve the plan for the project. But by doing so he was putting his life at risk, and the only hope he had of saving his life was if the archbishop could possibly protect him in some way.

Carlo thanked him, squeezed his shoulders, and assured the chairman that he would do what he could.

With that the chairman left and called an impromptu meeting of the board. They met an hour later, and Malatesta proposed that the board grant approval for the archbishop's project. To his shock, they refused. Only two board members out of six agreed to approve the proposal. Then the chairman realized what had happened. The Mafia suspected that he might try something like this, so its lieutenants "talked" to the other board members and made sure they would vote against the proposal if they knew what was good for them.

Malatesta resigned on the spot and washed his hands of the whole affair. That gave him some hope. Someone else could handle the problem. He could not be blamed if he were no longer there, could he? But still, would the Mafia want revenge for his faltering? Who knew what these people might do? He could take no chances. So he immediately went back to the archbishop's villa and asked to see him.

"The archbishop is having supper," the receptionist said. In fact, Carlo was having supper with the chairman's young relatives.

"But, please, it is extremely urgent."

"Come in and be seated here in the parlor, and I will talk to the archbishop."

When the receptionist told the archbishop who it was, Carlo realized immediately that the chairman was desperate, so he excused himself from his young guests, now his little family, and went out to the parlor to see him.

"Your Excellency, I am no longer the chairman of the city planning department. I brought your proposal to the organization, and it refused to budge. So I called a meeting of the board and presented your proposal and my willingness to compromise, but when it came to a vote, the members voted against it. At that point I knew the Mafia had got to them, as least most of them. I resigned. Now I am just Vito Malatesta, a desperate man obsessed about losing his life. Can you please help me? I'm afraid I'll be safe nowhere. Their goons will find me no matter where I go."

"Of course, I will help you, but now you are in a position to help many others as well. You can stay here with me and live on the third floor. There is only one way there, by elevator, and I will give you the code to get onto that floor. But, you must give me the information I will need to continue my struggle with these people."

"Your Excellency, I will do whatever you want. If you want names, I will give you names. If you need contacts, I will give you contacts."

"How about the lawyers and judges who are in their control"

"I can give you that as well."

"Good, now come with me and I'll show you the elevator and give you the code. There is a bedroom up there and a small kitchen with a refrigerator and stove, and food enough for you to prepare some supper. I don't want anyone to know you are here. So stay up there. Your young relatives are having supper with me now, and it would not be wise for them to know you are here, so adjust your thinking accordingly. I will be up later to talk with you. And one very important thing, do not turn lights on at night on that floor because we have never used it."

"Thank you, Your Excellency. I cannot thank you enough."

The archbishop conducted Vito to the elevator. He then went back to supper with the children as if nothing of any significance had transpired, though inside he was struggling with conflicting emotions.

16

WHEN THE CHILDREN RETIRED to their house, Carlo went up to talk with the former chairman.

"Bishop, I cannot express my gratitude for your kindness, which I know I don't deserve."

"We all deserve love, Vito. You are safe here. And you can help me help the homeless."

For a whole hour Vito poured out the names and details Carlo needed to execute his strategy. And when he finished, the archbishop knew all the key players.

Carlo was surprised to learn that his favorite cousin, Madelena, was one of the lawyers working for a judge who was tied in with the Mafia. Vito assured him, however, that she was in no way involved. She just did her office work and went home. She was never a part of their secret connections.

Carlo reminded Vito to make sure he kept away from the windows and did not turn on the lights at night. He would also have to eat whatever everyone else in the house ate, as they would be watching for any change in grocery orders. With that Carlo left and immediately called the pope. This time he talked to him in Swedish, as he appraised the Holy Father of the change in the situation. He asked if the Holy Father would speak to the highest officials of the federal judiciary to arrange for agents to meet with him in such a way that it would look like a meeting of family friends. Perhaps they could be dressed as priests.

Within a matter of weeks the whole plan was ready for action. The federal agents tapped relevant phone lines and cell phones. Carlo resubmitted the application for approval. The board rejected it. The archdiocesan lawyers sued, the case went to court and was heard in good time, and the judge upheld the denial of the permit to renovate the building.

With that, the federal investigators, using information from wiretaps and careful questioning of witnesses whose phones were tapped, were able to put together a case that was flawless. A trial was held, and the top figures in that Mafia family and their henchmen and the judges were convicted and given long prison sentences. Malatesta figured in none of it. As far as anyone was concerned, he was far away in a world of fear of his own making.

The court also ordered that the permit to renovate the building for the homeless by the homeless be given.

Soon after a letter of approval arrived at the chancery office, and a week later the homeless people were on the construction site, waiting for the architect and materials to arrive, eager to begin work. It would be a long project. A whole new piping system for heat and water for faucets was needed as well as an extensive electrical system. It was like building a medieval monastery, with private rooms and facilities for each person. There would be a common room for gatherings, television, and meetings, and there was a huge dining room.

Once necessary materials and equipment arrived, and each one was given his or her job, the work ran smoothly. The archbishop was even fortunate enough to receive funds from the government in Rome to help with the expenses for what was to be a pilot program to be imitated in other parts of the country. A modest donation also arrived from the Vatican, together with the pope's cautiously worded congratulations on the archbishop's accomplishment, in spite of obstacles that might have intimidated a lesser person.

The archbishop made sure that Vito Malatesta's wife learned what had happened to her husband. She was relieved that he was safe, although surprised at where he was living. She suspected her faithless husband must have had either the scare of his life or some crisis of faith to become so close to the archbishop. But who knows what miracles of grace are accomplished through prayer?

Mrs. Malatesta soon took her two children on a vacation to France and never returned. Through friends back in Taranto she was able to keep in touch with her husband, so that after they were safely settled in France, he could plan for his own departure and a new life with them. Everyone in town was certain that Vito had either slipped out of the country at the start or was long dead, so no one except the archbishop gave him another thought.

17

CARLO DECIDED TO VISIT his own family in Palagiano. It was too long since he had last been home. On this trip he decided to bring his adopted children, who were thrilled that they were going to meet their new extended family.

It was great fun. Carlo's mother was beside herself at seeing her son healthy and happy and none the worse for his encounter with the Mafia. The whole family came from all around to spend a few days for the occasion. When everyone was there, the celebration began and the dancing started. Carlo was happy to see his favorite cousin, Madelena. As usual the relatives chanted, "Carlo, Madelena, Carlo, Madelena!" until the two went to the middle of the dance floor to lead the *Tarantella Siciliana*, which nobody could do as well as that happy duet.

After the dance, they all sat down and attacked the food, spread out on tables strategically placed around the large yard. Carlo brought a plate of the foods she loved to his mother and the same to his father. Then he sat down with both of them.

"Now, son," his mother started out, "tell me all about yourself, but don't tell me about the Mafia. It makes me nervous."

"Oh, Mama," her husband complained, "you and your nerves! That's the best part. I'm dying to hear that part. Why should it make you nervous? He won the case, and they're all in jail."

"No! I still don't want to hear it. Son, you can tell your father later. I just want to know about you. You didn't have any health problems with all that battling, did you?"

"No, mother. I was very careful. I made each move in such a way that the organization didn't even know I was involved. The federal investigators did all the work. As far as the Mafia was concerned, the leaks came from deep within their own organization. And thank God everything worked out well."

"Now, Carlo," his father interrupted, "these new grandchildren we got here, where'd they all come from? You never told us about them before."

"Papa, I found these poor kids wandering the streets, so I adopted them."

"Che bella, son, I'm proud of you," his father added.

At that point Madelena came over and sat down with them. "I hope I'm not intruding," she said, "but I heard you talking about our new cousins."

"They are such well-behaved kids," Carlo's mother said. "So respectful and courteous."

Carlo then took a chance and opened up a subject that had been on his mind for a long time.

"The children have been a blessing," he said, "and they are so appreciative. They really take care of one another, and Francesco, the oldest, is very caring of each of them. But even though I try to be a father to them all, I know I can never meet all their needs. What they really need is a mother figure to balance out their lives."

"What about Madelena? She'd be a good mother," Papa said.

"You mind your business, old man," his wife retorted.

"Just suggesting. Carlo and Madelena have been best friends since they were kids. It would be good for everyone."

"I don't know how good I'd be," Madelena said. "And I do have my work. But it would be a beautiful ministry to care for such beautiful children. Since they are already so well mannered, it would be a joy to nurture the gifts and abilities God has given to them. Maybe Carlo and I could talk it over privately sometime. It's too personal to discuss in a conversation with all the family around, or they'll all have something to say."

With that, the conversation turned to Carlo's pilgrimage-retreat, and other family members came over and formed an audience while Carlo relayed some of the adventures of his year and a half spiritual escapade.

The family celebrated and enjoyed the time together. After two days they parted, and Carlo and the children returned to Taranto. The next day everything was back to normal. The supplies were being delivered to the construction site, and the homeless were thrilled about every detail of their work.

It was a whole week before Madelena called the archbishop to ask if she could come to Taranto to spend some time with the children, telling him that she was interested but could not make a commitment until she saw them in their normal setting. She had always been an academic and was not around children that much. With all their different ages, and her lack of experience, it would be quite the challenge.

She showed up that afternoon and had a chance to see the children working with Professor Giuliani. They were enthusiastic about learning their new profession; it showed in their happy spirit and their willingness to do the work, even though it was hard, digging with shovels and picks, and carrying heavy loads of balled and bagged shrubs and trees. And it was easy to tell that their teacher appreciated their help, as it made his work much easier. He just directed them, and they did the work, most of which he had previously been doing himself or with an occasional helper.

When they finished work, the children went back to wash up and dress neatly for supper at their adoptive father's residence. Carlo called Professor Giuliani and asked him to stop by for a chat with Madelena, who very much wanted to meet him after watching him work.

When Carlo met him at the door, the professor took off his cap, and when Carlo introduced him to his cousin, he took her hand and kissed it, saying how honored he was to meet her more formally.

Carlo led them into the living room, and the three sat in comfortable armchairs around a coffee table with hors d'oeuvres and tea.

Carlo wanted to get on with the meeting, so he got right down to business.

"Let's not be formal. Call me Carlo, and my cousin's name is Madelena."

The professor broke in, "And my name is Alessandro."

"Good, so now that we got that out of the way, Alessandro, I would like you to share with Madelena your opinion of the children you have taken under your wing."

"I wish they were my own children," Alessandro said. "They are so grateful. Even though they have some rough edges from living in the streets for so long, with no one teaching them proper manners, they more than make up for it by their appreciation for the slightest kindness shown them. Each one has his or her own personality. Granted, it does take time and patience to understand where they are coming from, but then it is much easier to accept them. With little suggestions here and there, they do grow, just like the flowers. They are trying hard to please, because they know it is not easy taking a group of kids off the street and being almost like a father to them. Not having a mother shows. Men cannot teach what mothers teach, and mothers have a way that men cannot even begin to understand."

Carlo smiled and felt he had to add, "Madelena, I haven't been talking to Alessandro about our discussion. What he said came right from his heart."

Madelena smiled and said, "I had the impression you might have primed him and prepared him for our little get together."

"Alessandro," she continued, "Carlo asked me to consider an offer that caught me completely off guard. By profession I am a lawyer. I have never married and have not spent much time with children, other than my own siblings and my cousins, of whom Carlo is one. Carlo asked me if I would consider being like a mother to the eight children who have been living here. Carlo has been like a father to these children, and, you have been a big brother to them, teaching them and preparing them for the future. Carlo and I have been close ever since we were children, so it would be easy for me to work side by side with him caring for these children. But I have to consider if I have what it takes to be a mother to eight former street children."

"Madelena, I would never dare suggest what you might do. All I can tell you is what I have experienced the past number of months. When Carlo first asked me to take them under my wing, I was not particularly happy, possibly for the same reasons you just mentioned. But after a week or so, they fit into my life like a favorite old glove. They show me more respect than most children show parents, because they appreciate all that is done for them. It is not my place to suggest, but, may I be bold enough to suggest that you stay here with Carlo for a while and see what it is like? Then you might have a better idea of whether you would feel comfortable taking up Carlo's offer."

"Thank you, Alessandro. That is probably the only way I could gather enough experience to make an intelligent decision."

"That does make a lot of sense," Carlo added. "If Madelena would like to spend some time here, she would be more than welcome."

They finished their tea and snacks. Carlo then asked Alessandro if he would like to join them all for dinner. He was delighted and said he would be back within the hour.

Carlo and Madelena accompanied him to the door and thanked him for his help and his insights. The two of them returned to the living room and waited for Alessandro and the kids to come over for supper.

At the long formal supper table, they looked like a beautiful family, complete now with father and mother. Little Vito looked at Carlo and spontaneously burst out, "Oh, Father, are we going to have a mother?"

That touched Madelena deeply, and her eyes got moist.

"Oh, I'm sorry, Ma'am, I didn't mean to make you cry."

"You didn't say anything wrong, Vito. What you said just touched my heart. Would you like me to be a mother to you?"

"Yes, very much. You are kind, I can tell, and I've never had a mother. She died and so did my father, and no one else wanted us, so it would be so nice to have a mother, especially one as beautiful as you."

Carlo could not help smiling, and when Madelena looked at him, she broke out laughing. "Vito, you and your family are precious. How could one not love you?"

During the meal, Madelena observed, "You children have such good manners at table. Who taught you?"

"The cook, Ma'am," said Radolfo. "She's been teaching us every day, so we don't embarrass our father. We know he's not our father, but he really is our father, and he will always be our father, even if we can't stay here for very long."

"Radolfo, please don't think like that," Carlo interrupted. "You will be able to live here as long as I am here. You are my family, and, yes, I am your father and will always be a father to you. Don't ever think otherwise. We will always be a family."

They all learned a lot about each other at that meal, and Madelena felt for the first time what it must be like to love as a mother and to be loved as a mother. How could she walk away from them? There was a need to respond to, and she was feeling the responsibility, and it seemed like both less and more than a burden.

After supper, Carlo and Madelena went to the children's house and stayed with them until bedtime. Then they tucked in the younger ones, saying their prayers with them for the first time, and after blessing them, kissing them goodnight.

On the way back to the main house Madelena said to Carlo, "How can you put those kids over there all by themselves. Don't you think that is telling them that they really aren't part of your life?"

"I never thought of it that way. I just thought that it would be strange to have eight kids living in an archbishop's house. I thought the house in the garden would be a lot better than wandering the streets."

"That's true, and I'm sure the children appreciate being off the streets, but if we are going to be a family, don't you think we should all live in the same house?'

Carlo laughed aloud. "You mean that you are already the mother and have made your first big decision as to how things are going to be done around here?"

"Well, we do have to have ground rules, and where we are all going to live should be first," Madelena said firmly.

Carlo realized what he was getting into. "Well, let's get together again and work out the details. This is new ground for me, and we will have to do things prudently, very prudently."

"When little Vito said what he said, that just did it for me, Carlo. How could anyone not respond to that precious plea coming right from his heart?"

"He's a charmer. He really wormed his way into your heart, didn't he?"

"How could I resist."

"You know who he is, don't you?"

"No."

"Vito Malatesta's nephew."

"God's got some sense of humor," Madelena said, shocked.

"Something we could all use," Carlo said. "Well, Cousin, are you going back to Palagiano tonight, or are you going to stay here?"

"I really should go home. I brought no clothes, nothing. I'll be back early tomorrow morning, and we can have a long talk as to how we should go about this. I have to admit I am panicky, but I will do it. I know that once I make a commitment to these kids, I will have to keep it. They have been hurt too much already."

They walked to the car, hugged goodnight and then Madelena drove off. Carlo went to his room, assured and relaxed, sensing that despite his clumsy efforts, God was seeing to it that all things worked out for good. It was something different, but God always made all things new. So, after reading a few pages of *The Lord* by Romano Guardini, Carlo went to bed and fell into a deep and peaceful sleep.

18

THE NEXT MORNING CARLO HAD an important meeting with the chancellor, Monsignor Arturo Sanpietro, to discuss a matter the archbishop had asked him to research before he left for America.

"In regard to your request," said Sanpietro, "let me put it briefly. In the philosophy years at seminary there is a series of talks on spirituality, and days of guided meditation. Spiritual directors are chosen for their own personal piety. In the four years of theology and scripture courses, it is much the same, except that being more mature, the seminarians are expected to work on their own spirituality. But now, with regard to your interest in serious studies on the person of Jesus and the human aspects of Jesus' life, like his emotional and psychological responses to various people and events and situations, there is *nothing*. The scripture courses are excellent, but they involve primary analyses of the text, and the historical and cultural background of the various books of both the Hebrew scriptures and the New Testament, particularly, the gospels. However, as you suggested, Your Excellency, this does not provide the seminarians with an in-depth understanding of Jesus and his inner life, as much as one can ever plumb the depths of Jesus' inner life.

"In doing that research I can now well understand your concern that the seminarians cannot be expected to imitate Jesus in their work as priests if they do not have a deeper understanding of the inner life of Jesus. With regard to my research into studies about Jesus and the values that were of greatest importance to him, I found two excellent studies. One is *The Mind of Jesus*, by a Scottish scripture scholar, William Barclay, whom I think came into the church before he died. And I know you are very familiar with the other, Romano Guardini's *The Lord.*

"Also, the writings of Hans Urs Von Balthasar are very mystical, but beautiful, as you already know. Another is *Le Mystere de Jesus* by Pierre L. Bernard, OP. There is an excellent analysis of Jesus' ministry entitled *The Public Life of Our Lord Jesus Christ* by Alban Goodier, SJ, and one by Henri Daniel-Rops entitled *La Vie Quotinienne en Palestine Au Temps de Jesus Christ.* And there is one I like very much, and that is by another French scholar, L. C. Fillion, SS. The title of that is *La Vie du Christ.* Another excellent one is by Father Ferdinand Prat, simply titled *Jesus Christ.* I had a difficult time finding good theological-psychological analyses of Jesus' life and the effects of painful events and religious enemies, and people's treatment of the poor had on him, as you requested. I have written all of this down for you, with summaries and suggestions, and have brought the books as well."

"You really did your homework, Arturo! I would like to discuss this matter at our next meeting with the whole staff. I am very grateful for your time and work putting together this material for me, Arturo."

"The pleasure was mine, Bishop. It was a very rewarding experience for me. In going through these various writings I learned a lot about Jesus that I never knew. I can see how it is very difficult to be a priest after the heart of Jesus, if we don't know him."

The meeting came to an end with a prayer.

After lunch, Madelena appeared with a car full of belongings. The receptionist answered the door and was surprised to see Madelena, whom she knew was the archbishop's cousin.

"Bishop," she joked, "there is a strange woman to see you in the parlor."

"Thank you, Gina."

Entering the parlor, he called out, "Where's this strange woman?"

Carlo was delighted to see Madelena. "Madelena, you made your decision already. I was afraid that after you thought it over, you might have had misgivings and changed your mind."

"Carlo, once I met those children and realized how beautiful they are and wondered how anyone could have left them to wander the streets, I knew I could not turn my back on them. They have been hurt too much already. Yes, my mind is made up, so you had better hang around here for a good long time, because we're partners in this one and we'll have to work together. Well, now that I'm here, where am I staying? There is plenty of room in this house for us to bring the kids over and have them sleep two or three in a room. The old servants' quarters have not been used in years. There's plenty of room for the children, and a large suite for me. You can still keep your own room on the other side of the house and your privacy."

"Thank you. That is so nice of you to allow me to keep my present room."

"Carlo, I didn't mean to be so pushy. I am just so excited about getting started. I can't wait to get things organized, so we can all relax. I promise I won't take over. It is your home, and I know you are very organized. I would never want to upset that. And I will have enough privacy at my end of the house to continue some of my pro bono legal work, as the children will be out most of the day. I can have lunch ready for them in our own kitchen and eating area in that part of the house. Unless, of course, you would like me to go over to where they are now and live there with them. I can do that, too."

"No, no. It would probably appear more proper that way, but how can I really be part of their lives if I am so removed from them? It is a lot healthier for them if we function as a family. I know it is unusual, but it can work. The people already know I took the children off the streets, and they thought it was a wonderful gesture, so they will understand that it is important for them to have someone besides me to look after them. This arrangement will work nicely. I bet you stayed awake all night planning how this could work out."

"I did, Carlo, and the changes I suggest are just a few practical ones."

"Good." Carlo went into his study and took an extra cell phone from his desk and gave it to Madelena. It was connected to the other cell phones, including Professor Giuliani's. He then called the professor to tell him that the children's new mother was here to stay and that the children were to move over to his house this afternoon as their new quarters.

The professor was excited that they were all going to be one family, with not only a father but a mother as well. He was happy and thought it was beautiful that an archbishop should be so caring. "Too bad there aren't more like you, Bishop. The Church would be the better for it."

"Just pray it works, Alessandro, just pray it works."

At mass the next morning Carlo shared with his early morning faithful that the new family was living with him. They all knew Madelena and thought it was a wonderful thing for that brilliant woman to postpone her career to be a mother to homeless children. This endeared their archbishop to them even more, and most thought little of them all living together in the archbishop's house, although a few had raised eyebrows.

After breakfast, which the family ate together, Carlo left for the cathedral hall for his meeting with all the priests of the archdiocese. There were over nine hundred, mostly older men, but still a surprising number of younger priests.

"My dear fathers and deacons, I appreciate your coming here this morning. I have always loved being your archbishop, and you have made my ministry here a joy because you have all been so helpful and so supportive. As you know, I took an extended leave of absence in an attempt to understand why Jesus was so obsessed with the poor, to the extent that he made our eternal salvation contingent on how we treat the poor. I can see helping those in need, but to elevate the poor to such a high status that our treatment of them would affect our salvation troubled me. I had to resolve that problem for myself, and I decided that for me to understand why Jesus felt the way he did about the poor, I would have to live among them, which I did for a year and a half."

"I finally understand, in my very marrow, what Jesus meant by teaching us to have the heart of the Good Shepherd. Since I came back, I have had an entirely different attitude toward the poor and the homeless. Last night I had supper and this morning breakfast with the new family you have heard of, eight homeless children who will be living with me in the bishop's residence. My cousin Madelena has graciously consented to give up her job at the law firm and be a mother to these children, as it would be impossible for me to give them all the parenting and time that they need. This morning, as I meet with you, Madelena is talking with the principal about their schooling. Later this afternoon I hope to join them while we shop for clothes. They still look like little street urchins.

"Now, my brothers, since this is a ministry that all of us as Christians must have a heart for, I encourage you all to look around your neighborhoods for homeless children and arrange for people in your parishes to help you care for them. You don't have to form a family as I did, nor would I even recommend it, but you can make your people sensitive to the plight of these unfortunate little brothers and sisters of Jesus and bring the resources of your parishes to bear.

"Another matter that I would like to discuss with you is your everyday parish ministries and whatever other ministries you may have developed. As I told you when I became bishop, I do not see your role as priests as servants of my role or as fundraisers for archdiocesan programs. I see myself as a support for *your* programs. I exist to help *you* further the kingdom in whatever way you need in your parishes. I am *your* servant. As my way of fulfilling that promise I made to you, I intend to visit each of your parishes and spend time with you, getting to understand your work and how I can help you. So, be ready for a call from my secretary asking for a convenient time for me to visit with each of you. And please do not think I am coming to investigate or criticize. I will be coming to ask how I can help you.

"Know that I love each one of you and pray every morning at mass that your ministries will make Jesus better known and loved. And I ask your prayers for me. Thank you."

The priests gave their bishop a standing ovation for two minutes. Then there was a time for questions, one of which was from a young priest: "Have you seen the newspaper stories about the priest up in Rome who is not in good standing and who is now homeless and spends his time working with the homeless? He said he was told by another homeless beggar that he is still a priest, and he can still minister to his fellow homeless, as they need a priest. Ever since then he has been an inspiration to the homeless in Rome. He said that the homeless beggar who spoke to him that day had changed his life, and he has been looking for him ever since. He remembers him only for the funny blue patch he had on his brown right pant leg. Have you seen those articles, bishop?"

Carlo blushed and said that he hadn't. The priest promised to send them to him. Carlo now realized that although people in Rome, including clergy, were aware of the events of his life as a beggar, fortunately, his identity was still a secret.

As the session ended, the group broke up and spent time chatting with one another while sharing refreshments that had been generously placed around the hall. The archbishop stayed too, listening to each one who came up to him, but in the back of his mind he was thinking about the afternoon shopping spree with the children for their new clothes.

 19

THE NEXT TWO MONTHS WENT BY smoothly. Carlo worked daily at the chancery, attended civic and church committees, did all the things a bishop must do, but still found time to spend at home. He also visited twenty parishes during that time, showing the pastors that he really was interested in the work that they were doing. A few, not believing he would carry out his promise, had nothing to show when he arrived, and Carlo was no one to be brushed aside by a heavy layer of hot air. Although always the gentleman, and respectful of the priesthood, he intended that his priests work hard, and for him, visiting the sick, evangelizing, and preaching Jesus were essential to that work. He let it be known in no uncertain terms that he would reschedule his visit and would expect a report on all that had been done to reach out to the people and to make sure they understood what it meant to be a disciple of Jesus.

Word soon spread to other parishes that he meant everything he said about the hard work of evangelizing and firing people up about their faith as Christians and that he wanted to see results. Their future positions in the archdiocese depended on it. He also suggested that priests work together, as some had more imagination than others, while others were good at preaching, but not very good at studying. Preaching Jesus and making him better known in his humanity was to be done on a regular basis, and the teachings of the faith were to be expressed through Jesus' message.

One afternoon during early summer, when Carlo, Madelena, and the children were eating lunch in the garden with the rest of the staff, a phone call was transferred from inside the chancery to the garden, and Madelena answered it.

"Carlo, it's for you."

"Hello, this is Archbishop Brunini."

"Your Excellency, this is the Holy Father's secretary. The Holy Father would like to speak with you."

"Carlo?"

"Yes, Holy Father."

"This is not a confidential call, so you can feel free to talk. Have you read the papers about that homeless beggar in Rome? Do you happen to know that priest who is working with the homeless?"

"Yes, Your Holiness."

"Are you familiar with the homeless beggar with the strange patch in his right pant leg?"

"Yes, Your Holiness."

"I thought you would be."

They both laughed heartily.

"Good job, Carlo. You kept your word and your identity between yourself and God. I am proud of you. And how is your new family?"

"Fine, Holy Father. Our family is growing. Professor Giuliani now lives with us, and together we all look after the children. Francesco is doing well in college and Eugenio, Giuseppe, Carla, Elisabetta and Radolfo, Marco, and Vito are in upper school and lower school. They are beautiful children, Holy Father. I hope someday that they can meet you."

The children beamed at hearing their names given to the pope. "Now even the pope knows us," they said to one another.

"I would like that, Carlo. Now to get down to business. I am at Castel Gandolfo for the summer. When will you be free to come here and visit for a few days? I have some very important matters to discuss with you."

"Holy Father, whenever you wish."

"In a day or two."

"I can do that. My friend Gianmatteo can arrange for me to go in his helicopter, and I can be there by tomorrow afternoon."

"Thank you, Carlo. Give my love to Madelena and the children, and my special blessing on you all. I am grateful to you for your important work and ask God to bless you in every way."

"Thank you, Holy Father. I'll be there tomorrow."

"You can land the helicopter in the inside courtyard. But, make sure you let the secretary know just before you are ready to land."

"Yes, Holy Father."

Carlo put the phone back on its crib.

"Arturo, my faithful chancellor, would you take care of everything while I'm away. It may be a couple of days, I think. I have no idea what it is all about, but I can tell he is happy with the way things are going here. I don't know how he finds out so much about this place when we are so far from Rome and he has the whole world to think about."

"Remember what you told us once, Bishop," Carmelo, the judge of the archdiocesan tribunal, said. "'The Vatican has eyes and ears all over.' It's the best intelligence network in the world, not only concerning what goes on in the church in every country, but in the political world as well. That's why the Chinese government is so afraid of the Vatican after what happened in Poland and in the Soviet Union. So, it's nothing for them to keep an eye on you."

After the luncheon ended and the staff went home, Madelena had a thousand questions. She waited to ask until the children went out to play.

"Carlo, what was that all about, if I may ask?"

"My dear, I have an idea it may be about diplomatic matters, probably in Iran, since the Holy Father thinks I'm an expert on the region. That's what I study at night when you all go to bed. I receive daily briefings from government officials in various countries updating me on the latest information about what is taking place in Iran and a few other countries, but mostly Iran. So I have an idea that the Holy Father has some concerns. He would like the church to have a better presence in that country so he can be in a better position to help the large Catholic population living there. He also has a lot of respect for the Iranian people and for their ancient culture."

"You don't think it will affect life here, do you?"

"I don't think so, but at some time in the future I'm afraid I will be asked to take an assignment as a papal nuncio or apostolic delegate to one of the countries I have been trained for. I may find myself a bishop without a real home once more."

"Oh, Carlo, I dread that day. I don't know how I could ever. . . . Is it something you have to do?"

"Madelena, leaving you and the children would be the most difficult thing I would ever have to do. I think of it every night before I go to sleep, and I try to focus on the words of Jesus, 'If you love father or mother or children more than me, you are not worthy of me.' I love you more than you could ever imagine Madelena. You don't know how my heart almost breaks sometimes, thinking that someday we may be separated. I didn't know I would feel that way. The only comfort I have is that these appointments don't last for too long, maybe a few years, and we can still find time to be together as family."

Madelena was silent.

Carlo continued, "My dearest, please know that you are the most important person in my life. Whenever I think of you, I think of God, and whenever I think of God, I think of you. Sometimes I almost wonder which of you I need more. I think God has bonded us together so closely that he has made us inseparable from himself. Whenever I leave you, I feel the pain deeply."

The two embraced but said no more. Then Madelena went to her room, and Carlo went to his office. After sitting quietly for a while, he called his friend Gianmatteo about going to Rome.

"Carlo, my dear friend. You don't have to be so shy. Of course, you can use my helicopter tomorrow. I will have my pilot pick you up. But you have to ask the Holy Father to pray for me. I have been having some little problems lately."

"What problems are you having? Can I help?"

"Nothing serious, just annoying. Don't worry yourself. You have enough problems. You can keep my pilot there. I won't need him, and he can do some sightseeing. What time will you be coming here?"

"How about twelve thirty? I have to be there by two. That should give us plenty of time. He can land in the inner courtyard. Thanks so much, Gianni. You're better than a brother."

"Niente, Carlo. See you tomorrow. Ciao."

"Ciao, car'amico."

The flight to Castel Gandolfo took a little over an hour, and after warning the Vatican officials of their arrival time, the courtyard was cleared, and the helicopter set down smoothly. The receptionist met them as they exited and ushered them inside, where they were met by some of the staff. The pilot felt like a visiting head of state, and asked Carlo if he was always treated like this. He was surprised that it was just ordinary routine.

"You must be important to them. I never realized. You always act just like one of us," the pilot said as they were being led into a sitting room.

"Well, that's what I am, my friend."

"Your Excellency," a monsignor said to Carlo, "the Holy Father will see you in about twenty minutes. How can we make you and your friend comfortable?"

"Could you show us around? I am sure we would enjoy that."

"That would be easy. I will have one of our assistants paged."

A thin, distinguished man in his early sixties entered the sitting room a few minutes later and asked the pilot and Carlo to come with him for a tour of the spacious, ancient residence. During the whole tour the pilot was wide eyed. He had never seen anything so impressive for a residence.

"I would love to be just a servant here," he said to Carlo.

"Sounds good, but the work is endless. You would soon realize how precious freedom is," Carlo responded.

After the tour it was time for Carlo's visit with the pope.

The monsignor who met them earlier conducted him to the pope's office. When Carlo entered, the Holy Father stood and walked toward him. The pope held out both hands for Carlo to take, preventing Carlo from bowing or genuflecting to kiss the ring of Saint Peter.

"Thank you for coming, Carlo. I hope it was not an imposition. I know you have added responsibilities now."

"I am glad to be here, Holy Father. I will always be available when I am needed. Don't ever give it a second thought."

"I am greatly concerned, Carlo, about the present situation between the United States and Iran. Part of the problem stems from the lack of knowledge on the part of U.S. officials to properly understand the Iranians. Can you share your intelligence on this matter? The Iranians have brought up the subject with our diplomats and have made overtures to see whether we would be interested in facilitating a dialogue between themselves and the Americans. Do you have an understanding of the history of the situation and why the Americans and Iranians can't work together?"

The two men sat on facing chairs. Carlo leaned toward the pope. "Historically," he said, "the Iranians have not had a problem with the Jewish people in Iran. That is important to know. In fact, there has been a large community of Jews in Iran for almost three thousand years, since the Babylonian Captivity, and they are a protected minority. The Iranian Jews even have one of their own as a member of parliament to represent the Jewish community.

"The Iranian politicians make a distinction between Jews and Zionists, and even the president, who speaks out continually against Israel and Zionists, donates money generously to the Jewish hospital in Tehran. It was the Ayatollah Khomeini who, after the shah was deposed, took up the defense of the Iranian Jews and insisted that they be legally protected.

"The problem the Iranians have with America, Your Holiness, is not with the American people but with various administrations. The issue goes back to the middle of the twentieth century, when Mossadegh was elected prime minister of Iran by 99 percent of the vote. He came from a very cultured, well-educated, and widely respected Iranian family, and he was very patriotic and deeply concerned that foreign oil companies controlling Iranian oil were taking an exorbitant amount of the profits and making it impossible for the Iranians to develop their own country and bring their people out of crushing poverty. When Mossadegh nationalized the oil industry, the British oil companies complained to Winston Churchill, who obtained American support from President Eisenhower to orchestrate a coup to overthrow Mossadegh and put the shah back into power. The Iranians have had a problem with Americans ever since, because the shah was a ruthless tyrant. Even after they overthrew the shah, however, when America asked their help to oust the Russians from Afghanistan, the Iranians cooperated. A few years later, when Iraq brutally invaded Iran, the Americans sided with the Iraqis and gave certain American pharmaceutical companies authority to send biological weapons samples to Iraq for development and use against the Iranians troops. The Iranians felt they could never trust the American government again. They also look upon the American government as collaborators with Israel in the ethnic cleansing of the Palestinian people and allowing Israel to develop an atomic bomb. That is the basis for the Iranian position on these issues, Holy Father.

"Another thing I need to mention, which is a concern to me, is the current leadership in Iran. Both the ayatollah and the president are difficult to read, and I cannot fully understand them. They have pulled off some underhanded schemes that have created chaos among the people and that makes me very wary of both of them. We have to be very careful, as no one can figure where they are coming from and where they intend to take their country. They are both enigmas. I think the president has an unstable personality, is totally undependable, and, even though we have to deal with them, it must always be with caution and great prudence at every turn."

"Carlo, you amaze me. With all you are involved in, you still keep up with these extremely complicated world problems. I have to remind you, my friend, that the time may come soon for you to be assigned as nuncio to help us in these troubled times. Do you think you are ready?"

"I try to be, Holy Father. I keep up on my languages and on current events in these countries."

"Which languages are you trained in?"

"Russian, Arabic, Farsi, French, Spanish, German, Swedish, and some Chinese and Japanese, but they cut those two short when someone decided that I probably would not be sent to either of those countries."

"How fluent are you in Farsi, Carlo?"

"It's my favorite. I love the Persian culture and their very respectful customs. They are so delicate in their diplomatic protocol and their way of showing respect; very different from most other cultures. The Iranians are a highly intelligent people. Their smooth diplomatic style is very similar to the Vatican's. They have a sensitive way of expressing their views on delicate issues."

"Thank you, Carlo. Would you mind staying till tomorrow, so we can talk again? There are some other matters about which I would like your understanding."

"I would enjoy spending the night here. It is a splendid place."

"A good place to escape the crushing heat and humidity of Rome for a few days. Carlo, would you concelebrate mass with me tomorrow morning?"

"I'd be honored."

"We have supper at seven this evening, and we pray Vespers at five. Can you make it?'

"Holy Father, I am embarrassed. I forgot my breviary."

"There are extra ones in the chapel."

"I'll be there."

As he walked out, the distinguished gentleman who met him earlier showed him to his suite so he could take a short siesta and freshen up before Vespers.

The room was stately and elegant, and since his experience as a homeless beggar, Carlo no longer felt at ease in such surroundings. He still could not shake the image of himself as a homeless beggar, and at that moment he thought, "What is a homeless beggar doing in such rich surroundings?" His stay there did not give him a comfortable feeling but made him feel almost guilty. The hour-long nap, however, was refreshing. He had to ask directions to the chapel, where other priests on the staff were already gathering.

The pope intoned the initial prayer, and the others took up to the verses of the psalms that followed. After Vespers the whole staff accompanied the pope into the dining room for supper.

After supper, they retired to a community room to relax and get acquainted with one another, as they all had different assignments, backgrounds, and experiences. Carlo enjoyed hearing all the exciting things others were doing. At one point the pope asked Carlo if he had had an exciting year. Carlo knew the pope was subtly teasing him because he knew full well that the pope had no intention of encouraging him to tell the story of his escapade as a beggar.

"You know, Holy Father, how boring my life is. Same thing day after day. I thought being a bishop would be an exciting adventure."

The pope laughed at Carlo's even more subtle response.

One interesting person in the group was a provincial of the Christian Brothers stationed in Israel. He told of the wonderful things that were happening at their Bethlehem University and how many Palestinian students would be graduating the next year. When asked if it was difficult for them in Israel, the brother did not feel it proper to discuss those things. All he said was it was very difficult for him to visit the seven communities of Christian Brothers under his charge as he was made to get permits for every place he went and had to stand in long lines at seven different checkpoints. "What I should be able to do in a day takes me close to four days because of all the red tape. The government is not happy that we are educating Palestinians and shows it in many ways. But we are still able to provide excellent academic training for students who might not have an education otherwise."

At ten o'clock the pope stood up to retire to his room and said good night to the others. Soon after, the group broke up and retired for the night.

The schedule was almost monastic. Everyone gathered for morning prayers and for mass. After mass and breakfast everyone went to his room to get ready for the work day, which began at nine o'clock. The pope's secretary relayed to Carlo that the Holy Father would like to meet with him at ten o'clock. After that meeting he could feel free to either stay for lunch or return to Taranto.

Promptly at ten Carlo presented himself at the pope's office and was ushered inside. Without formalities, the two sat down and immediately began their discussion.

"Carlo, I pondered over all you shared with me yesterday. I was quite surprised that you have been able to keep so completely current in your knowledge of the issues we discussed."

"I receive briefings practically every day, Holy Father, and I feel it is important not to miss any details, because seemingly insignificant things can show subtle changes in attitude or policy that we cannot afford to miss."

"Carlo, I am also concerned about Russia and about what drives its leaders. It is very difficult to read them, as they give conflicting signals almost daily. I visit with Mr. Gorbachev occasionally, and he has been very helpful in showing me how to interpret what is now taking place in Moscow. Of late he has become very close to the church, and he is a man of deep faith. But, I would like you to share with me your thoughts on the underlying feeling of the Russian leaders."

"Holy Father, it is not as easy for me to get inside information from my Russian contacts. My briefings are very carefully worded, and I have to read between the lines. I think that there are two emotions that drive the Kremlin leadership: fear and shame. By understanding that, one can understand almost everything they say and do. Since the Soviet Union disintegrated, Russia has lost everything: prestige, power, status as a superpower, pride, and whatever resources it had to build its huge army and strategic weapons arsenal. What makes the Kremlin even more insecure is that their former satellites are now allied to the West and to America. We cannot underestimate the paranoia that creates among Russians. The danger is that in their fears they may create their own nightmares, mistake them for reality, and precipitate a crisis in the real world. The fact that America already made one preemptive military strike in Iraq makes the Russians uneasy, and that precedent may prompt the Kremlin to do something similar in the smaller nations who were formerly part of the Soviet Union.

"What troubles me, Holy Father, is that a few of the Russian Orthodox leaders have aligned themselves with the Kremlin under the guise of patriotism and have pressured the Kremlin to come down hard on the Catholic communities in Russia. They know their own people have more respect for our priests because many of their Orthodox bishops and priests were used as stooges by the Communist rulers. The people could not trust them, especially in confession, and even today their confidence in their own clergy has not been fully restored. They feel more comfortable with Catholic priests and bishops, and their hierarchy knows it. Their bishops are now trying to use the political leaders to reverse this, but the people are very shrewd. They just bide their time. I can see, Holy Father, that you already know this, and you have been prudent in moving slowly in Russia and have been trying to help the Orthodox bishops feel comfortable with the Catholic Church in their midst. I think your strategy will continue to make progress, but it is going to be a long, long time before Russia changes. And the fact that alcoholism is a serious problem in Russian society, especially among the leadership in the military and government, cannot be underestimated when considering its political and ecumenical implications."

"Carlo, how do you see Russia and Iran—as friends or antagonists?"

"Holy Father, Russia and Iran have a complex relationship. The Iranians are very highly educated and are masters at diplomacy, especially because they have such subtle minds. The Russians cannot match them in diplomatic subtlety, so they would rather not be involved if they don't have to be. At the same time, they need each other and have significant trade agreements. The Russians can provide the Iranians with nuclear expertise, and they can safely form a partnership in that area, but the Russians also need the Iranians to help keep a balance of power in the area. They would very much like the Iranians to be their allies rather than allies with the Americans, but the Iranians would prefer to be close to the Americans if they can only find a way to work out some kind of a rapprochement. They would like to do business with the Americans. They desperately need international trade. This would give them greater prestige in the political arena. Iran is desperate for the rest of the world to recognize it for what it knows it is, a country with an ancient civilization and a highly developed culture, and a well-educated middle class with a very high percentage of scholars and well-trained scientists. Iranians are also shrewd industrialists and businessmen and, given a chance, have the potential to be the engine driving a powerful economic bloc in the Middle East. But the Americans have blocked them at every turn and have never forgiven them for holding U.S. citizens hostage in 1979, which really works to the detriment of the Americans.

"I think we have a better chance of expanding our numbers in Iran than in Russia, if we go about it carefully, and if Iranian Catholics concentrate on *living* their faith. Our belief in forgiveness is a powerful inspiration to others when they see it lived in real life. If our people live their faith in Iran, others will be able to see clearly the beauty of Jesus and how necessary his teaching on forgiveness is for healing the world. That teaching is not an option if we really want peace. The Iranians are intelligent and are more open than others in the Middle East."

"I am grateful, Carlo, for your thoughts on these issues. You seem to take more time keeping abreast of these matters than some of my staff who are so busy with their day-to-day work. I hope I didn't impose on you by insisting that you come here on such short notice, but we have been working on issues involving the Iranians lately and their relationship with Iraq. And I already mentioned to you that they have approached us about helping them develop a better relationship with the Americans.

"I may have to call you again, Carlo, so keep up to date on these matters. I also have little presents for Madelena, the children, and Alessandro. She is a real heroine for taking on that big responsibility. I have to admit, my dear son, that I worry about the two of you being so close. But, again, I trust you to be prudent. I am glad Alessandro is part of the family. He lives there, as well? "

"Yes, Holy Father."

A few minutes later the receptionist arrived with the pilot, and Carlo stood to take his leave.

"May I have your blessing, Holy Father, for myself and my family?" Carlo asked.

"May the blessing of Almighty God, the Father, Son and Holy Spirit, descend upon you and remain with you forever. Have a safe trip back home, and God go with you."

"Thank you, Holy Father," both men responded, and then they left. After saying goodbye to the secretary and the receptionist, who accompanied them to the helicopter, they boarded and flew back to Taranto. Carlo was eager to get back to his family and wondered what the pope had in mind for him next.

20

THE CHILDREN WORKING OUT in the garden with Alessandro heard Carlo's car in the driveway. They all ran out, even Francesco. In spite of being nineteen years old now, he was still like a child in his love for this man who brought him back to life. The only future he had had to look forward to was caring for seven children, who were not even his own, for the rest of his life.

"Oh, Father, Father! We're so glad you're back home with us. We missed you!" they all said, as they gathered around Carlo and hugged him.

"Oh, my dear children. I missed you, too, and I have a present for you from the Holy Father, which I will give you later. Elisabetta grabbed her father's diplomatic pouch and carried it into the house for him. Madelena met him at the door.

"I missed you too, Carlo." They hugged, then went into the kitchen and sat at the kitchen table, nibbling on snacks she had prepared for the two of them.

"How was your meeting with the pope?" she asked

"It was a good meeting. He needed me to fill in gaps, as his staff doesn't have the intimate knowledge that I have from my contacts in Iran and other places, all of whom have been dear friends for many years, and over time have worked their way up into important positions. Some of them are imams and ayatollahs now, and some are historians I became friends with in graduate school and have kept in touch with through the years. They provide me with valuable information that fills the gaps in what the secretariat of state staff collects."

"Did he mention anything about a new assignment for you?"

"No, but he did tell me to be prepared, for some time he may have to ask me to consider it, but hopefully Francesco will be out of college by then, some of the others will be considerably older, and a couple may be well on their way through college."

"I hope so," Madelena added." It will be difficult taking care of them all by myself if they are too young, but Alessandro loves the children and at least he will be here to help. The pope is not thinking of sending you on an assignment because of my being here, is he?"

"No, my dear, not at all. In fact, he was asking for you and said to give you his love and his blessing. I think he is proud of what we are doing with the children. He sent them all a little present, and a *Life of Jesus* for you."

He then took the beautifully bound book and gave it to Madelena.

"This is beautiful, Carlo. I must write and thank him."

"Madelena, if I am sent to Iran, it is possible that you and the children may be able to come, at least for a while. A couple of my friends live in villas, and either of them would be thrilled for you and the children to stay with them during my assignment there, and I pray that will happen. They could go to school there, and Francesco could do graduate work as well. We could be together as much as possible. I could not bear knowing you are far away, and I cannot be there to help you with the children. God has given us to each other for a reason, and he will always be with us. We cannot fear the future. God will always be part of what we are doing."

He reached across the table and put his hand on hers as they looked at each other. Their look expressed what could not be expressed in any other way. Carlo left and went over to the chancery to catch up on what he had missed the past two days.

Summer was already in full swing. The cherry trees in Alessandro's and the children's garden were drooping with fruit. The children's enthusiasm to pick the cherries was the most efficient way to win the war with the squirrels and the crows. They collected a beautiful crop—over four bushels. They had never had such an experience before. They liked this kind of work. In fact, they loved it. They had already picked raspberries and currants, and the children were happy to help Maria, the cook, in the busy job of preserving the fruits and vegetables and making jam. That was another delight that they never had when they roamed the streets.

The children were waiting most for the peaches to ripen, though they would have another month before they would be ready. The plums would be ripe a little sooner. They never dreamed working could be so much fun. They jumped with joy when they saw the first tomato turning red.

By the middle of summer Carlo had visited almost all the parishes in his diocese. While he was happy to see great progress in parishes where the pastors loved their work and where the other priests were zealous and creative in reaching out to people, he was shocked at how many had done little or nothing to make the message of Jesus real to their people. To those priests who had been enthusiastic in helping him carry out his dream of igniting the fire of faith throughout the diocese, he wanted to express his appreciation. This took the form of an extra two weeks of vacation. The archbishop arranged with the descendants of the Borromeo family for the priests to stay at their villa on Borromeo Island, in Lago Maggiore in the Italian Alps. Word soon spread that the archbishop could be very generous in rewarding those who were enthusiastic about their priestly work. The other priests soon got the message, and the parishes became beehives of activity in vying with each other in stimulating an interest in the spiritual life of their people. The people also caught fire when they saw their priests willing to stir up the life of the parish.

In the meantime, work on creating apartments for the homeless in the archbishop's huge building in Taranto was moving steadily, but not as rapidly as he had hoped. It was already July, and only about one-fourth of the construction was done. The chief architect was all apologies when the archbishop visited the site one day to view the progress.

"Your Excellency, we are moving as fast as we can, but you have to remember, we are working with a three-hundred-year-old building. When we remove inside walls, we take away the supports for the outside walls, so we have to tie them in with the walls opposite or with whatever stone columns there are inside the building. The engineers have been most helpful and we have been working as fast as we can. We hope we will have part of the building finished by late fall, with water, electricity, and enough rooms for two hundred people. If they can stand a friend or two in a room with them, we should be able to house everyone until we finish. That should be by February at the latest. We would like, with your approval, to use radiant heat embedded in the floors, with electricity generated by photo-voltaic cells built into the roofing. A major manufacturer of the most advanced and efficient units will donate them as advertising to show people how efficient they are. In this way, the cost for electricity will be nominal. To make sure of this, the exterior walls are well insulated, and since the old stone walls are so thick, need for air conditioning will be minimal. And if you like, we could also get a local well driller to donate his services to drill a very deep well to get pure water for the building, so we won't have to pay for water."

"Giancarlo, I am amazed at how you are going about this whole undertaking. I can now see why it seems to be taking longer. You are being very thorough and assuring the project will be as economical as possible," the archbishop commented.

"I also think, Bishop, that a major magazine is going to do a story about the project, since it is so energy saving, especially since the whole roof is covered with photo-voltaic panels. And I must say, these homeless people are something. I thought they might be lazy, but they are the most motivated workers I have ever had working for me. They are so appreciative of what you are doing for them."

"I am happy about that. And I am surprised on weekends when I see most of them at various masses. A lot of them are Muslims. People do appreciate what all of us, including you and your colleagues, do for them. And if you think we may be able to tap a deep well, go ahead. It will probably be better than the local water."

After walking among the workers and congratulating them on their work, Carlo had a thought. Leaving the site, he returned to his residence, changed into his old clothes, and went back to work with the laborers, carrying buckets of cement and boards and whatever else was needed by the craftspeople. The workers had never seen a bishop work before. Some were upset, saying it was beneath his dignity, and others thought it was a beautiful gesture of solidarity with the workers. After all, Jesus was a carpenter and worked with his hands. One of the engineers noticed the blue patch on the archbishop's pants and mentioned it to Giancarlo, reminding him what the newspapers said about the homeless beggar in Rome having a strange patch on the right leg of his pants.

"Do you think . . . ?" he said to Giancarlo.

"Interesting. He was away that whole time. I wonder, but it seems too ridiculous. It couldn't possibly be," Giancarlo replied.

But the thought was planted.

Carlo worked with the crew until the end of the day. When the children had finished their work with Alessandro, they went into the house, and when they couldn't find their father, they ran to Madelena. "Where's Father? We can't find him."

"He's out with the workers way up where they are renovating the old building," she told them.

They all ran out to find him. When they got there they couldn't see him, so Radolfo asked one of the workers, "Do you know where Father is?"

"Yes, son, he is over there," the man replied. "The man with the old clothes."

"Look, father's dressed in those old clothes again," Carla exclaimed, half embarrassed for him, yet proud that he was working with the homeless people.

"I think he feels at home with homeless people," Giuseppe remarked. "But he certainly doesn't look like an archbishop."

They ran over to him and surprised him. He turned and laughed, "What are you all doing out here?"

"We came out to find you," Elisabetta said. "We finished work early. We hadn't seen you all day, and we missed you, and Mother said you were out here, so here we are."

They each took their turn, even Francesco, hugging and kissing him. "We love you, Father."

The men had stopped what they were doing to watch, and as hardened as many may have become by life, they could not help being moved at such a beautiful scene, the group of homeless children they used to see roaming the streets begging for food now hugging and kissing their new father, the archbishop dressed in the rags of a homeless beggar. One older man broke down and could not help crying.

"What's the matter with you, Gino?"

"That is so beautiful! I never thought I'd ever see a bishop, not even a priest, and much less an archbishop being so humble, like Jesus himself, working side by side with us, and dressed like us, and his family of homeless children adoring him as the father they never had. It's just too much for me. I hope he becomes pope someday. We need a pope who feels the way we feel, but we'll never see that happen."

"Can we help, Father?" the children asked.

"I'm not in charge. Go over there and talk to the man standing at the drawing board and ask him."

Giancarlo saw them coming and looked over at the archbishop, who just smiled. Giancarlo picked up the message that it was okay to give them some little jobs. The other workers were still watching. One voiced their thoughts, "What a change in those kids! Ordinary kids would not be like that. What a difference love makes!"

Giancarlo gave them jobs like picking up the discarded boards and piling them neatly at the side of the building and putting the various tools into the shed. However, he treated Francesco differently. He showed him the plans on the drawing board and explained to him what they had already done and what they intended to do with the building. It made Francesco feel proud that an architect would treat him as someone special. The architect was either told, or knew, that Francesco was like a big brother to these homeless children, and for that he earned respect.

When work ended, Carlo and the children returned to the house. Madelena met them at the door. "What am I going to do with you people? Here it is almost suppertime and you are all dirty. All of you, take yourselves upstairs and wash up for supper."

"Mother, don't be mad at us," Elisabetta said, "we were just helping the homeless people working. We know them all from when we were homeless. They are our friends. They used to share their food with us when we didn't have any, so we were glad we could work with them. They were glad to see us, and they even cried when they saw us hugging and kissing Father."

"I am not mad at you, Elisabetta. It is beautiful what you were all doing. I just get emotional sometimes and try to hide it. That's all. So, go, wash up now and get ready for supper."

They all ran off to their rooms.

"Carlo, I was watching you all from upstairs with the binoculars. I saw everything that happened and was deeply touched myself. I guessed that those homeless people knew the children from before and were glad to see them so happy. It made me even more proud of what we are doing."

That day had been filled with so many exciting happenings that everyone was tired, more from the excitement than the work they had all done. Bedtime came early for everyone.

As tired as he was—probably because he was so tired—Carlo could not sleep. He could not put the thought of Madelena out of his mind. He wanted so much to go down to her room. Getting out of bed, he got down on his knees and putting his elbows on the bed he rested his weary head in his hands and prayed harder than he ever had in his life: "Dear Jesus, only you know how much I love Madelena. I cannot understand why we have to love each other the way we do. It is such a crucifixion. Sometimes I think my heart is going to break with the anguish of loving her and not allowing myself to show her my love. I am so torn between my priesthood and my love for this strong, beautiful woman. Give me strength, dear Lord, for I don't think my own strength is sufficient.

"Dear blessed mother Mary, I know you understand. You and Joseph had to have loved each other totally the way Madelena and I love, and Joseph had to have loved you, the most beautiful woman God ever made, as passionately as I love Madelena. The two of you remained chaste all your life. Dear mother Mary, please obtain from your son the grace for me to be chaste and to bless our love so it can become a channel of grace to those we must help by our love. Bless our love and give us strength.

"And bless these dear children, yes, these children of ours. Bless them, Father, and keep them in your love. Dear Holy Spirit of love and wisdom, guide them and mold their young lives in Jesus' image. Direct them through life so they may follow where you lead and accomplish your purpose for them in this world. And please comfort and bless my dear Madelena. I hope she is sleeping tonight better than I am. Good night, dear Father, dear Jesus, dear Spirit of love and wisdom, and dear mother Mary. Keep us always in your love."

21

THAT SUMMER PASSED QUICKLY. The children enjoyed working with Alessandro in the gardens and were so proud of their part in the construction of the magnificent display of flowers and shrubs, and fruits and vegetables. Their work was more fun for them than play. They were the happiest they had ever been in their young lives.

Carlo was becoming busier as the parishes were growing, due to the renewed interest of the priests. As a result, pastors were eager to have him come and talk to their people, especially as so many of the strays had become more enthusiastic about their faith. They asked their pastors if the archbishop could come and talk to them about Jesus. As a result these requests increased, and Carlo began to feel like one of the apostles, wandering from place to place telling people about Jesus and making him real in their lives. Even the priests enjoyed hearing him talk about Jesus as if he knew him personally. And it began to occur to them that maybe he did. Carlo's reputation among the priests grew, and their love for him also increased steadily. They had never known a bishop who cared so much for each one of them as well as for the people. They hoped among themselves that they would never lose him.

But that was not to be. The pope was calling on Carlo more and more frequently and having him spend more time at the office of the cardinal secretary of state, becoming more intimately involved in the work of the secretariat. Problems in the Middle East were an ever-pressing concern to the pope and to the diplomatic staff at the Vatican as reports from various papal nuncios and apostolic delegates became steadily bleaker. That had to be the most intense work in the Vatican as the secretariat of state had constant contact with most countries in the world on an almost daily basis, and there were problems everywhere, if not with governments unsympathetic or outright hostile to the church, then with countries where Catholics were progressive and pushing for change, or where Catholics were traditional and demanded no change whatever but pressured for a return to the old days. It became increasingly difficult for the Vatican to make the slightest decision without arousing a hornet's nest of resentment. Few men have strong enough egos to initiate change that they know is going to provoke violent reactions that can be long lasting and prevent other important work from being done.

One day the call came from the Vatican. It was the call that Carlo and Madelena knew would come eventually.

Carlo left two days later for Rome and was received immediately by the pope, who was most gracious and almost apologetic. "Carlo, my dear son, I appreciate your coming so promptly. I realize you have responsibilities at home. If I am correct, Francesco is almost finished college. Eugenio is in his third year, and Marco is just beginning?"

"That's right, Holy Father. Thank God, they are all doing well. And there are only five at home now. Madelena has more time to practice law again since the remaining five are much older now."

"Only five at home, my dear Carlo. You are the strangest priest I have ever heard of. You are either a saint or a very impetuous man. Word coming back to us from your priests is that they consider you a saint. Do you know the nickname they have for you?"

"No, Holy Father."

"It is San Carlo, the last of the apostles."

Carlo moaned, and the pope laughed heartily.

"They have a good point though, Carlo. They said you are the only bishop or clergyman, Catholic or Protestant, who brings Jesus to life in their hearts. They have never known Jesus so well as the Jesus you have given to them. You preach Jesus rather than church. That is a wonderful testament, my son. We have to make Jesus more real to our seminarians so they don't have to find him by themselves much later in life.

"Now to get down to church matters. Do you think you can bring this living flesh and blood Jesus to the Iranian people, not by preaching him with your words, but by the beauty of your life?"

"I would love very much to do so, Holy Father, but I am afraid I would fall far short of your expectations."

"Why the tears in your eyes, my son?"

"Holy Father, I am not a holy man. I try very hard, but I am so very conscious of how frightfully human I am. Please don't expect too much of me, as I am not what people think. I know what they all say, but they don't know me the way I know myself. All I can say, Holy Father, is that I will try to be as much like Jesus as my frailty will allow."

"No, Carlo, you will be as beautiful as God's grace will inspire you to be. Those people in Iran are a very special people. They are different from others, and if they meet Jesus in real life, they will respond. Believe me, my son."

"I respect you, Holy Father, so I accept your judgment, and your decision."

"Cardinal Magliore will prepare you for your assignment and will make all necessary arrangements with the Iranian government for the presentation of your credentials to their government and for your arrival there. The Iranian government is most happy that we have chosen you for the post. Many of the Iranians have been following you for quite a while. I understand you went to university with some prominent Iranians, and they have always sung your praises to others at home. So you go there with excellent references. I know you will be a credit to Jesus and to his church.

"And one last word, Carlo. You will in a true sense become homeless once more. Will Madelena be all right? I am concerned. You have both been so dedicated to what you have been doing."

"Yes, Holy Father, we have talked about this many times, and we both know what is important. She is a real saint, and being a Calabresa, she's tough. She'll be all right. I am hoping she and the children will be able to come once things get settled, but whatever happens, with God's help and a prayer from you every now and then, it will all work out."

"You can count on that, Carlo. Now, Cardinal Magliore is expecting you."

"Your blessing, Holy Father."

"Bendictio Dei Omnipotentis, Pater et Filius, et Spiritus Sanctus, descendat super te et tuam familiam et maneat semper." The pope pressed both hands firmly around Carlo's head, and then asked, "And may I have your blessing, Bishop?"

The pope went down on his knees as Carlo blessed him and bent over and kissed him on the head. Carlo helped the aging pope to his feet and when they looked at each other and smiled, there were tears in their eyes.

"God go with you, my dear Carlo. You will always be in my thoughts and my prayers."

"And you in mine, Holy Father, and in my heart as well."

The pope watched him as he left the office and wondered what the future might bring. He knew he was sending not just a diplomat but a very special envoy to a very special people—an envoy from God. The pope felt that it was not he who had made this appointment, but someone far above him. "What does God want from this strange and beautiful priest?" the pope wondered, "whom I cannot help but love, yet worry so much about him?"

PEACEMAKER

"Blessed are the peacemakers, for they
will be called children of God."
—JOHN 17:23

22

WHEN HIS PLANE LANDED at the Tehran airport, Carlo was met on the tarmac by the ayatollah and the president of Iran and other dignitaries, including staff from the papal nunciature. This welcome was not ordinary protocol. Not only has Iran had diplomatic relations with the Vatican for fifty-seven years, but they had heard that Carlo was a special kind of human being. Because of this, they greeted Carlo with unusual diplomatic courtesy, and rather than just shaking his hand, each one hugged him and kissed him three times.

"You are welcome here! Salam!" the ayatollah greeted him in Farsi.

They escorted him through the terminal, accompanying him directly to the limousines waiting out in front of the terminal with their own secret-service guards standing by. Carlo's luggage was handled separately by order of federal officials and taken immediately to the limousines. They then drove off to the nuncio's residence and informed him that they would like him to come for dinner at the ayatollah's residence later. They would send a limousine for him at that time. He could then present his credentials, and the dinner would be the formal welcoming of the papal nuncio and dean of the diplomatic corps. Carlo, ever looking upon himself as a homeless beggar, found it difficult to be treated this way. He really could not understand why anyone would want to treat him with such undeserved honors. He knew he was the Vatican's envoy, but he came to do a job, and had never fantasized being honored. His mind did not prepare him for this. But he graciously expressed deep appreciation for their kindness.

After being welcomed at the nunciature and introduced to the staff, he chatted for a few minutes, then was shown to his quarters, where he rested briefly and refreshed himself. He waited for the limousine to arrive to take him and others from the nunciature, who had also been invited, to the ayatollah's residence for the ceremony and dinner.

The limousine arrived at the proper time, and Carlo and his staff were driven to the ayatollah's residence, where again they were warmly received. Carlo was taken aside by the president and brought into the ayatollah's reception room where the ayatollah was waiting with other officials. The president of Iran, a small, wiry man with a growth of beard, took his place beside the ayatollah, and Carlo was formally asked if he had his credentials from the pope. After responding positively, the president asked if he would present his credentials. Carlo offered them to the president and they were formally accepted and read, then presented to the ayatollah for his approval.

Archbishop Carlo Brunini was then formally received and warmly welcomed as the papal nuncio from the State of Vatican City, with full diplomatic honors. At that point the Iranian officials all applauded loudly, and the whole group walked to the banquet room where there was a state dinner honoring the Vatican representative to the Republic of Iran. The dinner was a grand affair and, in spite of its formal nature, the Iranian officials were most gracious and relaxed with the representative from the Vatican, the home office of the Catholic Church. Carlo was impressed with the cordiality of these high Muslim officials toward the representative of what is in reality the Catholic Church. He was impressed because what he experienced was so different from the hostile and negative media publicity concerning Iran and Iranian officials. Carlo realized that the relationship of the Vatican and Iran was special, because the church had been in Persia for almost two thousand years and had always been an integral part of Persian, later Iranian, history. There was a special bond not shared with any other country, and with it went great mutual respect.

At the dinner Carlo was surprised to see Richard and Joan Zahedi, his dear friends for many years. They had maintained a steady correspondence although they had few chances to see each other. They had met in college years before, when Carlo was learning Farsi. Though they were Catholics, their family was highly respected in Tehran, and those who arranged the dinner were aware of their friendship with the archbishop, which explained their presence at the dinner.

The ayatollah told the archbishop that when he heard the Zahedis were good friends of his, he was introduced to them, and they shared so many wonderful things about him and his work that he felt he already knew him. That explained why he was received with such a welcome on his first arrival in Tehran.

As soon as there was a break in the dinner, giving people a chance to dance, Carlo walked over to their table and sat with them for a few minutes. He told Joan and Richard about his new family of homeless children and about his cousin Madelena, who cared for them.

They immediately asked him, "Carlo, why don't you have them come and live with us? There is plenty of room in our villa. They could even stay in the guest house if they wanted privacy. Please consider it. It would make us so happy."

Carlo was delighted that they had made the suggestion. He was sure Madelena would be happy at the prospect of joining him.

Talk at the dinner was light; nothing important or heavy was mentioned, not even by the president. In fact, during the break Carlo noticed the president sitting with Jewish people who were obviously friends and talking freely and light-heartedly with them.

In Iran for only a few hours, Carlo already liked the people he was introduced to and chatted with. Richard and Joan introduced him to another couple—the director of the Jewish hospital in Tehran, Dr. Jakob Ashrani, and his wife, Esther, and the evening passed pleasantly. He picked up a sense of what the important people in government and business were like, as least as to their spirit, though those invited for the archbishop's first dinner were carefully chosen to ensure a pleasant evening. This was Carlo's first experience of Iranian refined diplomatic sensitivity.

Before the dinner ended Carlo said a few words of thanks to the ayatollah and the president and expressed his great joy at having been assigned to a country with such an ancient and rich culture and highly distinguished history. He said he was certain his stay there would be not just an assignment but an enriching part of his life. He asked them to please pray for him as he would pray for them daily at his mass.

The ayatollah and the president also spoke briefly, and the ayatollah ended with a prayer to the God of Abraham, whom they all worshiped together—Christians, Jews, and Muslims. The evening ended with the orchestra playing the Vatican's national anthem and a group of singers singing the words in Latin. Totally taken by surprise, Carlo joined in with a big smile and sang along with them.

As soon as he returned to the nunciature, he called Madelena, who was waiting for him to call.

"Carlo, my dear, how was your trip, and what kind of a welcome did you receive?"

"It all went wonderfully. Guess what?"

"I can't imagine."

"My good friends Richard and Joan were there, and I chatted with them and told them about our new family and their first reaction was, 'Why didn't bring them with you? Bring them over and they can stay with us at our villa.' They told me to make sure I told you. I miss you all already. Can you come?"

"Well, yes, but wait . . . what about school? I think Francesco might prefer to finish his studies here first. Let me discuss it with the children."

"Yes, of course. It might be a wonderful education for the younger ones to live some time in another country. We can work it out when you are here, and Joan can help us."

"Is it nice there?"

"It is a beautiful country. I think you will love it here, and the people as well.

"It would be good for all of us to be together."

Carlo spent most of the next day being briefed on the day-to-day work at the nunciature. He was already getting phone calls from Catholic bishops and pastors around the country welcoming him as their new representative from the Holy Father and assuring him of their support.

His first call of the day was from Archbishop Ramzi Garmou, the archbishop of the archdiocese of Tehran. He called to welcome the nuncio, assure him of his support and friendship, and offer his assistance whenever needed. He also told Carlo that he would be honored if he would accept an invitation sometime in the near future to have dinner at his residence, where he could meet other clergy from various places in Iran. That was an important welcome, especially since the archbishop expressed a positive attitude.

The Vatican already had a long-standing relationship with the Iranians, and they had been of significant help to each other in tense situations involving other countries. That close relationship was soon called upon for an important mission. Two weeks after Carlo's arrival, the ayatollah called.

"To what do I owe this honor, Your Reverence?" the archbishop asked the ayatollah.

"I was hoping we could spend some time together to discuss a matter that troubles me deeply. I thought perhaps you could be of some assistance."

"I would be honored if I could."

"If you are free sometime this week, could I have someone pick you up and bring you to my residence?"

"I am at your service, Your Reverence."

"I respect your own need for space and for time to adjust to your new life."

"If it is urgent, I will arrange to be free and meet at your convenience."

"Can you come tomorrow for a light lunch, very private, just the two of us?"

"I would be happy to."

"My chauffeur will be there to pick you up at 11:30, Your Excellency."

"I'll be ready, Your Reverence."

"Thank you. May our compassionate God's blessing be upon you."

"And upon you and yours as well."

The next day the limousine arrived precisely at 11:30 and Carlo walked out of the nunciature at precisely the same time. Punctuality is a mark of highest respect, and Carlo was most strict with himself about being precisely on time.

When the limousine arrived at the ayatollah's residence, the ayatollah himself came out to meet the nuncio and usher him into the residence. They talked briefly in the reception room while waiting for the cook to announce that lunch was ready, then the two went into the dining room and, showing a delicate gesture of respect and friendship, the ayatollah sat, not at the head of the table, but across the table from his guest. This did not pass unnoticed, and Carlo expressed how gracious it was of his host to make such a gesture.

"You are a special person, Your Excellency. I assure you I do not do this for everyone. I want you to feel at home in our country. I have great respect for the pope, and he has been of great assistance in the past. It is deeply appreciated. All of us in Iran are grateful to him for having assigned you as ambassador to our country. A number of our important people have known about you for a long time through your Iranian friends, and it was our hope that you might one day be assigned here. God is good."

"I have the same feeling, my dear ayatollah. I admire your people and your beautiful culture. You are so much more advanced than most countries, and I hope to contribute to the recognition of your value to the rest of the world, which does not as yet know you."

"That is precisely the reason why I would like to speak with you, my friend."

Carlo thought it significant that the ayatollah did not invite the president to have dinner with them, but of course he did not raise the issue.

"Your Excellency, I have discussed this with the previous ambassador from the Vatican, and I share it with you now because it is on my mind and I am very concerned. It is the matter of nuclear weapons. I know that everyone today is concerned about nuclear weapons, and about nuclear bombs especially. I would like to assure His Holiness that I think atomic bombs are evil and their use immoral, and I am opposed to our government manufacturing such weapons. I oppose violence. I was opposed to the original tactics of the Hezbollah, but they have changed and are now a respectable part of the Lebanese people. Theologically, we may be stricter than other countries on these matters, and it is unfortunate that there is no way for them to understand that. If they did, they would not be so obsessed with fear of Iran's supposed interest in nuclear arms. Our government does insist, however, on other countries respecting our rights as a sovereign nation to continue our research and development of nuclear power for peaceful means, especially for energy. On this we will not compromise, nor will we allow it to be a condition for international discourse.

"When it comes to the matter of carbon fuels, we share the concern of the world that the use of carbon fuels must be minimized for everyone's benefit. I don't think the world understands. Though we produce a significant percentage of the world's oil supply, it is not to our benefit to use oil in the production of our own electricity, or for heating our homes, or running our automobiles. A clean atmosphere is essential for all of us. We have enough noxious pollution drifting in from other countries. We don't intend to make our air worse. It may be that we have purer motives in our policies about many issues than the world gives us credit for."

When the ayatollah finished, Carlo mentioned the public statements of the president of Iran about nuclear weapons, which makes it difficult for the world to understand Iran's intentions on the issue.

"I understand why the president speaks the way he does, and it often comes from frustration that our country is not given the respect from the United States that it deserves. The Americans accuse us of many things that do have some foundation but do not necessarily reflect the intent of our government. They accuse us of providing weapons to terrorists in Iraq. That there are weapons smuggled into Iraq is unquestionable, but is it the Iranian government that does that? The answer is no. And the reason is simple. We are Shiites, and the Iraqis are mostly Shiites. Why would we supply weapons to destroy the possibility of a majority Shiite government uniting the country? There are weapons smuggled into Mexico for the drug lords. Would it be correct to say that the American government is providing the drug lords with weapons? Of course not. It is this loose talk from all sides that poisons international relations and turns people against one another. It has to stop. And this, my dear friend, is the reason for my inviting you to talk with me. The Holy Father has the respect of the world, and it would be in the interest of humanity for the Holy Father to use his good graces to facilitate a formal dialogue among nations of good will. This could be a major contribution to better understanding of one another and, by calming over-heated minds, preparing the world for peace."

"I will do what I can, Your Reverence. It may entail a trip to the Vatican to discuss this, or it may entail your own visit with the Holy Father to bring this about. But, I will broach the subject and lay the groundwork and see where we can go from there."

"Thank you, Your Excellency. I will be very grateful if you can help to bring that about. And I know you are going to have a pleas-ant time in our country. Our people already like you. May our mutual God of Abraham bless you and make your work fruitful."

"And may our God bless you and give you long life. Your country needs your vision and your solid moral sense."

The two men finished lunch, and the ayatollah called for the chauffeur to take the archbishop to his residence. It was almost 4:30 when Carlo returned to his residence, and there were al-ready thirty phone calls that he had to return. One was from the Vatican secretary of state, concerned about his arrival in Iran and his reception by the Iranian government. The secretary was pleased that Carlo had a pleasant flight and was so warmly re-ceived. He was surprised, however, that Carlo had been asked to talk with the ayatollah so soon after his arrival. The phone call did, however, give Carlo a chance to share with the secretary the purpose and substance of the meeting. "An interesting sugges-tion," was all the secretary said in response, not giving a hint as to whether he would even mention it to the Holy Father. Carlo was disappointed and wondered as to why the secretary received such good news with such cool response. The lack of a positive response made Carlo, whose analytical mind sensed that some-thing was not right, consider the possibility that he could not trust the secretary. How much could he confide in the secretary, when he was reluctant to pass on something so clearly important and of interest to the pope? He now wondered whether the pope had concerns about the secretary's attitude toward Iran. Perhaps he doubted whether the secretary could be objective when it came to issues involving Iran. Carlo hung up feeling very uncomfortable about his own relationship with the secretary of state, who was his immediate superior and to whom he had to make his reports. This, he felt, was going to be his first crisis, and it was not with his hosts but with his own superior.

Being the kind of person he was, Carlo did not intend to put off a brewing crisis until it got out of hand, so he called the pope that night on his private phone, a phone for which the pope himself received the log of calls received and made.

"Carlo, is everything all right?"

"Yes, Holy Father. I have arrived after a pleasant flight and was warmly received by the government officials, including the ayatollah and the president of Iran. They had a dinner later that evening before which I presented my credentials. The reason I am calling, Holy Father, is that I have to share something with you that troubles me."

"What is that, Carlo?"

"Early yesterday the ayatollah asked if I could meet with him about something very important. We had lunch together privately, as he shared some very important matters that he hoped I could communicate to you, many of which we discussed when I talked with you in Rome a while back."

"Yes, Carlo, I remember."

"Well, the purpose of the meeting with the ayatollah was to ask you if you would consider hosting a meeting of the most important world leaders, and invite Iranian leaders as well, so the Iranians could show their interest in helping to play an important part in bringing about peace in the Middle East. When I told this to the secretary of state, all he said was, 'interesting.' I had expected him to at least say that he would communicate it to you, and when that was not forthcoming, I began to wonder if what I said to him troubled him."

"Carlo, I am reluctant to discuss this over the phone, but since you are so far away, and I am sure it is safe, I will tell you that I understand your concern, and that I think it is well founded. That was the reason I asked you to come to Rome that time, because I knew you would be very current on what is going on behind the scenes in Iran. You are right. I have reason to question the objectivity of the secretary of state on matters concerning Iran. It is not that I doubt his loyalty, but that he may be trying to be overprotective of me for fear that others may try to use me for their own purposes. But, Carlo, I assure you, I am shrewder than that, and I sense a devious ploy as soon as it raises its head. Carlo, let me handle this in my own way."

"Holy Father, this may be of interest. I mentioned to the ayatollah that he might consider meeting with you on some occasion, so that he could share with you directly what he shared with me. He was open to that, and I am sure he would enjoy meeting you as he has such respect for you."

"Thank you, Carlo. That is an excellent idea, and I think I can initiate that from here on my own. Would you tell the ayatollah that I would be very happy to meet with him? Tell him to contact me personally so I can contact him personally. Then there can be no confusion caused by our staff. I think this will work out fine. You are turning out to be what I always knew you would be, my dear Carlo, a very shrewd diplomat, 'innocent as a dove, and wise as a serpent,' as Jesus advised us to be. When I saw how you handled the Mafia, I knew you would be able handle this mission in the way I wanted it to be handled. With ordinary matters though, I want you to go through ordinary channels, through the secretary of state. I will work with you on matters that you judge to be sensitive. Thank you, Carlo, for bringing this to my attention. May our dear Lord bless you and your work."

"Thank you, Holy Father, and good night."

"Good night, Carlo."

When Carlo hung up, he was relieved, but he knew that his work was already complicated. He didn't know what to think of the cardinal secretary of state and felt uneasy about having to deal with him.

23

CARLO DID NOT SLEEP WELL that night. Once you know you cannot feel comfortable sharing sensitive information with your immediate superior, you realize you are alone and begin to wonder whom you can trust. You begin to suspect your superior and try to judge where his loyalty lies, and just what information you can safely share with him, especially when you are an ambassador in a country that has unclear relationships with so many countries. Carlo began to wonder if the ayatollah knew the secretary of state and if he did, what their relationship was. Was it cordial or strained? Was there more to it than met the eye?

Carlo had been invited to speak at a mosque, where a young imam was leader and spiritual guide. Mirza Diba had been a student of the Sufi Jesus mystics in Islam and tried to share some of their writings with his disciples. Knowing that the papal nuncio was not just an archbishop and a diplomat, but also a very spiritual Christian, he contacted Carlo within the first two weeks of his arrival in Tehran and asked if the two could meet. They decided to have tea and baklava one afternoon and ended by becoming friends. It was only a matter of time before they would work together, as they were so much alike in their understanding of what God expects of all of us.

One day, the imam called Carlo and asked if he would speak about Jesus on the following Friday night. This was no secret move on the part of either man to induce the people to accept Jesus, but rather just an opportunity for this holy archbishop to share his understanding of Jesus. Carlo was only too happy to accept, and the night was planned with a refreshment time after the service. It would be the first time that a papal nuncio gave a sermon in a mosque in Iran.

When that night came and the introductory prayers were all said, the notices of happenings and events read, the imam gave a gracious and warm introduction to his friend, the "highly re-spected ambassador from the Vatican to Iran, and deeply spiri-tual human being, His Excellency Archbishop Carlo Brunini."

Carlo arose to speak. The imam noticed five men in the back of the mosque stand up together and walk out of the building. He could tell they were very much disturbed by what was taking place. Carlo also noticed but began his talk as if nothing had happened.

"My dear friend and highly esteemed Imam Mirza Diba, and my dear children of Allah. I have been invited here this evening, not to convert you to Christianity, but to share with you the love that I already have for you, and to expand on what your saintly founder Mohammed wrote in your sacred book, the Qur'an, over thirteen hundred years ago.

"Indeed, what Mohammed has written about Jesus has always inspired me to a deeper understanding not only of Jesus, but of the rich spirituality of your sainted founder. Jesus lived his whole life for his heavenly Father and died out of loyalty to him; his death has benefited all of us, just as his teachings have been a blessing not only to his Christian disciples, but to his disciples in other religions. I am sure you are aware of the rich traditions in your own religion, especially the mystics in the Sufi groups among you. Their dedication to understanding the mind and vision of Jesus and the beautiful lives lived by these mystics have been widely respected by pious Muslims for centuries. The say-ings of Jesus about love of God and love of all God's children have made their lives a much-needed model for imitation today.

In fact, I think nothing would please our God, your God and my God, the same God of Abraham whom we both worship, more than our gathering together as his children and worshiping him together, and loving and respecting one another in his name."

Carlo continued in that vein, and at the end the whole congregation applauded loudly and joyfully, though there were some whom both the imam and Carlo could tell were troubled or confused by what had taken place, and a number of people walked out at different times during Carlo's talk.

Afterward, during the social hour, most of the people were very warm in their expression of welcome and appreciation to both the imam and the archbishop. When everyone left, Carlo and the imam spent time together at the imam's residence. He praised Carlo for his courage in agreeing to give the talk, assuring him that there is no Muslim cleric who knows and believes his theology who would find fault with anything he had said.

The two men parted that evening with mixed feelings, feelings of hope and joy at the thought that what happened that night would be the first ray of the dawn of a new day, where Catholics, and indeed, all Christians, together with their Muslim friends, could gather together to express their love and worship of their Father in heaven. The other feeling was based upon a premonition of dark clouds looming over their lives, a feeling that was indefinable but bearing with it a sadness that had no recognizable justification.

Word had spread throughout the Muslim community about the event at Imam Diba's mosque. His friends were very supportive, and among his friends was the ayatollah. Since there were some vocal complaints from radicals, he advised his friend to let things cool down before he attempted to discuss things like that again, just to keep peace. The ayatollah was aware of the Jesus mystics in Muslim history and respected that movement as an authentic expression of Islamic thought and theology, but he realized that with the radicalization of certain groups in these times, it might not be prudent to promote those ideas publicly. And the ayatollah was right.

A week later tragedy struck.

The imam's teenage son, Mohammed, was stabbed to death by a demented man, a radical, one of the men who walked out of the mosque the night of the archbishop's talk. The imam and his wife were devastated. This boy was kind and sensitive and an excellent student. He was everything a father and mother could want in a son, a son whose life was filled with the promise of a great future. And it all came to a tragic end due to a sick mind.

As soon as Carlo heard of what had happened, he immediately had his chauffeur drive him over to his friend's house to comfort him. Carlo embraced Mirza and, since it was not proper to embrace a Muslim woman, he embraced Zahra with his eyes, which expressed more compassion and sympathy than a physical embrace. He told them how sad he was over the horrible, senseless tragedy.

As there were so many friends and relatives coming to express their condolences, Carlo did not stay long, but before he left, Mirza asked if he could come visit him at his residence and talk with him, because he was afraid that in his grief he might be tempted to do something he might regret. Carlo told him he would be available at any time of the day or night, and on any day. With that he took his leave and promised his prayers for Mirza's son and for the family.

A few days later the imam called Carlo and asked if he could spare a few minutes for him to come over and visit with him.

"Come right over, my dear friend. I am not busy at all."

Actually he was busy, but when someone was in need, Carlo had developed the habit as a young priest to make time for the person. The imam appeared at the nunciature only twenty minutes later. He was escorted to the private sitting room for dignitaries, while the receptionist called the archbishop.

When Carlo entered the sitting room, the imam stood and the two embraced. Carlo held his troubled friend in his arms for the longest time as the poor cleric's body convulsed with sobs from the overwhelming grief that was consuming him.

"Carlo, my dear friend," the imam was finally able to say when he stopped trembling. "Carlo, I think I am losing my mind. I have not slept since that horrible nightmare. My wife is beside herself. When I see her pain, I want to kill the one who caused it. The thought that I could hate someone to the extent that I want to kill him frightens me. Help me, my dear friend, as I have no means within my beliefs that can give me strength and understanding to think differently."

The two men sat in armchairs facing each other.

"Mirza, anger and hatred are an inevitable response to the horrible crime that has been committed against you and your family. But even though it is a natural response, does it really comfort us or heal our pain? Our anger is painful, and destructive, not of anyone else, but of ourselves. It can eat away at our souls like a poison within us.

"I could never understand what Jesus meant when he told Peter to forgive always, as often as someone offends you, forgive. To me that never made sense, because Jesus came to heal, not lay impossible burdens on our hearts. For years I meditated on those words. Then one day when I was praying, the thought came to me, as if Jesus was telling me, 'What I said to Peter was not intended to be a burden but is the key to true inner peace. If you want peace in your soul, learn to forgive, and forgive endlessly.' And then I looked at Jesus' life. He was treated rudely by many, even those closest to him. Even when they had stripped him naked and nailed him to a tree, and his enemies were standing there ridiculing him, he looked at them with pity and cried out to his Father in heaven, 'Father, forgive them for they know not what they do.' I think the key for Jesus being able to do that is his ability to understand why people do mean and stupid things. Usually, it is because they are tortured inside. They have tortured souls.

"From then on, when people hurt me, I tried to understand where they were coming from, and what would lead them to do what they did, or say what they said. It was difficult for me in the beginning, but as time went on, I came to understand people better and found it easy, not only to forgive, but to go a step further, and not even take offense at what someone might do to me. Since then there is almost nothing that can disturb my inner peace."

"That makes sense, Carlo. It is logical. But I don't think my feelings want to follow what is logical. I will think about it, and read what Jesus said, and ask him to help me understand. One of the names of Allah, as you know, is All-Forgiving."

"Yes, Mirza, let's not waste time thinking about the killer. Your son was a beautiful young man. I could see his innocence from the first day I met him. He was and is a rare person, and now he is with God. You have a child who is a saint. How many parents can boast that they have a child in heaven, a child who died in such pure innocence. He died a true martyr's death, not a death while destroying another's life, but a true martyr's death, a victim of the honest and holy effort of his father to reach out to a better and deeper understanding of God. He shared your struggle for that deeper knowledge of God, who was there that night as we were all reaching out to embrace one another. It was that for which your son died.

"Mirza, your son is closer to you now than ever; so close that if you could put your hand through that thin veil separating us from heaven, you could touch him. When you talk to him, he hears you; when you need him, he will be able to help you. Your son wants more than anything for you to have peace. That is his only desire. My dear friend, work and pray hard for that peace."

"Carlo, I am beginning to feel a little of that peace from what you have said. God does heal. God does give peace. A comforting feeling!"

"If you would like, Mirza, I offer mass privately in our little chapel at 7:30 each morning. You and your wife are welcome to come, and we could pray together and then have breakfast."

"That would be wonderful. We will be here, not tomorrow, but the day after, if that is acceptable, a little before 7:30. Thank you, Carlo."

"I feel honored I could help. Please pray for me. God knows I need it."

The imam left, returned home, and told his wife what had happened, and when she saw the change in her husband she was happy that they both were invited back.

Later that day, Carlo got a big surprise. Madelena had arrived with the children and was already settled in at Richard and Joan's villa. When he got her phone call, he was totally surprised, and happy that they were together again.

She called from the Zahedis' villa, wondering if Carlo could come out in the afternoon and stay for supper. Carlo promised to rearrange his schedule and told her he would be there in the early afternoon.

He was particularly busy that day, as he had received a call from the cardinal secretary of state wanting an account of all the details surrounding the affair at Imam Diba's mosque and what ramifications, if any, were unfolding as a result of the event. Carlo explained everything, told him of the imam's visit earlier that day, and promised to send a complete written report as soon as he had a chance to put it together.

As soon as he hung up he wondered how the cardinal knew already about the affair, as he had not told him. He realized he had a person on his staff who was reporting to the cardinal, and this troubled him deeply. He would have to hire his own staff. He could not have someone working for him whom he could not trust. What had just happened made him even more wary about the cardinal and why, with all the nunciatures and delegations under his jurisdiction around the world, he was so focused on this particular one. What was his problem?

He managed to free himself after a light lunch and drove by himself to the villa, arriving there at a little after 2:30. It was a beautiful day, and everyone was sitting in the garden just off the courtyard. Richard was working and would be home later. Joan rushed over to greet him, with Madelena following, and then four of the children.

"Where is Elisabetta?" Carlo asked.

No one answered. Carlo was concerned.

"Did something happen to her? Is she all right?"

All of a sudden Elisabetta came running out from behind the shrubs, crying out, "Here I am, here I am." She ran over and threw herself into her daddy's arms.

"Oh, my Elisabetta, my Elisabetta! You had me worried. I thought something had happened to you."

Then Carla spoke up and said, "Daddy, would you worry about me if something happened to me?"

"Of course I would. You know I would. Come over here and give me a big hug, you silly little goose. You know I love you."

The boys just watched with odd looks on their faces, as if to say, "What's with them? Girls are weird."

Joan gave Carlo a warm welcome. "Carlo, it's so good to see you again! We really couldn't catch up on things at the ayatollah's house. You have to tell us about all your adventures. Tell us about the incident that has been all over the news."

"You've heard about it? It is so tragic. Imam Diba, a friend of mine, has been interested in the ancient Jesus mystics in the Sufi branch of Islam. He's been trying to introduce these holy people to his own disciples and asked if I would talk about them to his people, which I did a little over a week ago. Apparently, there were some in the audience that night who were passionate about not introducing change into their religion, and one person was so upset he decided in his own sick way to teach the imam a lesson by killing his son. It was all so senseless and so tragic. In fact, the imam came over to the house this morning to speak with me about his grief. The poor man is devastated. His son was precious to him, and he does not know how God could ever replace him. He and his wife are coming to the nunciature the day after tomorrow for mass. I hope I can be of some help to them. They are good people."

After supper they all sat around chatting. Carlo accepted their invitation to stay overnight. He spent time with Madelena and the children, asking if they liked their new home and their new country. The children were all excited, especially after Carlo told them that this was the country that the Magi came from. When the children went to bed, Carlo and Madelena talked for a while, and she told him she hoped she could see him more often as she needed him to help with the children.

"Madelena, if you knew how much I miss you, you would know that it is not easy for me to be separated. I'll be with you as many weekends as I can and as often as possible at other times."

The next morning he offered mass at the large kitchen table, with everyone participating. After breakfast, he drove back to the nunciature, as he had a very busy schedule ahead of him.

He was greeted by a stack of mail and several phone calls. One phone call troubled him. It was anonymous and threatening.

24

CARLO TRIED TO TURN THE ANONYMOUS phone call over to the Lord, but it still ended as the subject of nightmares, which made him bolt up in bed several times throughout the night. Whom should he call? Not the local police, certainly. Who knows, they may even be involved. He finally decided to call the Iranian State Department. Within fifteen minutes two secret police officers were at the Vatican nunciature, asking a whole battery of questions, most of which were either irrelevant or of little value, as far as Carlo could tell.

"Do you know anyone who might be upset about something you did or said at any time," asked an officer, "while you've been in Iran, or while you were in Italy, something that may have relevance to anything pertaining to international troubles, or to the Muslim religion?

"The only thing that might be pertinent is the talk I was invited to give in Imam Diba's mosque last month, shortly after which the imam's son was assassinated."

After a few other questions relating to that event, the agents felt they had sufficient information to begin their investigation. They thanked the archbishop for his prompt action and his cooperation, and then left. Within a few minutes the ayatollah called to express his sincere sorrow and deep embarrassment over what had happened and promised that the government would do all in its power to find who was responsible and bring that person to justice.

The archbishop thanked him for his concern and for the government's prompt response.

Several days later he received a phone call from a distraught Madelena. She was beside herself. She could hardly talk. "Carlo, Carlo, come immediately!"

"What happened?"

"Elisabetta has been shot. She is dying!"

"Oh, my God, no!"

"A deranged man came to the school during the children's lunch break. The children were outside because it was such a nice day. He must have been watching them for days. As soon as he saw Elisabetta, he ran across the street and shot her. She's in the hospital now, but the doctors are sure she won't survive. Please come before she dies."

Carlo called the president. The president was stunned and told Carlo to wait and he would have his helicopter pick him up, and the two of them would go together.

On the way Carlo explained the story of his homeless family and his cousin Madelena, whom he talked into being a mother to the little band of homeless children.

Madelena met the two men at the nurses' station and brought them into the child's room. Elisabetta was still alive, though barely. When she saw her father, she tried to smile. Carlo rushed to her bedside and bent over and kissed her.

"Father, I am so happy you are here," she whispered. "I think I'm going to die."

"No, no, don't say that, loved one."

"No, Father, I know I am going to die. When I closed my eyes before, I saw Jesus, and he smiled at me, and I am not afraid anymore. I want to be with him. He's calling me home. It's okay, Daddy. I will watch over you and Madelena and Carla and my brothers. I love you."

No one hearing the child speak that way could stop their tears. Carlo, usually so controlled, was crushed. He tried hard to hold back his tears, but could not. He tried to say something meaningful to the child before she died, but Elisabetta kept saying, "It's all right. I'm going home. And, you know, I don't hate the man who did it. I will pray for him the way you taught us to do when someone hurts us. Tell the man I forgive him."

At that point the nurse brought the other children in to say goodbye to their sister. They were all crying as each one went to her bedside and told her they loved her. To each one she whispered, "I love you. Don't cry. I'm going to be with Jesus."

Then the president walked closer to the child. "I will pray for you," he said.

"Jesus loves you too." she said.

Then Madelena and Carlo bent over her and kissed her. As she looked at them, all she said was, "Goodbye, Mommy, goodbye, Daddy." Then all expression in her face faded and her eyes just stared. The heart monitor showed a flat line. Carlo anointed the beautiful child whose soul was so ready to meet her Savior.

Later, outside the room the president looked at Carlo and Madelena and in carefully measured words, said, "I have a deep impression that I just witnessed the death of a saint, and what is so remarkable is that a child so young could possess such holiness as to forgive the one who has killed her. I feel blessed that Allah has so honored me, and I thank you for this experience. I know it will deeply affect my own life."

The president took them home. Carlo thanked him and went inside to call the Holy Father to tell him what had happened. The pope was stunned, expressed his heartfelt sadness over the tragedy, and promised to offer mass the next morning for Elisabetta and for the family, and asked if there was anything he could do personally.

"Your prayers and your mass, Holy Father, are a blessing to us. Thank you."

"Carlo, is it too dangerous for you to be there now?"

"Holy Father, I have never shrunk from my responsibilities out of fear, even when the Mafia threatened me. There is still much work I know I have to do here. We have already begun a dialogue about Jesus with a Muslim community, and there is great potential for that because the religious leaders here are intellectually open to such dialogue. And Madelena is of the same tough stock. With God's help we can weather the difficulties. We have long since realized that God has destined the two of us for work that we had to accomplish together. We know it is our destiny and that suffering is part of it. We both always knew that. We will do what we have to do."

"I think that would be the proper course. And Carlo, please call if you need me."

The remainder of the evening was spent making plans for the funeral. Clearly, this was not going to be an easy undertaking because Elisabetta was the adopted homeless child of the papal nuncio, the dean of the diplomatic corps in Iran, and dignitaries from many countries and clergy of many religions would be present at the mass. Arrangements had already been made for Francesco and Eugenio and Marco to come to Iran for the funeral. At the same time, the three boys decided they would move to Iran to be with their remaining little brothers and sister to protect them in whatever way they could. It was inspiring to see how these children were so deeply concerned about one another's welfare.

Finally, from exhaustion as well as grief, Madelena broke down and could not be comforted. Carlo was at a loss as to what he could do to console her. All the years he had known her, she had always been strong and disciplined in her display of emotion, even though he knew she was capable of strong feelings. He held her in his arms as she rested her head on his shoulder, crying uncontrollably. He knew she had really lost a daughter.

"Carlo, I am so frightened. I have never known such grief in all my life. Please don't leave me alone." Carlo held her and said not a word.

Early that morning, Carlo received a call from the ayatollah, expressing his deepest sympathy for the terrible tragedy that had fallen upon him and his family. He expressed a desire to be present at the mass, whenever it would be. Carlo was moved by the thoughtful gesture of the ayatollah, and said he and his family would be honored by his presence at the funeral mass.

Arranging the day for the funeral was a problem. Carlo wanted to avoid slighting anyone who might like to express sympathy by attending the mass. It would not be on a Friday as a gesture of courtesy to Muslims, or on the Sabbath as a courtesy to Jews, so the decision was made to have the mass on the following Monday.

Monday finally came. Carlo called the children together; Carla, Vito, Giuseppe, and Radolfo. They were still vulnerable and cried at the slightest tender thought of the happy, fun-loving Elisabetta.

No matter how their father tried to assure them, they kept coming back to the same theme, "But, she's not with us anymore. Nothing else means anything. Why couldn't God let her stay with us? We needed her. She always brought joy into our lives when we were wandering the streets hungry and lonely, and now she's gone. Why did God do that, Daddy?"

How do you answer such questions from innocent minds with broken hearts? Finally, Carlo said to them, "My dear children, all I know is that God did not kill your sister. Evil killed her. She died because Jesus was beginning to become real in some people's hearts nearby, and that upset some angry people. But Elisabetta is now one of Jesus' heroines, and the way she died will touch many other people's hearts as they see in her life and death the beauty of Jesus' presence in her and in your lives, too. She was a peacemaker. The world needs to understand Jesus' teaching on forgiveness, and when it does, the world will find its way to peace. Your sister taught that message of Jesus in a beautiful way, and her forgiveness of the troubled man who killed her will make Jesus real to these people and wonderful things will happen.

Your sister will be your guardian angel, always at your side, and in your hearts, so please take comfort in that, and rejoice that she is in heaven. Be happy for her, as she is happy."

The three college boys arrived, and though they were now sophisticated college and graduate students, they lost all their starch and cried unashamedly when they saw the body of their little sister lying in the coffin. She was always so full of life and in spite of their difficult circumstances she never lost her ability to love. When they wandered the streets and were hungry and cold and hurting, Elisabetta always tried to do or say something funny to make everyone laugh and be happy. It was even harder for them to understand than for the younger ones. When we get older, we are full of questions. Children are more open to accepting their parents' answers and believe what they tell them. It is easier for them to have faith, to dream of worlds they cannot see, and to rejoice when someone they love dies if they believe they are happy with God and other loved ones in heaven. That is why Jesus said that children are blessed.

The funeral had to be held at the Cathedral in Tehran because of all the international dignitaries. Archbishop Garmou was gracious in stepping aside and letting Carlo do the whole ceremony. For an hour before the mass Elisabetta's body lay in state so the well-wishers could pay their respects. Carlo and Madelena, the child's only real parents, stood beside the body, and her brothers and sister stood in a row. Everyone was crying. Knowing that Elisabetta and the others had been homeless children made the scene doubly tragic and heartrending. After the laypeople, dignitaries filed in and paid their respects, and took their seats in pews behind the family. Then Muslim clerics, the ayatollah, and Imam Diba and other clerics came up in procession and were conducted up into the sanctuary. Following them was the president, and other officials, and members of the Majlis, the Iranian parliament, including the Jewish representative in the Majlis.

Finally, behind them, a bedraggled man came up, looked for the longest time into the coffin, and walked over to Carlo, who was still standing near the coffin. Instinct or a light from God told Carlo that this was the man who had killed Elisabetta. When the man approached Carlo, trembling, Carlo hugged him and whispered into his ear, "I forgive you!" The man looked into Carlo's eyes, frightened and mystified. Finally he said, "You do?"

"Yes, from my heart."

The man whispered, "I am so sorry. I read that she forgave me and prayed for me. Is that true?"

"Yes, and she said it from her heart. She did not want you to be punished."

"That is why I came. To be punished."

"God forgives you. The rest is up to you. Thank you for coming."

The whole church wondered what was going on, especially as the man broke down crying as he walked to the back of the church and sat in the last pew. Carlo acted as if nothing unusual had happened and went over and kissed Elisabetta. Then Madelena and the children followed, while Carlo went to the sanctuary to begin the service.

"In the name of the Father and of the Son and of the Holy Spirit."

"Amen," many responded.

"The grace and peace of God our Father and the Lord Jesus Christ and the joy of the Holy Spirit be with you all."

"And also with you."

The funeral director closed the coffin and partially placed the white cover over it.

Archbishop Garmou walked over to the coffin accompanied by a priest and blessed the body with holy water that symbolized her baptism into Jesus' family, then took the edge of the white cover, with the words, "Elisabetta, I cover you with the symbol of your pure innocence before God, as we prepare you for entrance into his heavenly kingdom, a specially chosen soul, and blessed martyr."

The archbishop returned to the sanctuary and took his seat, as Carlo continued the liturgy. "Heavenly Father, we gather as your family to pray for our dear little sister, Elisabetta, whom you have called from this world. We pray that you will accept the gift of her life and bring her home to the joy of your heavenly kingdom where you live and reign with Jesus your Son and the Holy Spirit as one God, forever and ever."

"Amen," the congregation responded.

Carlo sat down in the chair for the presiding priest, on a raised platform, as the ayatollah rose to do the first reading from the Book of Wisdom. He had graciously suggested to Carlo that he would like to do something to show his solidarity with the archbishop and his family, and Carlo asked if he would like to do this reading.

"The souls of the innocent are in the hands of God, and no evil shall touch them. In the eyes of the heedless they seem to be dead, and their departure a tragedy, and the end of their existence; but they are at peace. They may seem to be punished but they are clothed in immortality. Though they pass through a moment of pain, they are presently surrounded with glory. Their brief trial has proven them worthy of God's presence so he took them to himself. They have been tested and have been proven to be purest gold, and their death a fragrant offering to the Lord. In time they will appear as brilliant sparks darting about the ashes of humanity, giving witness to the nations of the glory of God."

The ayatollah finished the reading with, "The word of the Lord," to which all responded, "Thanks be to God."

As the ayatollah walked back to his seat, Francesco walked up from his pew in the front row to the lectern and began the second reading: "A reading from the Acts of the Apostles: Stephen, filled with the Holy Spirit, gazed into heaven and saw the glory of God, and Jesus standing at God's right hand. 'I can see the heavens thrown open and the Son of Man standing at the right hand of God.' The elders were enraged. They took Stephen, dragged him outside the city and kept stoning him. Stephen prayed, 'Lord Jesus, receive my spirit,' and as they kept stoning him, he prayed, 'Lord Jesus, do not hold this sin against them,' and with that he fell asleep in the Lord. The word of the Lord."

"Thanks be to God," the people responded.

The deacon then went to the stand enshrining the Book of the Gospels and, holding it up in front of him, walked to the celebrant and asked for his blessing. Carlo stood and pronounced the blessing and then the deacon proceeded to the pulpit and read the following gospel passage: "How fortunate are the poor in spirit, theirs is the kingdom of heaven! How fortunate are the gentle, for they shall inherit the earth! How fortunate are those in sorrow, for they shall be comforted! How fortunate are they who thirst for holiness, for they shall attain what they thirst for! How fortunate are the merciful, for they shall find mercy from God! How fortunate are the pure of heart, for they shall see God! How fortunate are the peacemakers, for they shall be called the children of God! And how fortunate are they who suffer for what is right, for theirs is the kingdom of heaven!"

Then holding high the Book of the Gospels for the veneration of the congregation, the deacon proclaimed, "The Gospel of the Lord."

To which the people responded, "Praise be to God."

The deacon then proceeded back to the place where the Book of the Gospels is kept enshrined and put it back on its stand, while Carlo went to the pulpit to deliver the homily.

His homily was short.

"Our family loved Elisabetta. We will always miss her. I wish you could have known her and could have seen her gentle light. There is no doubt that she is with God, but her work here on earth is not finished. The beauty of her life and the holiness of her death will touch the lives of many people in Iran for years to come. Living here, and dying here, she can be considered a genuine martyr, a peacemaker, and an Iranian saint who died with love and forgiveness on her lips. There are already lives that have been radically changed during the past few days, and even this morning. On the day Elisabetta died, a beautiful glow came across her face. Through her pain she smiled, and as she talked to someone we could not see, we knew God was calling her home and telling her not to be afraid, that she would soon be with him. To ease our sorrow, she told us what Jesus had said to her and that we should not be afraid either. Then she told us that she forgave the man who hurt her, and that she would pray for him, and that her love would go out to him. She then looked at us, told us she loved us and quietly left this world. Now through our grief and our tears, we try to rejoice in the happiness our dear little Elisabetta enjoys in heaven with God."

Carlo went to his seat and Madelena left her pew and walked up to the lectern to lead the Prayer of the Faithful,

"For our dear Elisabetta, who died a martyr's death for the Lord, we pray to the Lord," to which the people responded, "Lord, hear our prayer."

"For all those who die for their belief in God, we pray to the Lord."

"Lord, hear our prayer."

"For all our friends and loved ones who mourn with us today, we pray to the Lord."

"Lord, hear our prayer."

"For our children, who suffer the loss of their dear sister, we pray to the Lord."

"Lord, hear our prayer."

Then, Madelena, following Carlo's instructions, added a little sermon in the form of a meditation.

"We witness here this morning a mystery, a mystery that I am only now beginning to understand. Why are we here in this beautiful country where we have been embraced with so much love by a people that only a few months ago we did not even know? This little child we are burying is not our child. She and the other children were given to us by God, and they became to us our precious gifts. The archbishop and I are not husband and wife, though we have been dear friends as first cousins since child-hood, and we have lived as friends because we know that it is a special design of God, and we have willingly allowed God to use us as he chooses. Our presence here in Iran is in some way tied up in the mystery of God's providence. In some mystical way God has bonded the Iranian people and our family together for some unknown but beautiful purpose that we will only under-stand as that purpose unfolds in the distant future. Our family has been blessed by your love, and I pray that our love for you proves to be a blessing to you and to your people as well. May we all continue to pray for one another as we celebrate the en-trance of our dear little Elisabetta into God's home!"

For the most sacred part of the liturgy the priests gathered around the altar and consecrated the bread and wine together, and at communion they all helped distributing communion to the large numbers who came to receive the body and blood of Jesus.

After communion the children took turns coming to the lec-tern and telling their own touching stories about their sister.

Vito was the first to tell his story. "We were eight brothers and sisters. We had no parents; we were all homeless; we wandered the streets hoping people would give us food. Some days we didn't eat. On days we did eat, sometimes it wasn't much. Elisabetta watched us and could see we were still hungry, so she made believe she couldn't eat all her food. She shared what she had left with all of us. It was probably most of what food she had. Since I was the smallest, she became my mother and took care of me. I feel as if my mother has died. She was the only mother I knew until our father the archbishop and mother Madelena adopted us, and they are the best parents kids could ever have. Now that Elisabetta is gone, I think my heart is broken. I don't feel the same inside. I wish she could come back."

The next was Carla. She was quite a young lady now and showed great poise and composure. "Dear friends, thank you all for coming. Elisabetta was very special to me, because we were the only two girls. Living in the streets we had to learn to take care of ourselves. Every now and then we would have to fight to protect ourselves. Elisabetta was usually ladylike and sweet, but when some strange kid would pick on me, Elisabetta could be like a tiger. She could run like a boy and punch like a boy. She would smile and laugh a lot, but she hardly ever cried. I think even when her heart was breaking she wouldn't cry. She was afraid that if she cried, it would make us afraid. She was not hard, but when she was hurting, she just looked like stone, like Daddy gets sometimes. She would just stare as if her thoughts were miles away. It was hard living in the streets. Elisabetta is gone now, and I don't want to even think about it. I loved her so much. At times she was all I had, and, and . . . " That was all she could say. She sat down.

The boys took their turns and shared much the same.

Then the ayatollah spoke a few words from his heart.

"This morning was for me a vast learning experience, the experience of a whole new way of life. I have been taught by little children, children who have spent much of their young lives as homeless wanderers. Today I saw something of the beauty of their lives. They teach all of us not only courage and loyalty and love, but perhaps the most important virtue of all: forgiveness. I am grateful."

The ceremony ended, and the funeral procession went from the sanctuary to the cemetery not far from the church. The family members clung to one another all the way.

25

THE PRESIDENT'S WIFE HOSTED the reception at their residence. It was elegant but simple. The president's wife was most gracious. She took the children aside and asked them if they would like a tour of the house. They were pleased, and her kind gesture took their minds off their grief, if only for a few moments.

The ayatollah and the president told Carlo how impressed they were with the ceremony. They wondered if all Catholic funeral masses were like that one.

"Pretty much so," Carlo responded. "The homilies will differ depending on how well the celebrant knows the deceased and what aspect of theology the celebrant decides to emphasize."

"Did you know that man who came up to talk to you when you were near the coffin?" the ayatollah asked Carlo.

"No, I had never seen him before. He told me he had read the newspaper and was deeply moved that the girl expressed forgiveness for the person who killed her and was even more impressed with her saying that she would pray for him."

When the reception ended everyone dispersed, and Carlo, Madelena, and the children went back to the villa with their friends. They spent the rest of the day recuperating from the stressful morning ordeal. It was a beautiful sunny day, and after freshening up, they gathered in the flower-studded garden, around the gorgeous, spring-fed pond with six majestic swans floating gracefully across its vast surface. On the opposite side of the pond two peacocks strutted to attract the attention of three females wandering nearby, very much aware of the presence of the stalking males and gracefully avoiding them.

Eugenio shouted, "Mother, look over there. There's a peacock coming out of those trees."

Everyone turned around to look, and Joan laughed, "Yes, they are part of our family, too. As beautiful as they are they can be a nuisance sometimes, especially when they fly up on the roof and make a racket. I think they do it to show off and get attention."

Before the day ended, the president called to tell Carlo that the killer of Elisabetta had turned himself in when he left the church and confessed to killing not only Elisabetta but also the son of Imam Diba. "I believe you knew that would happen." The president then assured the nuncio, strongly, in the ayatollah's name that they would have a speedy trial and would execute him publicly. Carlo thanked him for their speedy work but asked if he could meet with him as soon as possible and also asked him, as an extraordinary favor, not to do any harm to the person.

"This is very important to me, Your Excellency, and I ask your indulgence in this matter that means so much to our family as well."

The president had little choice but to agree to the meeting as he knew the nuncio would go over his head and obtain what he wished from the ayatollah.

Carlo shared with Madelena what the president had said and told her he had an appointment to meet with him in the morning. Carlo thought that especially while living in a Muslim country it was important that he practice what Jesus taught and forgive his enemies, which he would have done anyway. But as a representative of the church, it was even more urgent that he make a public statement of his forgiveness. This is the only way to have peace in the world, by teaching the world to forgive, and especially on so personal an occasion.

"Carlo, that is why I have loved you so much all my life. You were like that as a little child, but I must tell you, I am having a very difficult time forgiving that man. He was the one who came up to you in church, wasn't he?"

"Yes, and it's not easy for me either, but I am sure that the man is deranged. Hatred and ignorance killed our daughter. Reading what the paper said about Elisabetta forgiving him and praying for him made him realize he did an evil thing to an innocent and saintly child, and he knows what he did is wrong. He is truly repentant but afraid Allah will not forgive him."

"I understand. It's just hard."

All the way to Tehran the next morning Carlo too had a difficult time. Elisabetta's memories flooded his mind and haunted him all the way. How he missed that beautiful child who had brought such joy to his life. He knew he would miss her every day from that day on but would always keep the pain to himself as he did with everything else. He had learned early never to trust anyone with his most secret thoughts or feelings. This awakening of his memories made him think of Madelena and how much he wanted to belong to her completely. Though he never told her, she knew how he felt; his not telling her was his way of telling her. To put it into words, they both knew, would be disastrous, because then they would both break down and that would destroy the beautiful spiritual love they had for each other—the love that made possible the wonderful things they had accomplished together.

26

CARLO ARRIVED AT THE PRESIDENT'S OFFICE at a little after ten o'clock.

"Your Excellency," Carlo said, "I have struggled over my feelings about the person who killed my daughter. As a man I want him punished, but I know only too well what Jesus taught about forgiveness, and of late, I realize that what our sick world needs for healing is forgiveness—not condoning evil, but forgiveness and healing of all the festering wounds that make the world so sick. I would like to ask you and the ayatollah if we could make a public gesture to the world to show that even though we condemn evil in all its forms, what is needed more than ever today is to stop the chain of evil by breaking one painful link, by making a gesture that would please God and create a climate of healing that could change our sick world."

The president folded his arms, as if defending his own personal beliefs. "How do you propose we do that, Your Excellency?"

"By having a public trial of the man who killed Elisabetta, admitting his guilt and being condemned, and then both my family and I, and the imam and his wife who lost their son, will plead with the court to commute the death sentence requiring him to perform charitable works for the rest of his life under the surveillance of the court. I know the imam and his wife as if they were my brother and sister and am sure they feel the same

213

way. Hopefully, our doing this together, as Muslim and Christian leaders, will be a powerful statement to the world that we all have to learn forgiveness if we are to bring healing to our sick world."

"My dear friend, our law is clear."

"I know, and many of your people back what this person did and consider him a patriot for Islam, but you would not want to turn a person like that into a martyr."

"You are a fine logician, Your Excellency, and I treasure our relationship. It is not easy for me to accommodate you on this, as my readiness to punish this man was my way of expressing my respect for your grief. But, I do understand your feelings and respect your deep convictions. I will talk to the ayatollah and see what we can work out, although my heart is not in it."

"Thank you, Mister President. I also think the state of mind of the person is important. Could you find out if the person is sorry and also if he is mentally disturbed? I am aware that Mohammed would not approve of executing a person who is mentally sick."

The president smiled with his wry smile, "You are sly as well as sincere, my friend. You know he is sorry. He is the one who came up to you in the cathedral and said he was sorry. But I will talk to the ayatollah and we will see. I can see some possible good coming from such a gesture."

"Thank you. I am sure it would be a powerful message to the world if Iran and the Vatican sent a joint message that the only road to peace is by reaching out to one another in a spirit of forgiveness."

"Your Excellency, I can see why the Holy Father sent you here as his representative with such a high personal recommendation to the ayatollah and me. You are not only a master logician and a sly fox, but you are the most authentic image I have ever seen of the Jesus you worship. I promise to do what I can with the ayatollah."

"I appreciate that, and before I forget, would you accept an invitation to the nunciature for dinner some night at your convenience? I would really like to become more acquainted with the real man behind the title."

"Yes, I would enjoy that. Do you play chess?"

"Of course. Don't all statesmen?"

The president laughed.

Although they had not intended it, the two tough men, so vastly different from each other in polish and personality, hugged and kissed each other on both cheeks, and Carlo left for the nunciature.

Carlo had a mountain of mail including at least five thousand letters of condolence from people he did not know. Many were from people who read the story of the archbishop and his adopted homeless children. They were saddened and shocked that one of them had been murdered by a disturbed person in retaliation for a talk about Jesus that the archbishop had given in a mosque at the request of the local imam, whose son had also been murdered in retaliation for the same incident.

Carlo's attache came to his office and informed him the pope had called and would appreciate it if he would call him the first chance he had.

"Hello, praised be Jesus Christ," the pope answered the call in Latin.

"Now and forever," Carlo answered.

"My son, I am worried about you and Madelena and the children. Are you all safe?"

"Yes, Holy Father. I just left the president's office. I asked if he would talk to the ayatollah about forgiving the man who killed Elisabetta as a way of sending a message to the world, a joint message with the Vatican, that the only way to peace is by reaching out to one another for peace and forgiveness. And as evidence of their understanding of that message, the Iranian government would be pardoning a man who killed the son of an imam and the adopted daughter of the papal nuncio to Iran for discussing Jesus in their mosque. I could tell my request bothered him, as it is against their culture, but he promised to talk to the ayatollah and do what he could to persuade him."

"Carlo—then the pope switched to Russian—you have grown so much in the past few years. The matter you discussed with me about the Vatican working with other countries to open channels of communication with Iran has not been put aside. The staff has been working on that constantly, and we have some good news to report. The Europeans were the first to show interest, and the Americans lately have been warming up to the idea, so you can report to the ayatollah that he might be pleasantly surprised in the very near future. I do have to say that it was not an easy thing to pull off but persistence and prayer paid off. I expect much good will to come from it, and it might be just what is needed to bring peace to the Middle East."

"Thank you so much, Holy Father," Carlo said, "I was wondering how that was going. It will mean a lot to the people here. I can't wait to share with them what you just told me. In fact, I will call the ayatollah immediately. It will help to encourage him to go along with my request for the pardon, which I know is a theological problem for them, and a theological nod toward the forgiving Jesus, which won't sit too well with some. What you have done will be a big help, and the timing was perfect. Thank you so much, Holy Father."

"My dear son, continue doing your work. You have already accomplished much, and your beautiful Jesus-like spirit, I know from others, is touching many lives there."

"Thank you, Holy Father. I wish I could do much more. There is still so much lacking in me. I do need and appreciate your prayers."

"God bless you, Carlo. Feel free to call whenever you like, and give my love to Madelena and the children. I never thought I would feel comfortable saying that to an archbishop and a papal nuncio, no less, but you have made it such a beautiful expression of caring love. I can now easily imagine Mary, Joseph, and Jesus taking homeless children into their family when he was a child. Maybe they were the brothers and sisters mentioned in the Gospels." The pope chuckled as he said that, and Carlo did the same.

"Thank you, Holy Father, and may God bless your ministry, as well."

"Thank you, and peace."

The two men hung up.

Carlo left his office and went to the small chapel. He just collapsed on his kneeler in front of the Blessed Sacrament, put his face in his hands, and finally broke down and cried. He had been so strong for everyone during their grieving, he would not allow himself to grieve for the saintly, buoyant child he loved so much. He had loved her more than the others, most likely because he knew she was trying to be just like him in his love of Jesus. As much as he loved her, he never showed it, except for simple little gestures, like an affectionate wink, when no one was watching, or a gentle tender look when she looked up at him. His love for all his children would not allow him the luxury of showing favor to one over the others.

Now, alone in the chapel, he allowed himself to feel his grief and pour out to his little princess the love that he could never show her before. Then, having slept so poorly over the past few days, he fell asleep and dreamed of Elisabetta. She had walked over to him and with her happy smile hugged him and said, "Daddy, I still love you, and I always knew you loved me very much!"

"Oh, my dear, sweet Elisabetta!"

"Don't cry, Daddy. I will always be near you. I am so happy here with Jesus and his mother, and my own family. See this little lamb I am holding? Jesus gave it to me and called me his little lamb. Because of your goodness and all you taught us about Jesus, the hearts of many who do not know Jesus will be changed."

Carlo suddenly awoke, disturbed by a noise behind him in one of the pews. As he turned around, an old priest apologized for disturbing his conversation.

"But, Father, I wasn't talking to anyone. I was sound asleep."

The old man looked confused, then repeated, "I am sorry, Your Excellency, you may not have realized it, but you were talking to a little girl. I heard her talking to you too. It was all quite clear and so beautiful."

"I wasn't dreaming?"

"I don't think so."

"Father, can I trust you not to tell this to anyone?"

"I knew it had to be a sacred moment, and I assumed it must have been an angel or your little daughter God had taken home. You can rest assured I would never violate such a sacred trust."

"Thank you, Father. I think we have both been blessed in a very special way." The two men hugged, and Carlo began to laugh.

Carlo left the chapel and went back to his office to make the call to the ayatollah as he had promised the pope.

"Hello, Your Excellency, this is the nuncio. I appreciate your taking my call."

"I will always be available when you call, Your Excellency. My prayers have been with you and your dear family. The ceremony yesterday was most inspiring. I am sure the president told you about our arresting the culprit."

"Yes, Your Excellency, and I have already had a long discussion about that, which I am sure he will bring to your attention. But that is not the reason I called. I have just been talking with the pope, and he told me that he has had his staff working assiduously with leaders of European countries and the United States government about working together with your country. He had significant success to report to you. The first ones to respond positively were certain European countries, including France, Germany, Belgium, and Italy. As soon as his staff members receive more information, they will contact us with the news. They expect that any day now."

"Thank you, my friend. You don't know how much that means to me and to all of us. It is important that we be respected by other countries and accepted as an equal partner in helping to resolve these issues of peace, especially in our own region. I know your Vatican officials share our understanding of the fundamental issues confronting all Middle Eastern peoples. The Vatican does not think in political terms or in terms of years. The Vatican thinks in terms of decades and centuries. It has a long and profound understanding of the beginnings of problems and sees today's difficulties as symptoms of infections starting decades or even centuries ago. That is why we benefit from close relations with the Vatican."

"Our relationship goes far back, and we have always been a help to each other."

When the conversation ended, Carlo had a good feeling about the final decision concerning the matter he discussed earlier with the president, though what took place two hours after Carlo's conversation with the ayatollah was not as easy as Carlo may have hoped. The president did talk with the ayatollah shortly after Carlo's conversation with him. But the ayatollah's first reaction was negative—very negative—for Islam has stringent laws concerning punishment for serious crimes. Surprisingly, the president was so strongly convinced by the way Carlo presented the proposal as a gesture of human compassion and divine forgiveness that after some persuasion he managed to convince the ayatollah that it would certainly make the West stand up and take notice of Iran's potential for productive peace gestures. At the end the ayatollah gave the president permission to tell the papal nuncio that, although it was a difficult gesture to embrace, he could see great good coming from it.

When the president shared this with Carlo, he was delighted, and they agreed to work together so that it would be done in as sensitive a manner as possible. They wanted the people to see it as the only way to express properly the justice and compassion of God, as reflected in the best traditions of both Christianity and Islam. Carlo and the ayatollah spoke several times about how to accomplish their goal. They decided that the man, Farhad Morshedizad, guilty by his own confession, would indeed be convicted of the murders. But the fact that he had a history of mental illness and that he had been forgiven by Elisabetta herself and by all the parents would be taken into consideration. Because of the heartfelt and unselfish pleas of the victims' families, it would be the decision of the ayatollah and the Iranian Majlis, as well as the Holy Father and the Vatican, that the murderer would be spared the death penalty; instead, he would be required to do charitable service for the rest of his life in order to show adequate remorse for the pain and suffering caused to both families. The ayatollah would also express the truth that Islam does not condone the execution of a seriously mentally disturbed person.

Earlier the ayatollah had contacted Imam Diba, who wished for the same resolution as the nuncio, and invited the imam and his wife to consider being a part of the public expression of their solidarity. The imam assured them of his and his wife's support. Carlo also kept Madelena abreast of the plans, because she very much wanted to be part of the proceedings. Out of loyalty to their sister's dying wishes, the children also wanted to be part of this gesture for peace.

It was now just a matter of finding the right forum for the ceremony. The Vatican suggested that they choose the anniversary of the death of Dr. Mohammed Mossadegh. His death, shortly following the coup that drove him from office after having been elected by 99 percent of the people, was a very sore wound in the hearts of older Iranians. The coup, plotted by Prime Minister Churchill and President Eisenhower after Mossadegh nationalized the oil industry in Iran, put the shah back into power against the will of the people. That stroke destroyed the budding democracy in Iran in the late 1960s. Setting that day to proclaim the pardon requested by the imam and the archbishop for the murderer of the imam's son and the papal nuncio's daughter was significant because it also made a powerful statement that the Iranian people were willing to forgive those countries whose leaders plotted the destruction of their government.

The date was set and a massive communications program was organized for the Iranian people so they could become part of the forgiveness ceremony that everyone hoped would become the beginning of a new era of peace based on forgiveness, justice, and mercy.

When the day finally came, it turned out to be a beautiful sunny morning. The affair took place in a large sports arena, which was packed with dignitaries from many countries. From one aspect it was melodramatic, especially as the actual murderer was paraded (something he wished to go through as his own personal penance for what he had done) before the whole assembly and tried and convicted and sentenced to death. With this done, the judge then asked the ayatollah if he had any remarks.

The ayatollah then rose and took a prominent seat on the platform and asked Imam Diba and Zahra, and Archbishop Brunini, and Madelena and the children to come forward and make their requests known to the court.

In their brief speeches the imam and his wife expressed their grief over the death of their son. They told the assembled people that they felt deeply moved by divine grace to forgive the troubled man. Then Carlo and Madelena expressed their grief and asked that out of respect for the last request of their adopted child, Elisabetta, her murderer be pardoned. They requested the court to pardon the man and allow him to live in peace as he made his restitution to Allah for having snatched the lives of two innocent young people.

The court asked if that was a request the ayatollah could honor. The ayatollah delivered a beautifully moving address to the court, to his people, and to the countries of the world stating that by honoring the request he was, in the name of his people, and in the name of Allah, expressing forgiveness for the horrible crimes that had been committed against two innocent children, who in Allah's eyes were martyrs. He emphasized that Mohammed demanded mercy for persons who were mentally ill. "May this day be the dawn of a new era of forgiveness and pursuit of justice and peace based on justice for all the nations."

The ayatollah then asked the papal nuncio to read the letter he had received from His Holiness, the pope and bishop of Rome. Carlo rose and went the microphone, and began reading the pope's letter:

> *"To the Supreme Leader, and the Honorable President and the Majlis, and to the long respected people of the ancient culture and civilization of Persia-Iran, God's grace and blessings. I am honored to be present in spirit and in the person of my faithful ambassador, Archbishop Carlo Brunini, and to be part of this noble gesture for peace and reconciliation of the nations of the world. This joint statement by our two religious bodies is significant, not only because we represent practically the whole of the human race, but because we are also paying joint honor to two special children, one Muslim, the other Christian, who have died as martyrs because of a heroic act by two brave men who are seeking to find common ground between our two religions. I am moved to make the statement that Elisabetta, whose divinely inspired expression of love and forgiveness for the one who ended her life on this earth, acted under divine grace and evidenced beyond doubt that she is a special child of God. Not only might we pray for her, but we may also pray for her intercession with our heavenly Father. May the God of us all bless all of you present at the ceremony as well as those of you who are present in spirit."*

When Carlo finished reading the pope's letter, the ayatollah rose and, as had been arranged, made a statement declaring that the son of Imam and Mrs. Diba was a special child of Allah and could be considered among the blessed in heaven and deserved honor among the people. At that point the prisoner was called forward and was led to Imam Diba and his wife, Zahra, and to the Archbishop and Madelena and the children.

The prisoner burst into tears. "I am not worthy," he said. "I am so sorry."

To each he expressed his deepest sorrow for what he had done, and one at a time they reached out to embrace him warmly as they expressed their forgiveness and promised their prayers. At that point the whole assembly broke into loud applause, singing a powerful hymn of thanksgiving to God for his mercy and compassion. They saw that forgiveness could be a beautiful expression of authentic divine love and a release of horrible repressed feelings of anger over past injuries. The people's thunderous applause was a powerful attestation that the government had made a move that the people of Iran understood and heartily approved.

TEACHER

Just then a man came up to him and asked, "Teacher, what good thing must I know to get eternal life?"
—MATTHEW 19:15-17

27

IMMEDIATELY AFTER THAT REMARKABLE EVENT, responses began coming back through the media. The US president and administration welcomed the heroic gesture that had been made to the world. Most Americans were moved, but some were cynical, saying that Iran would have to do more than that to show it was prepared to make such gestures in ordinary dealings with other nations. Reactions from European countries were also mixed, though the Eastern European countries were more positive. People who were hoping for a change in tone and policy from Iran's leaders were not as skeptical and were willing to give them the benefit of the doubt. Time would show if they were sincere. The important thing was that the precedent had been established and that the precedent had come from the Iranians. The challenge now was for others to match that noble gesture in some way other than by cynical remarks that merely hinted at their own bad faith.

As time passed, Carlo's relationship with the ayatollah and the president continued to be friendly and productive in many ways, such as in allowing Catholics more freedom to function and hold more outdoor celebrations. Because of the good relations Carlo had developed with the leaders, ordinary Muslims felt freer to be friendlier with Catholics and vice versa. Their presence at each other's public celebrations was much more common than ever before. Imam Diba felt comfortable enough to invite Carlo to give other talks at his mosque about the Sufi mystics who had such a devotion to Jesus in their prayer life and in their form of mysticism. Gradually the imam's followers were adopting that form of Muslim spirituality for their community as an expression of their gracious attempt at ecumenism.

During this time the Vatican released a stunning statement indicating that the pope was about to call a consistory to invest newly nominated cardinals. The list was quite extensive and comprehensive: one from Japan, two from China, one from Indonesia, one from the Philippines, one from the United States, one from Scotland, one from Germany, one from Lebanon, one from Syria, a Palestinian from Israel, and three from Italy. The American was a heroic priest from the diocese of Albany, New York, named Peter Young, who had worked with the homeless and addicts all his life.

Of the three from Italy, one was Archbishop Carlo Brunini.

The Iranians went wild with delight. The ayatollah was the first to express his personal joy and congratulation, and the president could not contain his joy when the media interviewed him. He said it was as if his own brother had been made a cardinal, and even though he would miss the archbishop terribly, he was happy for him and wished him only the best. "Yes," he said, "I intend to be there to witness and celebrate the event if I am invited." Mirza and Zahra were also thrilled. Madelena could not contain her happiness, and the children were so proud. Right away they said it was the work of their sainted sister, who probably pestered God, which inspired this. Richard and Joan were thrilled at the honor bestowed on their friend.

Carlo's time in Iran had gone by more quickly than he had expected. Francesco had received master's degrees in engineering and biotechnology, and another degree in computer science. Eugenio had also graduated with honors, and Marco was about to graduate. Two of the other children were now in college, and the two youngest were in their last years before college.

Where this little family would be living was again a trouble-some concern. Carlo learned he would soon be asked to work in Rome in some capacity. Finding an apartment for his family would be a problem, as he had not amassed any kind of financial resources. What little he did receive in income and gifts was spent mostly on the children and Madelena, who had abandoned her full-time professional work to care for the children, except for small cases she handled for people who were aware of her reputation as a lawyer. In Rome it would probably be important for her to work, since cardinals' salaries are not great, the cost of living is high, and children's expenses never end.

Leaving Richard and Joan would be difficult, as they had become close and had gone through painful times together. Parting with friends who are so loyal and so much a part of your soul carries with it a special kind of grief.

Wondering for weeks where they would live when they arrived in Rome, Carlo was shocked when he received an invitation from the trustees of the Villa Borghese offering him and Madelena and the children residence there for as long a time as they needed to get themselves settled. He could not help but wonder if someone there found out that he had spent time there as a homeless beggar. He could feel his face flushing with a rush of blood.

The trip to Rome was anticlimactic. Carlo had accepted the invitation to stay at the Villa Borghese. When the family arrived there, they received a surprisingly cordial welcome. Carlo could not understand why the hosts were so gracious to one who really was a stranger. It was only after he had been there a few hours that the mystery became clear. The director came to meet Carlo when he arrived, and on seeing him, called out, "Carlo, Carlo Brunini!"

Carlo looked up and recognized one of his old seminary class-mates, Paolo Di Franco. They hugged each other, happy to see each other again. Paolo had left the seminary, obtained his degrees in architecture and the history of ancient buildings, and had begun restoring old Roman buildings. One day he was asked if he would like to maintain and operate the Villa Borghese for the board that administered the estate. The day that Carlo had visited there as a homeless beggar, Paolo had recognized him, even in his beggar's clothes. But because he did not want to embarrass him or invade his privacy, Paolo made no attempt to talk with him. In fact, he was the one who called the attendant when Carlo tried to enter the Galleria but had no money.

Paolo did not tell his friend all those details, but they had a wonderful time going over memories of seminary days and all the fun they had had way back then. Carlo introduced Paolo to Madelena and his little family. Paolo could not resist the comment, "Oh, my, we finally have a good old-fashioned Renaissance cardinal-archbishop and his woman and children back in our modern church!"

Carlo laughed, realizing that that was just about what people must think. He then mentioned that Madelena was his cousin, his first cousin, in fact, and the kids were adopted. By that time the kids had wandered off with their luggage, following the attendants who were showing them to their rooms.

"Let me show you your quarters," Paolo said. "Of course, you will be staying in the country house itself, the home of Cardinal Scipione Borghese himself, whose ghost still roams the place."

"Paolo, you don't have to be so generous. All we need are some simple rooms."

"Well, I feel I have to make up for my rude treatment the last time you were here."

"What do you mean, the last time I was here?"

"The night you slept out among the shrubs as a homeless beggar."

"Paolo! How did you know that?"

"I thought I recognized you when you first came here. Then, when I read that newspaper article in the Rome paper, about the homeless beggar with the strange patch on the right pant leg, I was certain. So this is my chance to make it up to you, even though at the time I was trying to respect your privacy."

"Paolo, I am so embarrassed. I'll tell you the whole story sometime."

As the three walked over to the casino, as the main house was called, the attendants picked up the luggage and carted it over to the house. Along the way Madelena commented on how beautiful the gardens were. She could not believe that there could be so many awesome varieties of plants and flowers on one estate.

"Yes, the place is stunning in its beauty. The flowers are brought in from all over the Mediterranean. Some are annuals; some are perennials. I expanded many of the gardens when I first came here years ago. Since then, they have been more spectacular each year."

When they arrived at the residence, Paolo took pride in showing them around what really was a palace. The guests were overwhelmed and could not believe they would be staying there. After they had seen their rooms and the children's rooms, Paolo reminded them that after the investiture ceremony at St. Peter's, the reception was going to be held right there at the house.

That made Carlo a bit nervous, because he intended to invite some of the homeless in Rome. When he broached the subject, Paolo responded that he thought that that was what his friend would do, so he was ready for it.

"Carlo, just tell me how many homeless you will be expecting, and I will find clothes that will fit them. We can dress them and feed them, so none will be the wiser as to their identity."

"Paolo, you are so thoughtful. We are all grateful to you for being so concerned. You'd make a wonderful priest."

"I've been thinking about it. I had problems way back when we were in theology together. My wife died a number of years ago, and I've been thinking hard about it ever since. I'll call you about it when everything settles down. You were always my role model, you know."

"You honor me, Paolo."

Not only had Carlo invited the homeless from Taranto, but he
sent invitations to Marty O'Dea and his family of homeless in
New York, and also to Father Labita on Long Island.

The day for the investiture ceremony and the bestowing of the
red hat came soon enough. The basilica was filled to overflowing, with people from every continent and all colors and cos-
tumes. The pope was most gracious to each one as he invested
him and spoke kindly and with hope for each one.

The ayatollah and the president of Iran were present, as well
as the archbishop of Tehran, Imam Diba and Zahra, and Richard and Joan Zahedi. It was only after he had seen his friends
from Iran and the few others from other countries that Carlo had
a chance to see his own family. His mother was so proud. His
father still kept his reserve, always trying to offset the fact that his
wife had always looked upon Carlo as her baby even though he
was now over fifty years old. Carlo's father was still trying to
make his son stand on his own, not realizing how independent
he was and capable of handling life's most difficult problems,
even those that had involved the Mafia when it opposed him. In
his father's eyes he was still just his mother's baby.

When the informal reception ended, somehow all Carlo's
friends and relatives managed to find their way across town to the
Borghese Gardens for the real celebration. Some two hundred
homeless men and women were quietly ushered into a section of
the house where they could be taken care of and dressed up in
every way, if they so wished. Fortunately, they were so appreciative of being invited that they rose to the occasion and accepted
all the fuss made over them. Most of them were friends of the
homeless priest, "Peppino" Anastasi, whom Carlo had met when
he was a homeless beggar in Rome.

Carlo spent time with every individual who came. He knew
each one by name, even the homeless, as they had been introduced to him by their homeless priest friend. The party lasted for

over five hours, though the dignitaries and other friends from Iran left after a couple of hours. They were awestruck by the magnificence of the celebration, which enhanced Carlo's image in their eyes. What impressed them was the credit Carlo gave to his friend Paolo, saying that if it were not for him, he would not have had such an elegant reception and would have had only a modest reception for family and a few friends.

By the end of the day, even Carlo's family and friends from Palagiano left so they could get home by a reasonable time. Only Richard and Joan Zahedi, and Imam Diba and Zahra remained; they had been invited to spend the night since they had a flight the next day. Marty and Maureen O'Dea and their children as well as Carlo's homeless family were also there, but they had to get back to their hotel, where Carlo had already visited them the day they arrived and had a wonderful time reminiscing and laughing over all the good times they had together.

The following day Carlo went to the Vatican to see the pope. The Holy Father was very gracious and asked about Madelena and the children. He was happy to have had a chance to meet them, and he told Carlo how proud he was of what he had accomplished with those children.

"There should be more priests with a heart like yours, Carlo. But enough of the nice talk. Let's get down to business. I would like you to become Secretary of the Congregation on Christian Life. That involves everything that pertains to the vocation of being a disciple of Jesus and how we should carry out that vocation in our daily lives. I think it is the most important facet of our work here, and I know it is something very close to your heart. Do you have any problem accepting that assignment?"

"Not at all, Holy Father. In fact, I am honored that you entrust me with such a task, and I will try to fulfill the responsibilities to the best of my ability."

"I know you will, Carlo. Also, I would like you to report to me each day, as there are many things I would like to discuss with you and share with you. I have not told anyone of this yet, but I have not been well, and the doctor is concerned. There is so much unfinished business, and I am hoping that if anything happens to me, you may be able to use whatever influence you have later on to promote some changes that are very close to my heart and that I have not been able to accomplish due to strong opposition on the part of some here. You are like a son to me, Carlo, and I trust you with the most important dreams I've had ever since I became pope but could not push through on my own because of the opposition. Whoever dreamed secretaries could frustrate a pope, and obstruct his orders?"

"Holy Father, I am overwhelmed. I feel so humbled by your trust in me. I always felt you were like a father to me, and I tried never to disappoint you. And if it is your wish that I assume this responsibility, I will accept it with honor, but not without considerable trepidation."

"I knew you would, Carlo. I have already informed the staff of the congregation of your appointment, so they will be expecting you. You might stop over there now and introduce yourself. They are very conservative, which is probably my fault, so you will have your work cut out for you, but if you could outfox the Mafia, you can do a good job with the congregation staff as well. Good luck, and I will see you tomorrow. May the Holy Spirit guide you in all you do!"

28

CARLO WENT DIRECTLY TO THE OFFICES of the Congregation on Christian Life, made his introduction and was welcomed by each of the staff. They were gracious and proper. They insisted on speaking in Latin, rather than Italian, even though Carlo spoke to them in Italian, but since there were Germans and French and Spanish as well as other nationalities on the staff, he then continued conversing with them in Latin. He was already beginning to understand the pope's concern about a power struggle, right from the first day.

Carlo asked them the substance of the projects and the programs. They named a few. The one with top priority concerned the approach that lay Catholics should use in building up a more solid faith in the young people. It was centered on a deeper knowledge of the doctrines that all Catholics should know almost by heart. It reminded Carlo of the catechisms they used many years ago in teaching the children their religion, except that these programs had more scripture in them. Teaching the children the proper theological terms and their precise meanings was an important part of these new programs.

Carlo asked if he could have a copy of the programs. This created consternation, as if he were wandering into territory that was classified and could not be released, as if he were an intruder and not their new superior. They didn't argue but made it clear they did not feel comfortable with the request, which made Carlo even more suspicious. He didn't push the issue, because it was not his way. His strategy in this kind of a situation was to allow enough leeway for people to put themselves in a jeopardizing position with no way to back out. He knew these fellows had friends higher up to whom they reported and who were dictating to them the material to be incorporated into their documents. By appearing to allow the staff members to have their way, he was allowing word to get back to whomever they were reporting that he was a pushover and could be manipulated.

For weeks this chess game went on, and the staff members became more and more comfortable with their ability to sidestep any requests made by their new secretary. Little did they know that they were slowly working themselves out of a job. But in the process they were doing Carlo a big favor by letting their patrons higher up think that the new cardinal was easygoing and rather simple. Carlo was at the same time getting acquainted with other cardinals, some of whom he knew from seminary, who were happy that he was now one of them. They enjoyed telling him the rumors about him and his inability to understand the work of the congregation he was heading. They added that some of his staff made him the butt of jokes with the cardinals to whom they were reporting. He was learning fast, and he would make his move when he had enough information about which cardinals he could feel comfortable with and which ones he had to be careful of. As gentle and loving as Carlo was, he was no fool. "Be wise as a serpent and innocent as a dove" had been his mantra ever since his confrontation with the Mafia. Like a cobra watching and waiting calmly and patiently for the best time, he would strike without warning.

For months this game went on, and Carlo found out much about many of the cardinals and bishops and functionaries in the Vatican. From his former classmates and their friends who worked in the Vatican, he learned much and became acquainted also with the group who controlled the staff in a number of the Vatican congregations. They were adamantly opposed to change and were determined by their influence over staff in various offices to prevent changes from being made and disseminated to the dioceses around the world. These staff members were to be well rewarded for their loyalty to their patrons when they had even greater control over the administration of the church.

Carlo was beginning to see clearly what the pope had told him. He wasn't scandalized, but he was learning much. The pope was grateful that Carlo was willing to take on the responsibility of promoting what the pope was unable to accomplish because of the devious obstruction techniques of those who considered that any changes were dangerous to the faith and to what the church was supposed to be, *in their eyes.*

One of the issues that was dear to the pope was that divorced and remarried Catholics who did not have annulments would be allowed to receive the Eucharist. His thought was that if Jesus could give communion to the apostles at the Last Supper, before Judas left to betray him, it was a clear sign that Jesus intended to embrace sinners in the Eucharist. The Eucharist is not just an award for holiness but medicine for sinners and those most in need. The pope had suggested this at a synod, but it had fallen on deaf ears as well as deaf hearts. Another issue that troubled the pope was the critical shortage of priests. He was quietly considering ordaining married men, but he knew opposition was too great, and the obstructionists would do all they could to prevent it from ever happening. Carlo recalled a day not long ago when the pope had encouraged him to dream great dreams for the catechism and act on them. Carlo smiled and asked, "Holy Father, why do think I am going to have any better success than you have had?"

"Carlo, my son, you don't realize what God has given to you. I am a theologian. I am not a diplomat or even a good administrator. My gift is my honesty, but you have been blessed more than you even realize, which is why those close to me here have such high hopes for you. How many priests could have fought the

Mafia and won—and survived? And your stay in Iran showed your diplomatic skills, especially when you preached Jesus in a mosque and orchestrated that ceremony of forgiveness. So, whatever God has planned for you, I know you will do your best to promote what is loving and good and necessary for the church."

"Holy Father, I am not at all what you think I am. Ever since I experienced being a homeless beggar, I learned to understand my true self, and I have never been able to see myself in any other way. When I look in the mirror, all I can see is a homeless beggar, stripped of all those things that others see in me. And I know I see the real me. So, please, Holy Father, don't try to see in me any more than what I really am."

The pope walked over and embraced him. "Carlo, you have experienced Jesus' heart through your own pain, but it has separated you so much from others that they will never be able to understand you. Your future will be very lonely, my son. Trust no one. There are people here who need to find evil in the most beautiful of God's gifts. They have been my cross all my life. I tried to be like Jesus and put up with them, but you may find that it is wiser not to be so tolerant."

"Thank you, Holy Father. I will remember what you said, but I may not be in a position to do anything. I am learning from experience what you are saying. I will be careful, 'innocent as a dove,' as Jesus said, 'and wise as a serpent.'"

The pope smiled. "Jesus was no fool. He knew he had to be the scapegoat for our sins, but you will not need to be a victim. Be strong in making decisions when you know they are inspired by the Holy Spirit, Carlo."

"I don't understand, Holy Father. In my mind I just try to be a good priest."

"One day you will understand. Carlo, I must rest now. Go in peace and confidence."

The two men hugged and Carlo took his leave.

The next day Carlo spent the whole day at his office conferring with the staff. When he asked to see a copy of the work they were finishing, the monsignor overseeing the project said that it was being reviewed by others before publication.

"Who are those people who are reviewing your work?"

"The ones who have been advising us through the whole project. They said that since you were not here from the beginning, you would not appreciate the fine theology that went into all the work these past months." But he would give no names.

"The only one you should be concerned about reviewing your work is the secretary of this congregation. That is me. So I want those documents on my desk before your siesta."

"But, Your Eminence, those documents are across town."

"I am sure you will have no problem finding updated copies and having them on my desk shortly."

Fifteen minutes later two staff members came to Carlo's office, announcing that they had "found" copies in their office. They offered him the documents.

"I want the version that is being worked on by your advisers. This copy is out of date."

"But we'll have to send a special courier, Your Eminence."

"Good. Couriers are running around here all day long."

Finally, five minutes before siesta time, the current documents were on Carlo's desk. He spent the whole day reading the material, and the more he read the more upset he became. It could have been written in the sixteenth century. He thought, "No wonder people are leaving the church. With fossils of another age pushing out this kind of stuff, it's no wonder people feel that we do not understand the real-life problems and crises that they face daily. It's not what they need to know."

It was not in Carlo's nature to be mean or vindictive, but he had given his staff plenty of time to show some willingness to cooperate with him, especially since he had expressed concern about the substance of the material in their documents. They still had pushed to get the documents finished as soon as possible and get them to the printing office *before* Carlo could do anything about it. Realizing their temporizing had become a critical problem, he decided to make his move.

The next morning he called the whole staff into his office and told them that he was not at all happy with the game they had been playing. He needed a staff that would be loyal to him.

There was nothing any of them could say, because they realized he knew what was going on behind his back. They would never again be trusted in the Vatican once word got around. They also realized that even their patrons would not want them around because it would look bad for them, too, especially if they were to hire them to work for them.

The men tried to explain that what they had been doing was just normal procedure because their previous secretary had been busy with other matters.

"That is no excuse, gentlemen. When I came, I made it clear that I would be very involved in this work and expressed my interest in working with you. I gave you plenty of time to work with me. Now it's too late. I will expect your resignations by the end of the day."

Carlo got up from his desk and accompanied them all to the door, closing it after them, and returned to call one of his classmates at another congregation.

"Pietro, this is Carlo."

"Carlo, my dear Carlo, I heard you were here. Welcome aboard! What can I do for you."

"Pietro, I just fired my whole staff. They were working with . . . "

"You don't have to tell me. We all know about it. They've been working behind your predecessor's back, too. That was why he quit. They were scheming with Cardinal Scalzo and two other cardinals. Those three live in the Middle Ages and are determined to bring the church back there, too. Carlo, I think I know what you need–a staff you can trust. If that is why you called, I think I can help. There are two excellent priests I was hoping I could hire, but I have a full staff already. There is also a woman theologian who is brilliant and has her doctorate in canon law from the Angelicum. And I think Matteo–remember him?–has one or two experts in ancient Semitic languages he could loan to you for a while. I'll give him a call and see what he says."

"Thank you so much, Pietro. I knew you could help. You're still a beautiful, faithful friend. I would appreciate you calling Matteo. I really need two good scripture people, two top theologians, and gospel specialists, men or women."

"What are friends for, Carlo? We're thrilled you are with us. It has been a lonely place for a long time with all the people from previous centuries."

Carlo laughed. "Thanks, Pietro. You have been a tremendous help. I'll talk to the staff's secretaries and find out all the projects these fellows have been involved in besides the documents that they were supposed to have almost ready for publication. We must tell the people about Jesus."

29

CARLO IMMEDIATELY WENT TO WORK with his new staff. He explained what he wanted in the document he asked them to begin working on. He was insistent that the church, and the teachings of the church, not be the subject of evangelization but that Jesus be the sole focus of evangelization. Jesus is the Message that should be taught, and not the church, which is the vehicle for the message. The church's teachings could be easily woven into the document as expressions of who and what Jesus is and how he thinks and reacts to people and events. The Christian people have to get to know Jesus, and they are not going to do that by studying theology alone. They have to meet the real Jesus, as close to the real flesh-and-blood Jesus as possible, and realize that Jesus is all about relationships.

"This project," he told them, "has the personal interest of the Holy Father. He is very much concerned that we finish it as soon as possible."

Hilda, a scripture scholar, spoke up, "I love that man. He came from my hometown, and I am sure we will all work double time to do our very best, so we can present our finished work to him as a present."

Carlo spent that night reading Dr. Marlis Schroeder's manuscript about Jesus. It was in German and written as a scholarly document. Carlo was disappointed. It was not what he had in mind. He had envisioned a document that would appeal to ordinary people, but he realized that there was probably no one in the Vatican capable of writing like that. He was impressed with Dr. Schroeder's in-depth analysis of Jesus' emotions and his most probable reactions to the whole range of situations and encounters Jesus faced during his life. From that perspective, it was a masterpiece of psychoanalysis of Jesus' inner life and the interaction of both his divine and human natures to all the complex realities he encountered daily. As Carlo read he realized that such a scholarly document was important also, and then he began to wonder whether the staff could produce two documents, one for theologians and scripture scholars, and one for the ordinary laypeople. The material for both manuscripts could come from Dr. Schroeder's work. Of course, the others on the staff would have their own ideas about what was important in developing a realistic portrait of Jesus. So, ultimately they would have to work together so that they could all feel that they had made a significant contribution to the document. Carlo finally went to bed with the thought that the staff could be considering the scholarly document, but their first efforts would be to create the document for the laypeople, one that would read easily so that everyone could understand it and be able to fall in love with Jesus while reading it. His time spent with the homeless beggars had taught him how to speak to the humble, childlike people, with whom he had felt most comfortable ever since that bizarre but life-changing pilgrimage-retreat. That is the tone he wanted for the document. He fell asleep praying for all those dear friends whose life he shared in those beautiful humbling days.

Days passed. Carlo had not heard from the pope, and he did not know what to do. He knew the pope loved him as a son, but he also knew his boundaries. It did not seem proper for him to make a friendly call just to see how he was, yet the pope is human, like everyone else, and might be pleased just knowing that Carlo cared. Finally, he decided to call.

"Hello, this is Cardinal Brunini. I had been expecting the Holy Father to call for me to come so he could share some important things with me. Not having heard from him, I am concerned. If possible, I would like to speak with him."

Fortunately, it was the pope's secretary who answered and knew that the pope would like to make that decision himself, so he excused himself while he talked to the Holy Father. Then he came back to the phone.

"Hello, Your Eminence. The Holy Father would like it very much if you could come to visit him. He is looking forward to seeing you."

"Thank you, Bishop. I will be there is a few minutes."

When Carlo arrived, the secretary accompanied him to the pope's apartment. Carlo was shocked to see the pope in bed. The secretary placed a chair beside the bed so the two men could talk. Then he withdrew, so they could be alone.

"My dear Carlo, I am so glad you came. First of all, I would like to make my confession. Would you please do me the honor of hearing my confession?

Carlo was taken back, but said, "Holy Father, I would consider it an honor that you would trust me with such a responsibility."

The pope paused, then said, "Bless me, Father, for I have sinned. It has been three weeks since my last confession. For a long time now, I have felt that I have not been a good Christian, and I have the frightening feeling that God is terribly disappointed with me and my failure to accomplish all that I know he had been expecting of me. I know I have failed my responsibility as the successor of Peter. I should have been stronger, but in my weakness I allowed myself to tolerate those who frustrated every attempt I made to bring about change that I knew was needed for all the hurting sheep throughout the world. I have not been the good shepherd that he demanded of me. Father, I know I have failed miserably to answer his call."

He hesitated, then said, "Carlo, I deserve what I am feeling, that in the loneliest time of my life my God has abandoned me, has turned his face away from me and turned me out from his presence and left me alone in my hour of darkness. This is my greatest sin, that I have failed him. Father, if you think I am worthy, I ask you to forgive me in God's name."

"Holy Father," said Carlo, "though you fail to see your own goodness, I know you to be a priest of God, the most saintly I have ever known, and a faithful successor of Peter, whose fault was not his failure to accomplish what God demanded, but his humility and ability to forgive that allowed him to tolerate his enemies. Your weakness is not in refusing to do God's will—that is your great virtue—but in not knowing how to counter devious people at every turn. As brilliant as you are, you are like a child in a lair of foxes. Your calling may not have been to change the world but to show that same forgiveness and love that made it possible for you to reach out far beyond the limits of God's flock and touch the hearts of others who could be a far greater danger to God's flock than the foxes who worked their way into the sheepfold. Your heritage is the heritage that God intended for you, not what you think he intended."

Carlo squeezed the pope's hand. "Your feeling of abandonment by God is not unique to you. Very few saints escaped that horrible desolation before God took them home. Do not be afraid, Holy Father. God has not abandoned you. God is giving you a precious chance to show that you can remain loyal to him even though you feel that you are on the brink of hell itself."

"For your penance, say to God, with Jesus, from the depths of your soul, 'My God, my God, why have you abandoned me?' Say it once slowly, meditating on each word, and know that the blessed Mother is by your side, interceding for your peace of soul. And once God draws from your soul your final desperate commitment to his will, you will find a profound peace."

As the pope expressed his sorrow for his sins, Carlo gave him absolution: "Ego te absolvo, in nomine Patris, et Filii, et Spiritus Sancti."

"Thank you, Carlo," the pope said through his tears. "I knew I needed you to accept my confession. But you are too understanding. I thank you for judging me worthy of God's forgiveness. Now I must rest. Keep me in your prayers, my son."

"I will offer mass tomorrow morning, Holy Father, and I will make sure that my staff has that document done in record time. I intend to use Marlis Schroeder's manuscript as the basis, but I will make sure that in its final form it will be written in a way people can appreciate."

The pope smiled, and said in a weak voice, "I expected you would."

Carlo kissed him on the forehead, and left to do what the Holy Father expected of him.

30

On leaving the pope's chambers, Carlo had a heavy heart. He went immediately to St. Peter's to pray for his friend, asking God to give him many more days to continue his dreams of what he saw his work to be. Thinking of what the pope had said, Carlo realized he could have been more help to him, if he had only known, but it was a burden the pope had shared with no one.

Back at the office, the members of the staff were hard at work on their new project. Marlis had copies made of the introduction and first five chapters of her manuscript and gave all the workers a copy so they could review it and add their own comments. They were all impressed that she had done such a remarkable job of psychologically analyzing so many details of Jesus' life, thus creating an entirely new dimension to an understanding of Jesus at a much deeper psychological level. The other members of the staff were able to contribute to the document in those areas in Jesus' life in which they specialized. The Russian priest, Father Vladimir, concentrated on the life and customs of people in Jesus' day. Hilda focused on the attention Jesus paid to all the details in nature: the flowers, the seeds, the grain, the vineyards, the sheep and other animals, and the signs in the changing weather. Father Flynn specialized in Jesus' knowledge of the Law and the Prophets, which added still another dimension to the document. Marlis emphasized the delicate way Jesus communicated with people and put even the simplest people and sinners at ease.

As Carlo walked past their offices, he did not disturb them. He was happy they were working so hard. It had been decided that at the end of each day, each team member would bring a copy of the day's work to his office so he could go through them in the evening. And what they could do each day was considerable, as these people were not amateurs. They had been studying their subject for years, so it was not a matter of burdensome new research. They were long past that and had a massive amount of knowledge ready at hand when they sat down to begin work each day. Coordinating each facet of Jesus' life into a synthesis having as the final product a study of Jesus that had never been accomplished in such a way was the most difficult part.

At lunch each day they discussed the progress they were making, and Carlo explained in detail precisely what he hoped to see: "a very clear realistic image of what the Jewish people saw when Jesus came walking down the street in one of their villages. What was it that made the ordinary people, especially well-known sinners and outcasts, feel so comfortable with him and fall in love with him?" That was his goal, to understand these questions. He was happy with the progress they were making so far and told them he could not have a better team working on this most important project.

Reading the results of each day's work, he could see the group worked well together and had a good feeling about where each was coming from. The material came to him in separate documents representing each person's insights into Jesus' life from his or her assigned perspective. In the end one of them would meld all of their contributions into one carefully harmonized symphony of beautiful thoughts and insights into the mind and heart of the Son of God. Then the whole staff would go over that draft and make whatever changes or recommendations they could agree on. When that was done, Carlo would go over the finished document and either accept it or make suggestions for further changes. Each one on the staff would sign off on it, and Carlo would present their work to the pope for his approval. Once approved, the document would be released to the whole world, eventually translated into every major language and, Carlo prayed, into every heart.

As the days moved on, Carlo grew ever more grateful for the enthusiastic spirit of this staff, so different from the one he had inherited when he first arrived. These people were real professionals and experts in each of their fields, and they loved Jesus and wanted to follow him. It was a joy working with such people.

While doing his work at the office, Carlo was sensitive to his responsibility to Madelena and his rapidly maturing family. He was constantly reminded how fast the years were passing by and how quickly the children had grown into young adults. Conscious of how busy he had been of late and how much time he had been in effect "homeless" while close to home, he was now trying to go home at least every night, even though it took almost an hour to and from the villa each trip. He knew that many people working in Rome spent more time than that commuting each day.

He felt he was now being a better father to the children and was happier spending more time with Madelena. She had given up her whole life to be a mother to these eight children who were not even her own. Carlo knew he was the only real adult in her life, and he was rarely there for her. Had she loved him less, she might have complained, but her love and respect for him were so deep she bore her loneliness stoically without him.

The weeks passed, and the pope's requests for Carlo to visit became less frequent. Finally, one Monday morning, when Carlo came back from his weekend at the villa, Dr. Schroeder asked if she could see him. When she came to his office, she looked downcast.

"Marlis, you look so sad. What happened?"

"It's the document, Your Eminence. You will not believe this, and I don't really know how to break this news to you."

"You have me worried. What has happened?"

"I might as well tell you, Your Eminence," she continued very slowly and solemnly, and after a long pause, "we have finished the project over the weekend, and I am presenting the finished manuscript to you!"

"Oh, Marlis, you almost gave me a heart attack! I thought the pope had died or something had gone terribly wrong with the manuscript. You really put on a good act!"

With that the other staff members, who had been outside the door, walked in with the manuscript and gave it to Dr. Schroeder, who presented it to the cardinal. Carlo was close to tears.

The title was simple: *Jesus, Filius Dei* (Jesus, the Son of God).

As Carlo knew, the manuscript contained a carefully written biography of Jesus with an in-depth understanding of his life, his feelings, the interaction of his divine knowledge with his human knowledge, and his reactions to events and people of all types whom he encountered each day. It spoke of the complexity of the thousands of relationships in his life, as well as an explanation of complex life situations he encountered, as daily life flowed from season to season, and also a detailed analysis of political life and how it affected the lives of the people. The team had managed to merge all their contributions into a seamless fabric so that the life of Jesus flowed smoothly, and simply, and still with great depth. They described Jesus' life and explained his teachings in a way that made his talks a powerful expression of just how well he understood people's very difficult lives. The manuscript would prove to be a masterpiece, and Carlo's first thought was to take it immediately to the pope so he could be the first one to read it.

Carlo thanked Dr. Schroeder and the staff for the remarkable work they had done and assured them that, based upon his daily readings of their progress each day, he knew that the work was a great achievement and would affect the lives of billions of people. It would show very dramatically how Jesus' Way is so sublimely different from every other way of living.

Carlo told them he had a big surprise for them. "You can have the next month off for a well-deserved vacation and come back here refreshed."

They were all ecstatic.

As soon as the team left his office, Carlo called the pope's secretary and asked if he might talk with the Holy Father.

The pope came on the line. "Carlo, I am happy that you called. I have not been well, and the doctors have insisted that I rest and not have visitors."

"Holy Father, I have some good news."

"What is it, Carlo?"

"Dr. Schroeder's team has finished the manuscript. Would you like me to bring it over to you?"

"I've been thinking about that so often. I was hoping they would finish before it was too late for me to read it. By all means, bring it over! I will see you when you get here."

Carlo left immediately, and when he arrived at the pope's rooms the pope was resting in a reclining chair.

"Carlo, Carlo, my dear brother, I am so glad you came. That manuscript you are carrying, is that it?"

"Yes, Holy Father."

"I hope it's not written in too scholarly a fashion, or I might fall asleep before I get very far."

"Holy Father, the team wrote it so everyone can enjoy reading it and can get to know the real Jesus and fall in love with him."

"Just what I was hoping, just what is needed, getting back to preaching Jesus and making him real for people. I cannot wait to read it."

Carlo put the manuscript on the pope's lap, and knowing how excited he was to receive it, asked the pope if he could leave to give him a chance to start reading.

"Go ahead, Carlo. I can't wait to get into this. I will call you when I get a few chapters read and let you know my feelings about it."

Carlo took his leave, concerned about the pope's failing health. He stopped at a restaurant to have a plate of risotto and salad, then returned to his office for his afternoon meetings. As soon as he returned, his secretary told him that Imam Diba had called and asked if he could please call back.

Carlo called immediately. "My dear, dear friend, it was so nice of you to call. I have been thinking of you and your dear wife, and praying for both of you."

"We have been doing the same for you, my forever friend. I have the joy of telling you before anyone else. My wife is pregnant."

"What good news!"

"But that is not the only reason I called. I have had a request from a mosque in Rome to speak to them about Jesus and introduce them to the Sufi mystics. They also asked if I would consider being their spiritual leader. They heard of our gathering in Tehran that beautiful night, that wonderful night for which we paid such a high price. But Allah has brought much good out of it, and now more and more people want to learn about the Sufi form of Islam. They think it is so beautiful and healthy."

"When are you supposed to visit?"

"Not for three weeks, and I was wondering if we could get together."

"Why, of course. I would like nothing better. Please stay with Madelena and myself and the children? There are only two at home now."

"That would be wonderful, as long as it is not an imposition."

"Not at all, and there is plenty of room, so please feel free to bring Zahra and anyone else whom you would like."

"Wonderful! I can't wait to see you and your beautiful family. I may bring another friend, a young ayatollah whose family is very powerful in Iran. He is also interested in learning more about Sufi."

"Very good. You are all welcome. I can't wait to see you! May God bless you and Zahra and the child she carries."

Carlo was so happy his friend had called. They were indeed forever friends, sharing a loss that would remain in their hearts until they died.

31

AFTER READING A FEW PAGES OF THE MANUSCRIPT, the pope called Carlo to his apartment, and after a moment of deep thought, said, "My dear son, this book can change the whole direction of Christianity for the next thousand years. It introduces Jesus again after five hundred years of conflicts. We have been teaching the medium and not the Message, who is Jesus. We have now found Jesus again. I am so happy that as I am about to die, Jesus comes back to life in our hearts. I can now rest, knowing that I am going home. The responsibility is now yours, my dear son, to make Jesus real. This manuscript is just the start. Thank you for this wonderful gift! I am honored to be able to sign this document with my approval for its publication."

"Holy, Father, I don't know what to say. Thank you."

"I will continue reading. It is so beautiful," the pope said with tears in his eyes. "It expresses love, Carlo. We have finally done justice to Jesus, although this is just a start. Hopefully the church will develop on this foundation as our civilization slides into the Age of the Unknown. Don't be afraid of the future. The Holy Spirit still guides us. But always remember, 'Be wise as serpents and innocent as doves.'"

"My only ambition is to do my work well and be a good shepherd. You still place too much confidence in me. I am comfortable just being what I am, a homeless beggar. That is where I felt and still feel most comfortable, as though I've found a shoe that fits. I will never feel comfortable seeing myself in any other role."

"Carlo, you are impossible. Get out of here before I lose my patience and throw a shoe at you, you and your homeless beggar. If you only knew . . . "

Carlo laughed, took the pope's hand and kissed it respectfully, then left as the pope raised his hand in blessing.

Carlo left with a heavy heart. The pope tried to act strong, but Carlo could tell he was weak and might not be around much longer. When he returned to his office, he did his work, but his heart was not in it. The pope had been not only his defender and friend, but was like a second father to him, and he was already beginning to feel the pain of loss that he could sense was imminent.

In fact, a few days later the message came to all the cardinals in Rome that the pope had died during the night. His last words were, "That Jesus will come alive again in our hearts."

The news, though not unexpected, hit Carlo with such force that he fell into the armchair near where he was standing and sat there, overcome with grief.

"Are you all right, your Eminence?" his secretary asked.

"He was like a father to me," Carlo answered. "I've lost a father." He sat up. "I must call the cardinal secretary of state and ask if he needs me. There are so many details that have to be taken care of."

Before calling the cardinal, Carlo called Madelena to tell her the news. She knew that Carlo was hurting, as she understood the beautiful friendship between the two men. She asked if there was anything that she could do to help him, to be of some comfort to him.

Carlo knew he needed Madelena now more than at any other time in their long lives together. She knew it, too, but there was nothing either of them could do.

At a time like this the whole machinery of the Vatican goes into operation, and the ancient ritual begins efficiently, methodically, with everyone knowing just what his responsibilities are. The camerlengo, or papal chamberlain, certifies the death of the pope. The body is removed, and the papal apartment is sealed. The dean of the College of Cardinals notifies world leaders, the diplomatic corps, and the other cardinals around the world of the pope's death. The cardinals are to come to Rome at once.

The heads of all the Vatican congregations, or dicasteries, automatically lose their positions, except for the camerlengo and the major penitentiary concerned with complex moral issues, who still have duties to perform.

All cardinals under eighty come to Rome. Those over eighty may come but will not vote. The cardinals then meet daily in general congregations to make preparations for the dead pope's funeral, which is held between four and six days after his death.

People from all over the world came for the occasion, including kings, queens, members of royal families, heads of state, ambassadors. For this pope's funeral the president of Iran and the prime minister also came, as well as the ayatollah, Iran's spiritual leader.

They had come not only because Iran had had diplomatic relations with the Vatican for over fifty years, but also out of gratitude for the help the pope had given them in response to their requests for assistance on a number of occasions and out of respect for Carlo, who had been their personal liaison with the pope.

The crowd at the funeral filled the vast piazza of St. Peter's and flowed into the side streets and down into the Via della Conciliazione. The death of a pope, especially a pope who has made a dramatic impact on the world, is a significant historical event and an impressive moment for those fortunate enough to be present.

The funeral mass was a gloriously joyful liturgy celebrating the resurrection of Jesus and the grace of the resurrection that he has shared with those who accept him. The death of a pope is celebrated with great pageantry and joyful music as God receives the soul of the deceased into the joyful life of his heavenly home.

After the ceremony, the pope, clothed in his vestments, with a certified death certificate, key documents of his papacy, coins and medals struck during his papacy, and the destroyed Fisherman's ring, was buried in the crypt below St. Peter's basilica.

Carlo and Madelena had managed to find each other after the funeral. Just those few minutes were a comfort to them both. It is times like this when love is so powerful in healing a grieving soul and expressing the true meaning of selfless love.

Immediately after lunch Carlo gathered with the other cardinals to discuss what further details had to be undertaken before the conclave. It is the custom that a series of masses is offered on the next eight days for the repose of the soul of the departed pope. After that, the cardinals enter the Sistine Chapel for the beginning of the conclave. Impressive seats for the cardinals have been constructed for the event and set into place. All is ready for the election of the next pope. A two-thirds majority is required for a pope to be elected. There are two votes each morning and two each afternoon until a new pope is elected.

When that day finally came, the cardinals were locked inside the Sistine Chapel and the first vote took place. As the votes were counted, it was clear that they were spread out among twenty-five cardinals. The second vote was much the same.

After each of the votes, a fire was started in the little stove to send the black smoke out signaling to the people waiting in the square that no pope had yet been elected. The third vote, which took place in the afternoon, was divided among nineteen cardinals. On the third vote, Cardinal Carlo Brunini received one vote. On the fourth vote, Cardinal Brunini received five votes, Cardinal Albert Helliger received two votes, Cardinal O'Connor received four votes, Cardinal Yamazaki received sixteen votes, Cardinal Altamessa received four votes, Cardinal Ming received thirteen votes, Cardinal Maloney received fourteen votes, and seven other cardinals shared over seventy votes. No one had anywhere near the required majority.

After the second afternoon vote the cardinals retired to a special residence on the Vatican grounds, where they had no contact with anyone but themselves. The next morning the voting started again. The cardinals wrote down their vote on a ballot. The ballot was then folded in half and carried high in the air by each cardinal to a paten resting on the altar, then dropped into a repository.

On this, the fifth ballot, Cardinal Maloney received thirty votes, Cardinal Ming twenty votes, Cardinal Helliger twelve votes, Cardinal Szatkowski five votes, Cardinal Brunini thirty-eight votes, and the remaining votes were spread among three cardinals. The sixth ballot sifted out most of the cardinals; there were only four remaining: Cardinal Szatkowski had thirty-one votes; Cardinal Maloney, thirty-four votes; Cardinal Ming, ten votes; and Cardinal Brunini, fifty-two votes.

The cardinals backing Cardinal Maloney were part of the bloc of strong traditionalists, among whom were those who were controlling the theological staff that Carlo had inherited. They believed that Carlo was not very bright and could be controlled if he were elected pope. The cardinals who had voted for Cardinal Altamessa were most likely friends of Carlo, and Altamessa was a cardinal whom Carlo also knew from seminary. The first votes were just to get some sense of what everyone was thinking, because each person fit into some kind of theological category. Now, for the seventh vote, the lines were drawn. The cardinals with strongly traditional views who had favored Cardinal Maloney now realized that Maloney would not be able to get enough votes to catch up with Cardinal Brunini. Also, Carlo's friends, those who really knew him and knew of his brilliant mind and shrewd way of maneuvering in extremely difficult situations, now saw his chance to gather most of the votes.

So, on this, the seventh vote, there was a dramatic change: Cardinal Maloney, eighteen votes; and Cardinal Brunini, one-hundred-and-ten votes.

Carlo put his head in his hands and said silently, "O God, how could you do this?"

The dean of the College of Cardinals then asked the newly chosen pope, "Cardinal Carlo Brunini, do you accept your canonical election as supreme pontiff?"

Carlo was stunned. He almost said, "I am only a homeless beggar. This can't be happening." But he did say, in a weak voice, a voice that expressed his disbelief of what was happening, "If that is what God wants, I must accept."

"You are now the bishop of Rome, and the successor of Peter. By what name do you choose to be known?"

Carlo, never thinking that such a thing would happen to him, had never considered a name should he be elected. But he only had to think for a moment. "Athanasius, the father of the church who struggled to teach the true Jesus to the world."

A young cardinal started a fire in the stove and white smoke went up through the chimney announcing the election of a new pope. The crowds outside cheered.

Carlo was conducted to a separate room where he discarded his cardinal's robes and returned to the Sistine Chapel wearing the white papal robes and miter, with crozier. He was seated to receive the honor and obedience of the cardinals.

He then was led through the halls to the balcony of St. Peter's basilica, where he waited for the senior cardinal deacon to announce in Latin that a new pope had been elected. "Habemus Papam, Carolus Brunini, Sanctissimus Suus Papa Athanasius!"

The vast crowd went wild. "Viva Il Papa, Viva Il Papa, Viva Il Papa!"

Although Carlo never wanted to be a public figure, people knew him throughout Italy as the archbishop who fought the

Mafia and survived, and as the papal nuncio to Iran who preached Jesus in a mosque in Tehran, and as the archbishop who had adopted eight homeless children. Though Carlo never took credit for these things or felt pride when he read about them in the newspapers, the stories of these happenings had spread all over Italy and beyond. It seemed like a beautiful dream, a fairy tale, to all those people that such a man was elected pope.

A few minutes later the new pope appeared on the balcony, again to the thunderous applause of the huge crowd representing every country in the world.

As they became quiet, Athanasius raised his hands in benediction and sung in solemn fashion the blessing of God upon the people present and upon the world, "Benedictio Dei Omnipotentis, Pater et Filius et Spiritus Sanctus descendat super vos et maneat semper."

The crowd thundered "Amen!"

SERVANT

The greatest among you will be your servant.
—Matthew 23:11

32

ONCE INSIDE AND AWAY FROM THE PUBLIC EYE, Carlo immediately asked the cardinals surrounding him if he could please have a few minutes of privacy to go to the chapel. There, before the Blessed Sacrament, Carlo knelt and then lay prostrate. "Father, how could you do such a thing to me? You made me realize that I am nothing more than the homeless beggar I see in the mirror every day. Why have you done this to me? I don't know what to do or even where to start. This is all your doing, Father, so all I can do is be dumb and inept before you and depend upon you completely, because you know what you have in mind and you alone understand this horrendous responsibility that you have cast upon me. I am so frightened and so unprepared. All I can ask, Father, is that you send your Holy Spirit to guide every move I make, as it is going to be only too easy for me, if left alone, to make the clumsy and tragic blunders that could bring upon your church even more abuse than it is suffering already. I am in your hands, dear Father. Please help me and be with me. Thy will be done!"

Even though Carlo asked for privacy, the cardinals could not resist, out of concern, watching and listening from a side door not far from where Carlo prayed. As the new pope rose from his prayer and walked outside, his assistants were waiting for him. They conducted him to the papal apartments, not so he could rest, but so he could have a few minutes of privacy and ready himself for introductory meetings with various high-ranking persons. They also had to brief him on what appointments had to be made to set the whole Vatican machinery in motion again, as every official had lost his job on the death of the previous pope.

Even though there was pressure on him to reappoint practically all those who had served to their previous positions, Carlo appointed only those who were absolutely needed for the day-to-day work to proceed smoothly. This ruffled the feathers of those who had held positions for years, and not a few were very unhappy over it. But Carlo remembered the words of the Holy Father who had preceded him. He also knew that the first thing he had to do was find a few of his old classmates who were veteran Vatican insiders and appoint them as advisers, as they knew everybody and where their sympathies and loyalties lay.

After the necessary meetings and introductions were finished, Carlo went to his apartments and called Madelena immediately.

As soon as she heard his voice, she broke down crying.

"Madelena, Madelena, why are you crying? Are you all right?"

Through her tears, she tried to talk. "Yes, I am so happy for you! I knew in my heart that God was preparing you for this all along. I could see it coming, and am so happy but also so afraid you won't be with us anymore."

"My dearest Madelena, don't ever fear that. You and the children are the most precious people in my life. Our lives have been bonded by God since we were children. There had to be a reason for it. That is not going to end just because I am pope. Our lifelong friendship is no obstacle to the work God has called us to do. And we still have responsibilities to the children. That obligation is sacred, and I intend to fulfill it. I know it is going to be very difficult for me to leave this prison, as I no longer can move about as I choose, but I will find some way of seeing you and the children. And you and they will visit me here. I'm homeless again but not without a family."

"It is going to be difficult and lonely without you, Carlo, or should I be calling you, 'Holy Father'?"

"Don't you dare."

"I know it would not be proper for you to hire me, but I would very much like to use my legal expertise in the service of the church. It would be purely voluntary, so keep that in mind. The children are almost grown. I could be of some useful service to God in this way."

"Madelena, I will alert my new secretaries as to who you are and that when you call that you are to have direct access to me. When you come to visit, they will extend to you proper courtesy. It is going to be difficult and painful for us to have to live this way, but I hope you can bear with it. It in no way affects my love for you. That is not negotiable. I love you, Madelena."

"I love you, Carlo."

Carlo then called his two cardinal friends, Pietro and Matteo. It happened that they were together discussing Carlo's election as pope, so they both got on the speaker phone. "Congratulations, Holy Father!" they both said together.

"Cut it out, you guys. Don't start that stuff."

"Carlo, we're serious." Pietro said. "You have to get used to it. We don't intend to take it lightly. You have to learn to respect your office. It is not just you anymore, and as much as we love you, we intend to make sure you yourself accept your new position with grace. We know it won't be easy, but we can't take your position lightly."

"Well, right now I need you two."

"We know what it is," said Matteo. "You have to fill all the vacant positions, and you don't even know where to start. When do you want to see us?"

"Right now, if you can."

"Give us fifteen minutes. At your apartments?" Pietro asked.

"Where else? Nobody will let me out of here. It's like a prison."

"Get used to it. It's a life sentence," Matteo quipped.

"You're great for my morale. See you soon."

As he waited for the two cardinals, Carlo called Marty O'Dea to tell him the news and to invite him, his family, and his homeless family to come for another visit. Marty was beside himself, saying he and the homeless had watched the whole proceeding on television, and they were all thrilled at his election.

"Marty," Carlo said, "I also have a request to make of you."

"Anything, Holy Father."

"It will demand sacrifice."

"I don't care."

"Well, I do want you to think about it. You see, I value your love of family and church, and your intelligence and passion for justice as a lawyer. I am going to put together a team that will gather all of the documents relating to the clerical child-abuse scandals throughout the world. I would like to bring you and your family to Rome for a year so you can head up the team and ensure, as best you can, that justice is done not only for the victims and their families, but for the many priests who have been unjustly accused and have seen their reputations destroyed. We need more than closure, Marty. We simply have to do the right thing, once and for all. Will you help me?"

Marty did not think twice.

Carlo's friends Pietro and Matteo arrived dressed properly in their cardinals' garb and everyday cassock and zucchetto. When they arrived at the papal apartments, the three men could not contain their joy in seeing each other. They had seen each other only in passing since the death of the previous pope and had done no politicking during the conclave. So, now their outburst was genuine.

"We brought over a bottle of Felipe II brandy, like the old days, and some homemade cookies to toast your election."

"You guys haven't changed one bit, still like the *ragazzi* you were thirty years ago. We had such good times together. Well, let's get down to business. The interim caretakers are pressuring me to make appointments, and I don't know a soul."

The three men went down the list of appointments that had to be made, and since the two friends had been in the Vatican for enough time to know everyone, they made suggestions as to who would be supportive and who would be more of a hindrance to getting important things done. After three hours they had pretty much given Carlo enough suggestions to provide him with what he needed to fill most of the positions.

By that time they were hungry. Matteo suggested they go to an out-of-the-way restaurant and have a supper.

"Do you think it's possible?" Carlo asked, looking at Pietro, who was the more serious of the two.

"Well, I don't think there are too many people who really know you yet. We could give it a try."

Carlo put on his old cardinal's cassock rather than the papal white one.

As they approached the entrance, the Swiss Guards stood at attention and politely reminded the Holy Father that they were not permitted to allow him to leave without adequate security.

"But we're just going to a restaurant for supper."

"I am sorry, Holy Father, but you must have security."

"So, how do I get security?"

"I will call the officer on duty to appoint plainclothes officers to accompany you."

Within minutes two officers arrived and accompanied the three to a restaurant that Matteo suggested. When they arrived at the restaurant, Carlo blanched.

"We can't go in there," he protested.

"Why not?" Pietro asked.

Carlo didn't answer, but followed his friends inside.

When the main course came out, the owner, as was his custom, served his guests. When he arrived at the table and greeted the three, he looked at Carlo, and Carlo put his head down and took a sip of wine. The man then asked, "Your Eminence, don't I know you? I distinctly remember your face."

"How could you know me? I have never had supper here before," Carlo said politely.

The waiter gave his boss each plate, and the owner placed it before each of his guests, a nice gesture he performed for all his guests. Having wished them "buon appetito," he went back into the kitchen and immediately told his wife, who was helping with the cooking, that there was a cardinal out there whose face was very familiar, but that he could not remember where he had seen him. He told his wife to go out and welcome them all and see if she knew him.

A few minutes later she casually walked over to greet the three men and welcomed them. Then she looked at Carlo, and asked, "This is your first time here, your Eminence?"

"For supper, yes, Signora."

"I hope you enjoy your evening, all of you. And please come back again."

"*Grazie*," the three said in unison.

When the woman went back into the kitchen, her husband asked her if she recognized him.

"Of course I did, you damn fool. I have seen his picture on that wall for the last nine years! I'm sick of looking at it!"

"Which picture?"

"The one of the beggar that you cut out of the newspaper and boasted that he came in here one day and you had him scrub the floor!"

"That's ridiculous. You should get your eyes examined."

The man took the picture off the wall and scrutinized it. The more he looked at it, the more he remembered, and he then remembered the news and turned on the television, for the same news was flashing all day. Sure enough, the cardinal at the table and the homeless beggar with the patch on his right pants leg, and the new pope, were one.

"Oh, my God, what have I done? I can't believe it. And here all these years I have been boasting about that famous beggar in the newspaper years ago scrubbing my tile floor, and now he's the pope. If people find out what I did, they'll never come in here again!"

"I always told you that you had a big mouth. Maybe now you'll learn and won't be such a buffoon," his wife said.

When the three friends finished their meal, the owner came over, brought them a cordial, and told them the supper was on the house. Then, looking at Carlo, he bowed slightly and said, "I have owed you this supper for a long time, your Holiness, and I hope you can find it in your heart to forgive me."

Carlo was embarrassed, but he looked at the poor humbled man and said, "There's nothing to forgive. You taught me things that God wanted me to learn, and I am grateful to you for it. And don't worry. I will visit your restaurant again. We are grateful to you for our supper this evening. The food was delicious, much better than last time," he said with a smile. "I will gladly recommend you to my friends."

"Thank you, your Holiness. This is the greatest honor of my life and also the most embarrassing moment of my life. Please pray for me."

"Only if you promise to pray for me."

"That I will, and I will start going to mass again. I think God is teaching me a lesson, too."

The three men left, and Carlo's friends asked what that was all about. But Carlo merely said that it was a secret that he would never share with anyone, but he hinted that the man had done him a great favor many years ago."

"Carlo, you're a saint. A man does you dirt, and you say he did you a favor, and you ask him to pray for you," Matteo said.

Pietro asked Carlo what dreams he had for the church now that he was Athanasius.

"Well," Carlo said, "as they say, 'man proposes but God disposes.' I will do what I can to see that spirituality becomes a priority in the church. We'll soon have the new life of Jesus and what he means to us, and I hope that will be a beginning. I will also—and you will keep this to yourselves, my friends—ensure that some of the changes my dear predecessor envisioned come true."

"Pray tell," Matteo said. "I will keep it in my heart."

"Good," said Carlo, "or I'll have to have you killed. A Swiss Guard's halberd in your heart."

Matteo feigned dying. "Awwww, et tu . . . "

"Cut it out, Matteo," Pietro said. "Carlo, please tell us more."

"Well, one of the first things I'm going to initiate is a complete review of the laws on the relationship between the Eucharist and the sacrament of marriage. It doesn't make sense that over 40 percent of the church's members are deprived of the Eucharist because of complex and impractical laws that were largely a reaction to upheaval caused by the Reformation. If Jesus gave the Bread of Life to Judas, would he want us to deny the Eucharist to good people struggling to live good lives? Is the Eucharist only a reward for holiness, or is it not also medicine for the sick? Do people go to church because they are holy or because they are in search of wholeness?

"We'll also take a take a fresh look at the priesthood. Remember how St. Paul insisted that men of proven virtue, married only once, and with stable families, be considered for the priesthood? Don't you think the people are ready for it? We already accept Episcopal priests who are married and become Catholic. The church has to be sensitive to the delicate movements of the Holy Spirit and recognize a true vocation in whomever the Holy Spirit clearly manifests a calling. Celibacy is wonderful when it's clear that an individual has a genuine calling from God, as we'll always need priests totally dedicated to the work of the church who have the freedom to go wherever they are needed, especially when spreading the gospel in dangerous areas in the world. But it's also imperative that we look at all options and not be afraid. The Holy Spirit must be our guide."

They talked long into the night.

The walk back to the Vatican was quiet, and the conversation lighthearted. At the entrance Carlo invited his friends in, but they declined.

"I am grateful to you both for your help tonight, and I really enjoyed our last supper." They all hugged and knew it would not be their last. They would find some way to have fun together again.

33

CARLO'S JOY WAS TINGED WITH LONELINESS as he walked past the Swiss Guards and entered the ancient building, reminding him more of a museum than a home. As he walked the steps, he experienced a profound aloneness. "Oh, Jesus, please stay near me. I feel like I am being buried in a vast tomb. Nobody lives here but me and the few who help. Help me to be helpful to *them*. I don't know whether I will be able to do this, Lord. I need people. I need my friends. It's like being homeless in a different world."

Arriving at his apartments, he entered and went into his chapel to spend a few minutes before the Blessed Sacrament. "You are really my only comfort, Lord. I won't even have the comfort of Madelena being near me anymore. Please bless her, Lord. She has been such a source of strength during these difficult years. We shared everything, and now she has to carry on alone with the children. Bless them all, dear Lord, and give her strength. Send your Spirit to mold Jesus in the heart of each of them. They are such beautiful children. Protect them and keep them innocent of the world's meanness and deceit. Help me to be a good shepherd. Help me not to disappoint you. Good night, dear Lord, and dear Mother, please keep me close to your Son."

Carlo's sleep was not restful. Too many things rushed through his mind all night. He rose early the next morning and went to his private chapel to pray, but now more to *listen*, as the previous pope had advised him. He did not know what to pray for, so his prayer was a prayer of waiting, waiting for God to tell him what to do within his heart. Though he did not lie on the floor, in spirit he lay prostrate before God, waiting for his directions. How does a mere human know how to spiritually guide and direct over a billion people without causing scandal or rebellion somewhere, when so many cultures and so many languages and so many ancient customs and traditions are involved? A pope was to be "the servant of the servants of God," and that was Carlo's deepest wish.

The next day, when the staff gathered, Carlo suggested they start with mass, and suggested he would like to begin each day having mass together. After mass and breakfast, they collected their paperwork and returned for their first meeting.

Carlo surprised them by having a complete list of names to fill the positions in all the congregations.

"Your Holiness, I never dreamed you would have been able to put together the whole staff in one sitting. We thought you would surely need our suggestions as to whom you might consider for each of the dicasteries."

"Well, gentlemen, why don't you share with me your suggestions? They might be better than the ones I had in mind. As you explain the reasons for your choice, that will be a great help to me in getting a better knowledge of each of the congregations and the work they are doing."

As the staff expressed their choice for each office, Carlo said nothing, just listened, and recognized each one from his friends' briefing. Now he was getting a good picture of the mentality of the transition staff and where their loyalties lay. He had never known firsthand that the relationships among the Vatican cardinals and bishops were so complicated, divided among traditionalists, progressives, neutrals, rigid legalists, centralists, and only a few who really understood Jesus' good news.

He listened patiently to each suggestion and made notes to incorporate certain individuals for positions on the various congregations so that the transition staff would not think that they were just wasting their time. The meeting took the best part of the morning, and then they broke for lunch. Within a week Carlo had contacted the persons he had selected, had all the positions filled, and had distributed folders containing the work he wanted done by each congregation.

The work of the congregations is the key to changing the direction of the church throughout the world. If directed properly and efficiently, and with sensitivity to the feelings of the people, it can gently change the face of Catholicism. Carlo had learned much from his pilgrimage-retreat, and the most important of his insights was the realization that it is essential to make Jesus the focus of the church's life and not the institution, which unfortunately had been the emphasis for the last several centuries. The church is merely the vehicle for bringing Jesus to the world.

Carlo realized that the countries of Europe have turned secular mostly because the people are tired of hearing about church. They hunger for spirituality and intimacy with God, and all we give them is church. Carlo was determined to make Jesus real again for the people, knowing from his own experience that when he preached Jesus to the people, it changed their lives. It is what they had been looking for, and the crowds at his masses proved that. Now was his chance to make that happen throughout the whole world, and it was his plan to start with the seminaries. The congregation governing the seminaries would prepare a course on Jesus. The book that Carlo's special staff had just finished would become the resource material for making Jesus real to seminarians studying for the priesthood throughout the world. They would no longer be trained as lawyers, masters of moral law, liturgical law, canon law, the natural law. They would be molded in the image of Jesus, the Good Shepherd, so different from the masters of the old law, the scribes and Pharisees.

While the cardinals were still in Rome, Carlo held his first meeting with them as pope. The rumors and divisions among them were already beginning to circulate. Many of the traditionalists saw significance in the name he picked, Athanasius, the staunch defender of orthodoxy of belief. They felt he would be one of them. Those cardinals who knew him, especially those who were in the seminary with him, knew of his far-reaching intelligence and his warm, playful personality. They knew he picked Athanasius because Athanasius was the only bishop who had the courage to fight most of the other bishops, and even the emperor, in defending the real identity of Jesus. They also knew he would be a people's pope and also a man of prayer. On more than one occasion in the seminary, some of his classmates had caught him so deep in prayer that they were convinced he was in ecstasy and that God was communing with him. When they mentioned it to him, he never prayed by himself in chapel again, only in the quiet of his room or when walking in the garden alone.

What he said to the assembled cardinals was very simple.

"I appreciate the confidence you have shown in me, and I pray that I will not disappoint your hopes and dreams. I am a simple man, and I may be a disappointment to many, but with your prayers and support I will try my best to be a good shepherd after the heart of Jesus. I look upon, not the church, the institution, as our religion, but upon Jesus, the Way, the Truth, the Light, as our religion. He will be the touchstone of my ministry.

"Jesus' love was for people. They were his prime concern. The law was made for the people, not people for the law. The law must be at the service of God's people, not a painful and difficult burden that only too often keeps God's children at a sad distance from his loving embrace. If Jesus chose to go out and look for sinners and lovingly pick them up and carry them back home, then we must allow Jesus to embrace sinners and not tell them they are unworthy of his embrace. The intimacy of that relationship is between each individual and Jesus himself. If Jesus chose to give the Eucharist to Judas at the Last Supper, maybe we should try to understand his theology. He is clearly teaching us something. The Eucharist is not just a reward for holiness. The Eucharist is also medicine for sinners, who need to be embraced by him if they are to be healed. It is the mind of Jesus that must guide us. That will be the light that will guide my pontificate. What would Jesus do? How would Jesus treat people, like the lawyers of his day or as the Good Shepherd, reaching out and embracing sinners? A beautiful image of the Eucharist."

The cardinals were listening intently. They were not hearing what they had expected to hear.

"I am sure that all of you have always approached your ministry in this way," Carlo continued, "and that you have a profound understanding of how Jesus thinks, so with prayer for each other and good will and a generous willingness to work together, we can do much to heal deep wounds that have been inflicted of late on the body of Christ. I thank you all and assure you of my love and prayers. Also, if you need to talk with me, you all have my phone number."

The group laughed in appreciation.

"No one will be turned away. I will always be here for you, my fellow apostles."

A few weeks after settling in, Carlo did what he had wanted to do from the start, visit St. John Lateran, the cathedral church of the Diocese of Rome. In that vast palace, built in the time of Constantine, were located the diocesan offices. He told the vicar in charge of the diocese that he would be spending one day a week there, as he wanted the message to go out that he was taking seriously his responsibility as the bishop of the Diocese of Rome, and the successor of St. Peter, its first bishop. During that day each week he would make himself available to the priests of the Diocese of Rome and involved laypeople to discuss their concerns about important pastoral matters. And while there were more problems than could be discussed during only one day a week, it made those involved in such a difficult diocese realize that their bishop really cared and appreciated the work they were doing and understood how complicated their work was in such an extraordinary diocese. He also stressed that no matter how confusing their work might be at times, the first priority must be compassion for the people and their difficult lives. When in doubt, they were to let the mentality of the Good Shepherd be their guide.

Another item that had been on Carlo's mind for a long time was the priest who worked with the homeless beggars, the one he had met on the street so long ago. Carlo decided to send two of the Swiss Guards to circulate among the homeless and inquire about the priest who lived among them. At first the homeless were wary and suspicious, but as the two guards became familiar and the homeless felt more comfortable, they told them where he usually hung out. It was not far from the park where Carlo had met him years before. That was the place where the homeless knew they could find him whenever they needed him.

The two guards found the priest and told him the pope would like to see him at his office at St. John Lateran on the following Monday. When asked what it was about, they merely told him that the pope wanted to ask his help for something he was planning.

When that time came, and the priest showed up, he was still dressed as a beggar. Strangely enough, even though he had been invited with other homeless beggars to the formal reception at the Villa Borghese and now was ushered into Carlo's office, he did not recognize the pope as the homeless beggar whom he had befriended many years before. Carlo had been apprehensive about that. He was still trying to keep secret that episode in his life.

As the homeless priest entered the office, Carlo came from behind his desk and welcomed his visitor. "Father Peppino, I am grateful for your coming. Please sit down so we can have a little chat."

The priest made a gesture as if to genuflect and kiss St. Peter's ring, but Carlo reached out and shook his hand. Then both men sat down.

"Father Peppino, how are your parishioners?"

"Never much of a Sunday collection, Holy Father, but all week long they share what little they have with one another. Church is not much comfort to them, but I try to make Jesus real to them, reminding them that he also was a homeless beggar. And we all find our comfort in knowing that Jesus is one of us, and like us, often slept out under the stars."

"You have a beautiful ministry, Peppino. If I asked you, would you trade it for work in a parish, or to help me?"

"I am sorry, Holy Father, there is no way I can abandon them. I am all they have. Without a shepherd, they would all be lost again. I could not do that to them. I love them, my lost sheep, and I could never leave them, though I am grateful to you for asking."

"Peppino, Christmas is fast approaching, and I would like to celebrate Christmas with your homeless flock."

"Holy Father, do you know how many there are? There are almost two thousand."

"I understand that, and I do not want just the homeless in Rome. I want to invite all the poor from as far away as they can come. I don't care how many there are. I want to show them that in spite of how the world treats them, they are precious to Jesus. I intend to invite them all to St. Peter's on Christmas Day for a special mass and for a party afterwards. A huge feast. Will you help me with this?"

"Holy Father, I do not know what to say. I am just a simple priest. I am not a big organizer. But I have access to all the homeless, and they can help to spread the word among the poor. They can reach each other more effectively than anyone else."

"Spread the message far and wide and among the homeless from as far as the word can reach, and not just the homeless but the poor from the whole surrounding area."

"Holy Father, that will be tens of thousands, maybe over a hundred thousand, and they are not all going to be Catholics! There are many Muslims from North Africa, and atheists, and a number of Zoroastrians from Iran, plus some who are just plain crazy people!"

"Sounds like my old diocese," the pope said with a laugh. "That's fine. They are all God's children. And I will have some good news for them when they come."

"Holy Father, I will be more than happy to do what I can!"

"Do you know if there are any musicians among your homeless?"

"Yes, quite a few, surprisingly, all playing different instruments as well: violins, accordions, oboes, trumpets, French horns, two women who play the harp, some flutes, others drums and some harmonicas, and we all sing, but some we have to tone down; they don't blend so well. The problem is that most of the musicians had to sell their instruments for food."

"Let me know what you need, and I will provide them. And Father Peppino, do you offer mass for your parishioners who may no longer be believers?"

"I haven't, Holy Father."

"Don't you think it might be a good idea, even if you don't do it every week?"

"It had crossed my mind, but I never did it."

"Think about it, and if it is something you consider workable, you have my permission. I once offered mass with a group of loggers, with the stump of a tree trunk as my altar, and a plastic cup as my chalice, and, as I had no vestments, I felt it was much the same as the Last Supper, which Jesus performed around a dirty table full of lamb bones and grease, bread crumbs, and spilt wine. He intended it to be an intimate part of our lives."

"As you feel it is important, I will, Holy Father. I see things the way you see them and your encouragement fills me with joy. Thank you!"

The next six weeks were busy for Father Peppino and his homeless as they scoured the city and the outlying villages with the pope's invitation to their special feast.

Carlo went back to his office for a few more appointments, then went back to the Vatican, where he met with the ambassadors from two countries that were almost at war with each other. Carlo did not feel comfortable with these meetings. The ambassadors were dressed with such trappings, how could they act with plain humble humanness? He invited the two men to come with him to a little residence out on the Vatican grounds.

This residence was small and simply furnished, with a little kitchen and comfortable living room and two bedrooms. Carlo took off his white cassock and asked if the two ambassadors preferred tea, coffee, Arabic coffee, espresso, fruit juice, or just plain water.

The ambassadors suddenly felt embarrassed at the pope serving them and asked if he minded if they took off their coats and ambassadorial sashes.

"Not at all, gentlemen. It's easier to talk when we're relaxed."

Stripped of the trappings that made them feel important, there were now just three simple human beings discussing problems that they knew needed to be resolved.

"Now, my friends, let's look together for clarity. Bertrand, you were saying that your country is ready to go to war over an incursion of troops from Silvan's country because they have occupied a piece of land that belongs to your country? Is that true?"

"Yes, your Holiness," Bertrand replied.

"Is that true, Silvan?"

"Holy Father, that land had been ours for centuries before it was overrun by our neighbors, and we have contested it ever since, but to no avail. It was our outlet to the ocean."

"So, what you really are looking for, Silvan, is a piece of land that will give you an outlet to the ocean."

"Basically, yes. But we want Bertrand's country to acknowledge that it took that piece of land by force."

"Your Holiness, Silvan is forgetting that years ago his country occupied a piece of our land that is rich in minerals!"

"Is that true, Silvan?"

"But, that was a very long time ago, your Holiness."

"It seems that both situations occurred a long time ago. But even so, does that mean that changes cannot be made and situations rectified? Could the two of you, for the sake of peace and to prevent further losses in life and financial resources, agree to *exchange* pieces of land so your country could again have access to the ocean, Silvan, and Bertrand's country could benefit from mining minerals that will help its economy?"

Neither man could think of an intelligent way to disagree, so all they could do was stutter and then admit that the proposal had merit, even though it seemed so simple that it embarrassed them. The stalemate both governments could not resolve was so complex that neither country would agree to anything. The pope's solution was so simple they wondered why it had eluded them during all their previous wrangling. They agreed to discuss the pope's recommendation with their superiors.

They agreed to break for the day and meet again the next day. The three donned their finery and walked out through the gardens and back to the Vatican offices, where they said their goodbyes and left. The two diplomats shared with their superiors what they had discussed with the pope and outlined the pope's suggestion. Their superiors saw the value in resolving the issue as the pope suggested, as both countries would benefit greatly, and they could finally have peace between them.

The next day the meeting at the pope's residence in the garden lasted less than an hour. Both ambassadors signed the agreement, shook hands, and shortly after were shocked to learn that the pope had prepared a simple lunch for the three of them.

One of the ambassadors commented, "Servus servorum Dei [the servant of the servants of God]. You truly live that in real life, your Holiness."

"That's all I am in real life. I am what I am, God's servant, and yours as well. I just hope that my cooking pleases my guests," Carlo said with a grin.

"It's delicious," they both agreed.

He served a simple meal of linguine with a homemade arrabbiata sauce, homemade wine his family had brought as a gift when he was appointed cardinal, and homemade gelato from a recipe a friend had given him.

"Holy Father, if you ever get fired from your job, you can always open a restaurant."

"Judging from the reaction of some over the way I do things, I may have to consider that some day, but I'll need a few more recipes."

The men left and shared with each other their shock over the new pope's casualness about protocol. Both being Catholics, their original thought was that he should have kept his dignity and not come down to the level of the laity, but then they realized that it was his humility that touched their hearts and made it possible for them to be more willing to listen to him when he made suggestions, suggestions that made such good sense. They shared their experience with colleagues in the diplomatic corps, noting especially that the pope met with them in his little residence and cooked a delicious lunch for them.

Carlo knew what he was doing and wanted to spread that message. His strategy was simple. He wanted ambassadors and government officials who came to meet with him to see him and respect him not as the head of the church, though he knew they would do that anyway, but to know him as he is, an approachable human being with whom they can talk as a friend and feel free to share their problems, whether problems of state or personal problems.

As pope, Carlo now had a chapel nearby at all times and spent time each day and late at night in quiet meditation. He listened. He learned. He knew peace.

34

CARLO WANTED TO BE IN REALITY, and not just by title, the bishop of Rome. He wanted his diocese to be the model for the rest of the world and a reflection of what Jesus would have it be. He had the chancellor of the diocese send a notice to all the priests in Rome to come to the hall at St. John Lateran for a special meeting with their bishop.

When the day arrived, every priest from every parish and school and hospital and every other institution in the diocese arrived. Priests from the various religious orders also came. The meeting lasted for only two hours. Carlo spoke to them and later worked his way through the crowd and made sure he embraced and talked to each one of them personally.

What he expressed in his introductory talk was his vision of the mission of the church, and especially of the Diocese of Rome. "In brief, there are two things that are important for all of us as shepherds of Jesus' flock. First, we as his priests must make Jesus real to all our people. I know in the past many of you have been stuck in rectories, waiting for the phone to ring, caring for the material work of running a parish. But that is not what we have been ordained for. We have been ordained to preach the gospel, which means to make Jesus real to the people, and not just to our own people, but to people who have never heard of Jesus. So, we must not stay holed up in our rectories. We must be about our real work. We must be apostles.

"We may need a guide in doing this, so the Congregation on Christian Life has published a book put together by a remarkable staff of theologians, scripture scholars, psychologists, and historians. It is an extraordinary analysis of the life of Jesus and will be available to you within two months. Please use this as resource material in making Jesus real to your people.

"My second concern is for the poor and the homeless of our diocese. The poor and the homeless are our parishioners. They are the hidden treasure of not only the church, but of society. The genius and talent and potential holiness locked in the minds and hearts of the poor must be brought to blossom. It is God's plan for them. It is God's plan for us. In the days after Jesus there were fewer and fewer poor and homeless in the Christian communities. They were taken care of by their Christian brothers and sisters. It is important that our diocese be the model for the rest of the world for our care of the poor and the homeless. Each parish should have a committee to identify the homeless in its boundaries and to provide shelter for them, so there will be no homeless in any of our parishes. This is a something that I would like to see started immediately. I will be personally involved in this work, and I will be kept informed of the progress in each parish. If any of you have questions or problems, you should call the chancellor. We will help. But I expect you to work assiduously on this project. As you may have already learned, my eight adopted children were previously homeless. They were at one time beggars wandering the streets of my diocese. Now they are lawyers, architects, engineers, and one is about to receive his medical license. One is a saint in heaven, having been martyred because of her family's dedication to Jesus. So do not be deceived by what you see in the homeless. They are a rich treasure of precious undeveloped gifts. Treat them with love and gentleness. They are Jesus walking your streets.

"I thank you all for coming today, and I support you in your efforts to bring Jesus back to our people."

The applause was immediate, overwhelming from some, faint from others. Carlo knew beforehand that many would not take kindly to his making homeless beggars a pastoral priority, but like a bulldozer in low gear, he was determined to change priorities among his flock, especially among its shepherds.

Behind the scenes at the Vatican, word had spread about the pope's unusual negotiating style with the ambassadors and with other warring government officials, and it enforced the idea of many of the cardinals that the pope was a simple, unsophisticated farmer from a backward family, an embarrassment to the church. When some of these cardinals met the pope walking down the corridor or even at a meeting, they ignored his title as Holy Father and merely addressed him as "Signore" to show their contempt. Had they only known, this pleased Carlo to no end. He cringed when the others called him Holy Father or your Holiness. He wanted to earn respect by what he was and not because he had a title that demanded respect. When they called him "Signore," he merely smiled back in recognition. What he didn't know was that they were plotting to undermine his attempts to change age-old customs and practices.

When word spread that he was planning a Christmas mass and dinner for the homeless beggars of Rome, many of them laughed at his stupidity and claimed he was demeaning the role of the papacy in international society. But the homeless, he had always said, were his family. He felt more at home with them than with some of the cardinals, saying that the homeless beggars were the secret treasure of the church, most beloved of Jesus himself. As the day for their celebration approached, Carlo's joy seemed to increase. He was so happy that he felt it would be selfish not to share the experience. So he invited any of the cardinals who would like to celebrate with him to come. Out of the thirty around Rome, only twelve accepted.

In preparation for Christmas, Father Peppino, the homeless priest, distributed the musical instruments Carlo had donated, so the homeless musicians could practice for a Christmas concert. The best musicians in the group were men and women who had emotional or psychological problems and would rather roam the streets than live with family, but who were nonetheless extremely talented. As long as they were playing music, they were stable and at peace. In fact, when Carlo realized this, he told them they could keep their instruments, so they could work together giving street concerts, live with a little dignity, earn some income, and share with other homeless who had no such productive talents.

When Advent came, Carlo gave a service every night on the Hebrew prophecies describing what the Messiah would be like when he came and when and where he would be born. He also showed how the Holy Spirit had been preparing the pagans as well through the more sensitive and pious of the Greek and Roman philosophers for the coming of a savior for humanity. He went into great detail in portraying Jesus' mother as a chosen vessel of election, specially created by the Father for his divine Son. God gave her graces and gifts he had never given to any other human being. Carlo went on to describe Mary as the only creature who had an intimate relationship with each of the three Persons of the Blessed Trinity: bride of the Father, mother of the Son, and overshadowed by the power of the Holy Spirit, making the sacred incarnation of the Son of God and the Son of Man possible. Who else had ever been so honored by the Almighty?

Christmas finally arrived.

Carlo first offered a Christmas Eve mass in St. Peter's and explained that the little baby in the feeding trough for animals possessed the mind that designed and controls the whole vast machinery of the universe. His birth in a stable teaches us how beautiful we can be if we live and treat others with humility.

Madelena and the seven children, now so grown, spent Christmas morning with Carlo. He had breakfast ready for them at the cottage when they arrived at the Vatican. A beautiful Christmas tree next to a fireplace bathed the room with soft colors of red and green. Presents were piled beneath it. It was the most beautiful Christmas they had ever had. Who among them would have ever dreamed that their father, and for Madelena, her dearest love, would be pope, and they would be celebrating Christmas privately with him inside the Vatican in that special little cottage!

While they were having breakfast, Carla, who was now in her twenties, asked her father, "Papa, we all know that you and mother have always loved each other. It would be so beautiful if you could marry."

Carlo and Madelena looked at each other, their eyes glistening. Carlo said, "My dearest Carla, your mother and I have always been married in a spiritual way that God understands. It is a bond of love that we have shared from childhood, a bond from God, a bond that has never been broken. We both had missions to accomplish, and we have always been there for each other and have been helpmates to each other more wonderfully than most other relationships. It was God's plan that it be this way so you could become our children, which would not have happened otherwise. Isn't it wonderful how God has planned every detail so we could all be a family?"

"God *is* beautiful, isn't he," Vito said.

"Yes, she is," Carla said.

The family was eager to go to the great mass for the homeless and poor scheduled for one o'clock.

More than fifty thousand poor and homeless had already gathered in the vast piazza of St. Peter's Basilica the night before Christmas, with musicians nearest the steps of the church playing Advent hymns, and the growing crowd singing along. All night they streamed in from all sides and by dawn the number had increased tenfold!

An altar had been set up and beautifully decorated with a manger scene in front of it and life-size figures expressing the joy of new life. The weather was beautiful, and even the air felt like the breath of God.

By noon the piazza was filled to capacity, and the peaceful crowd extended down into the Via della Conciliazione and beyond like a great cross of life. Father Peppino's estimate was surpassed. More than a million poor and homeless had streamed into Rome from all the neighboring towns, villages, and cities!

The loudspeakers now were amplifying the music as the orchestra broke into Christmas carols, which everyone knew. The effect of a million voices singing "O Come, All Ye Faithful" was breathtaking.

Television cameras stationed on top of St. Peters brought the mass to Catholics and non-Catholics in every country of the world.

Birds flew back and forth across the blue sky in every direction.

As the procession emerged from the side of the portico, the whole crowd clapped in a tsunami of appreciation, which prevented the musicians from starting the entrance hymn. But after a few minutes the clapping stopped and the music began.

The mass began as the musicians played the entrance hymn, and everyone sang. To the surprise of the clerics, as well as to their own surprise, the music was astonishingly beautiful, especially when another choir of about three hundred homeless children started singing.

The procession arrived at the altar, and the pope began the prayers in Italian: "In the name of the Father and of the Son and of the Holy Spirit." Speakers carried his voice to everyone.

The crowd roared, "Amen."

After men and women selected by Father Peppino did the readings, and the deacon read the Gospel, Carlo walked to the lectern and delivered the homily.

"My dear brothers and sisters, you would be surprised if I told you that I am one of you. But I am one of you more than you think. You have been in my heart in a very special way for the past fifteen years at least. You may be homeless, and you may be poor, but you have gifts and talents and have been blessed by God in ways that are hard for mere human beings to even begin to understand. You are the secret treasure of the church and of society itself. You are the key to heaven for all of us, because our heavenly Father has made our eternal salvation dependent on our appreciation of you. You are walking images of God in our midst. I know that among you there are Muslims, and Hindus, and Buddhists, and Zoroastrians, as well as Christians of all kinds, and that is good, because that is the kind of crowd that followed Jesus every day. They were not only Jews, but people from all the surrounding countries who came to him daily for healings and to learn–Philistines, Romans, Greeks, Persians, and many others, and those who believed in their own gods.

"Jesus' message to them all was, 'Do not be afraid, little flock. Your heavenly Father loves you.' You are poor; so was God's Son! Look at him in that stable. None of you were so poor that you had to be born in a stable. You may have been driven far from home. He was born far from home and soon was hunted down to be murdered, and his family was forced to flee to a foreign country. You are homeless. One day a man asked if he could follow Jesus, and Jesus' reply was, 'You want to follow me; I do not even have a place to lay my head, but if you are willing, you are welcome.' So, see, you are the ones who follow him! Don't ever feel alone, because Jesus is by your side and in your hearts as you welcome him each day.

"Today we celebrate his birth. When you look at the baby in that crib, you see only a baby, but in that baby's brain resides the divine mind and the divine will that controls this vast universe, and that baby comes to *you* today. So, welcome him into your hearts and allow him to comfort and bless you and share with you his peace. He comes to you today as your savior. Open your hearts to him each day and live with him. Jesus said that he lives in the poor. What an honor! So live your lives in such a way that people will be able to see Jesus living in *you*, and one day he will welcome you into his heavenly home where you will live in glory with him forever.

"I invite all of you—all of you—to receive him today!"

There was no applause, just holy silence.

At communion, more than three thousand laity from three hundred parishes gave out communion, which had been placed strategically near the eucharistic ministers throughout the vast crowd, so it took no longer than an hour to serve all those who wanted to receive. The music and the singing and the silences made it seem timeless.

When mass ended, Carlo told the vast crowd that there was food being served by staff from all the restaurants in Rome at strategic places all along the sides of the piazza and down the Via della Conciliazione and all along the Tiber. "So please be patient and orderly and find a seat at a table next to your brother or sister in Christ. I wish you all a blessed and holy Christmas for the rest of your lives!"

For more than a mile the crowd responded in a long, thunderous greeting of gratitude and Christmas joy.

After removing his robes, Carlo put on his homeless clothes.

He and the cardinals worked their way through the crowd and down to the very end of the Via della Conciliazione as far as the Tiber, serving the poor and homeless with their affection and respect, and then back up again to greet those they missed.

Even with the generosity of restaurants and cafes and hotels throughout Rome and beyond, there was not enough food for a million people. But everyone ate, and everyone was filled.

35

It wasn't long before Lent came around, and Carlo fasted each day and stayed up praying in his private chapel till late. Then he went to bed, after what he felt were simple messages Jesus had shared with him, messages in the form of changes to be made, or things to be done, or attitudes to adopt. He felt the Holy Spirit was guiding him in this way, and it made him feel as if God was changing the course of the church in little ways, one at a time, so as not to create shock waves and polarize the worldwide flock.

Each night as he prayed, he read a few pages of the newly published book about Jesus, from which he learned more and more about Jesus' inner life and spirit. Each day his insights into Jesus deepened, and his awareness of what Jesus expected of him grew more poignant, as his motto, "Jesus living in me," became a vivid reality to those around him whose minds and hearts were open.

Not everyone was able to understand the way Carlo did things, or even the way he thought. He had become, without realizing it, an anomaly, a beautiful anomaly, but different, and for some difficult to understand and appreciate.

His first synod of bishops showed this in a dramatic fashion. As the bishops from around the world came and held their conferences, his introductory remarks were simple and clear. He wanted to have input from the bishops, including the Orthodox and Lutherans and Anglicans who came, since they were the ones dealing on a daily basis with people from their own cultures and who understood their people. Their input into the synod was valuable. He suggested, however, that they might think of filtering their considerations about important issues in light of what is important to Jesus rather than from the perspective of what is good for the church as an institution.

That emphasis annoyed some of the bishops and indicated to them that the pope was a radical. He wanted to shift their thinking away from the church and onto Jesus, who is the heart of religion, and indeed, *is* the religion. That was disturbing to some, whose dedication was not to God but to the majesty of the church, which was the source and basis of their own self-importance. Following Athanasius's lead would be self-defeating, because it would make their living like princes look ridiculous. Sadly, they didn't even understand the contradictions in their thinking.

Carlo knew that he would have a problem with that mentality but realized he had to face it and at least encourage those individuals who felt that way to consider that there could be a different way of thinking. In the meantime, he stressed the importance of the bishops making Jesus real to their priests and people and encouraged them to offer mass in their cathedrals on as many weekends as possible and talk to the people about Jesus and the rich facets of his life and thinking. If people are drifting away from religion, it is because they crave intimacy with God, and the churches are not providing the guidance to find that intimacy. It is only by making Jesus real to the people that people can again find comfort and strength in their church.

The synod went by quickly, and most bishops felt blessed by the new emphasis and the lively discussion held around the pope's opening remarks. Even some who originally were taken back by his remarks changed their thinking when they experienced the discussions and the good sense some bishops made out of those opening remarks. Some conservatives recalled that Pope Benedict XVI as Cardinal Ratzinger, often said, "The church speaks too much about structures. It needs to speak more about God." The synod was a success, and Carlo was pleased with the attitudes and thoughts as well as the suggestions expressed by the bishops. He tried to talk to as many of the bishops personally as he could, and he assured them all of his support and appreciation. He reminded them that he and they, not the Vatican staff, were the ones guiding the church, as he and the bishops were the successors of the apostles and that is where authority lies. And for that reason it was critical that they learned to think like Jesus. The bishops applauded loudly when he said that.

Carlo was not naive enough to think that he could make changes easily just because many of the bishops were impressed with the discussions and voted positively on matters important to him. The real test would be if they implemented the course about Jesus in their seminaries when they returned home. Already the Orthodox from Russia and Greece, the Lutheran and Anglican bishops, and bishops from other denominations were enthusiastic about implementing his directive in their territories.

On the last day of the synod Carlo offered mass with all the bishops. His sermon was touching.

"My dear brothers, this has to be one of the happiest days of my life, gathered here with you, and with Jesus as our main celebrant at this breaking of the bread. The spirit I felt over the past few days must make Jesus happy. He prayed so hard on that last night of his life that all his apostles and disciples would be one. What has happened to his church must have broken his heart, seeing it torn apart for so many centuries, marring the witness of his image to the world. Seeing your goodness and openness this past week was encouraging. I had the strongest sense of the presence of the Good Shepherd being in our midst touching the hearts of each of us, as if he was bonding us to see as one through his eyes, his heart, and his mind. It is only through him and in him that our family can again become not only friendly but find each other in love, and where there is love, unity of thought and belief will come as the spontaneous gift of his grace.

"I ask you all to bring that blessed spirit back home to your people, so they may feel the peace and grace that we have all experienced. And remember I am your brother, and I am here for you, so feel comfortable sharing with me your deepest concerns. Go in peace with the blessing of God's spirit, and with my love for each of you."

When he finished, each one felt that this holy man really was his brother. When they returned home, it was well into Lent, and many shared their experiences with their people, filling their hearts as well with a new hope and a blessed vision of the future.

Holy Week arrived. For Carlo, this had always been a special time spent in deep meditation, living in his mind the events that took place during the last week of Jesus' life. Though he was walking around the Vatican and working constantly, his mind was continually focused on the presence of Jesus.

On Holy Thursday, a day that recalled a spiritual revolution, Athanasius celebrated the liturgy of the Last Supper at St. Peter's. The Vatican cardinals and bishops and priests were all there, as well as all the officials attached to the Vatican and thousands of laity, who overflowed onto the street. Representatives of governments and other officials were also in attendance.

After his homily the pope told all the cardinals to remain seated and asked the master of ceremonies to bring into the sanctuary those who had been previously invited. At that point a group of homeless men, women, and children walked into the sanctuary and took their places in chairs specially arranged for them. While this was taking place, the pope was divesting himself of his liturgical vestments, and to the shock of the whole assembly in that vast basilica, he walked around to the front of the altar dressed in the clothes he had worn as a homeless beggar, with a large towel draped over his arm.

The whole crowd was awed into silence. Almost everyone there knew about that homeless beggar who had wandered the streets of Rome years ago dressed in old clothes with a mismatched patch on the right pant leg. Many prayed, thinking of when they met him in the streets years before and how they had treated that homeless beggar, now their saintly, revered Pope Athanasius I.

The acolytes brought a bowl of water to the pope. He knelt in front of the first cardinal, who had already taken off his shoes, waiting for the pope to wash his feet. The scene was moving because it was so mindful of the Last Supper when Jesus, dressed as a slave wearing only a loin cloth, got down on his knees and washed the feet of the apostles, who had only shortly before been arguing as to who was the greatest and most important among them. Here the pope, dressed as a despised homeless beggar, the image he had of himself, was washing the feet of these important princes of the church.

Then, after washing the feet of the cardinals, he washed the feet of the homeless.

They all understood the symbolism as this humble pope washed the feet of each of them. The whole congregation was in tears. No one had ever seen anything like it. And the same reaction must have taken place in every living room around the world where people were glued to their televisions sets.

Then, something happened that was totally unrehearsed. One of the homeless—a teenage girl in a shabby dress—deeply moved by the pope's humility, jumped up before the pope returned to the altar and took his towel and asked him if he would please sit in her chair, so she could wash his feet. The pope, caught off guard, and touched by the extraordinary gesture of this young girl, did as she asked and sat down in her chair, took off his shoes, and let the girl wash his feet. After she dried them, to his embarrassment, she bent down and reverently kissed them, and with tears in her eyes, looked up at the pope and said, "Thank you, Holy Father, for all you do for all of us. You are truly our father, and the father I never had. I love you."

The homeless beggar belonged everywhere and to everyone.